STONE

COLD

DEAD

STONE COLD DEAD

B. PAYTON SETTLES

LEVEL
BEST BOOKS

First published by Level Best Books 2022

Copyright © 2022 by B. Payton Settles

This novel is entirely a work of fiction. The names, characters and incidents portrayed in it are the work of the author's imagination. Any resemblance to actual persons, living or dead, events or localities is entirely coincidental.

B. Payton Settles asserts the moral right to be identified as the author of this work.

First edition

ISBN: 978-1-68512-102-0

Cover art by Level Best Designs

This book was professionally typeset on Reedsy.
Find out more at reedsy.com

For Tiernan Settles & Kaitlyn Huntoon

Prologue

When that terrible summer finally ended and Jewell's biggest problem was how to keep Lois Lane from chewing holes in Mr. Plougher's slippers, she couldn't help wondering,

How did I get drawn into the Stone family's tragic history? Why didn't I run like hell when the truth surfaced about that mansion? I was scared—terrified—almost from the beginning.

Was it the mansion's similarity to my grandfather's home in Kansas? I still remember the day I realized I'd never be allowed to even visit that prairie-style Victorian, let alone live in it. I remember, even now, the snapshot daddy showed us when he returned from grandpa's funeral. Daydreams about that house got me through the pain of my childhood.

So, that was part of it. Not all, though. After bunking with Caroline and Hank, I sorely wanted my own place. When that room became available, I didn't think twice.

Should I have cut my losses when 811 Radish's problems began multiplying? Of course. Instead, the McDunn family stubbornness took over and I dug in, determined to protect my four walls no matter what.

I think the dreamer, the maybe-I'll-win-the-lottery side of me, rejoiced when I saw that peaked roof, those old leaded windows. From the beginning, the house keyed right into the lost little girl within. I felt welcomed in some odd, unexpected way. The house's soul reached out to me.

In retrospect, I was very lucky. I'm still alive.

Chapter One

The Civic rocketed out of the G.I.s Joe parking lot, narrowly missing a shiny red Corvette just pulling in. In her rear-view mirror Jewell McDunn saw the driver, an athletic-looking, gray-haired man. He was shaking his fist.

Oh, dear God. I think I just pissed off Uncle Leo.

Thirty minutes earlier Jewell had parked in the shade across from the camo-painted coffee truck, nothing more important on her mind than the morning's latte served by her friend, Beth Anne Stone.

"You in there, Beth Anne?"

From within the coffee truck's interior a voice called, "Be right out, Jewell," and the barista, Beth Anne Stone appeared. "Sorry; I was on hold with our baker. The usual?" Although she was in her early twenties, Beth Anne could have passed for a sleep-deprived. underfed teen-ager.

Jewell pushed back the damp ringlets of brown hair around her face. "Gonna be a scorcher today." She leaned against the truck. "I should know better than to break in new shoes in this heat."

"I hear you." Beth Anne pulled levers on the espresso machine.

"Are you okay?" Jewell squinted curiously at her friend. Although she didn't look it, Jewell was old enough to be the girl's mother, barely, and Beth Anne's red, puffy eyes brought out her maternal instincts. "You working too hard?"

"Well, yeah, but mostly I'm worried about Bob. The stress is really getting to him." Beth Anne sighed. "How's it going with you?"

"Could be better. Carolyn's new boyfriend stayed overnight a month

1

ago and he's still there." Jewell's shoulders sagged. "I don't care during the week—I'm on 24-hour shifts Monday through Friday—but weekends suck. I can't turn around without tripping over giant gym shoes."

"I met him once—the boyfriend. Hank something, right? Not bad looking." Beth Anne grinned.

"Oh, he's a cutie," Jewell nodded. "He's like a stray dog, though—found shelter and won't leave. I've told Carolyn he's taking advantage, but she won't listen. Been rescuing strays since she was nine years old."

Beth Anne ran a wet cloth across the counter. "Those stray-dog types can spot a soft-hearted woman a mile away." She yawned. "Since we added sandwiches to the menu we've tripled our business. I'm worn out, but we need the money—the interest on our loan from Bob's aunt is killing us." She looked speculatively at Jewell. "Say, you know that big-assed Victorian over on Radish? Aunt Doris lives there and she has a room for rent. Want us to put in a good word for you? It would get you out of Carolyn's way and make some brownie points for us, too."

Jewell had to smile—that Victorian was way out of her league—but before she could say no, a customer honked for service. While Beth Anne traded coffee and scones for money, Jewell thought about her situation in Carolyn's cramped apartment. *Maybe the Victorian's not such a bad idea.*

When Beth Anne's customer drove away, Jewell put out a feeler. "Is that the place where someone died?"

"Oh, you know." Beth Anne avoided Jewel's stare. "There's bound to be stories about any place that old. It's beautiful inside—it has an amazing front staircase."

Jewell downed the last of her latte. "You're right about one thing: I do need to change my living space. It was great at first—Carolyn needed help paying off her credit card debt and I needed to build up my savings—but everything changed when Hank showed up."

As Beth Anne nodded agreement, a late-model SUV pulled up next to G.I.s Joe and a man with an eagle tattoo on his shaved scalp climbed out. He swaggered over to the counter and slipped an arm around Jewell's waist. "How's my second-favorite girl?"

Jewell blushed. "Bob, the way you go on!"

Bob gave Jewell a squeeze and smiled at Beth Anne. "You want to do the rest of the errands, babe? it's cool in the SUV."

"You don't have to ask twice." Beth Anne stepped inside the coffee truck and reappeared a minute later, popping a baseball cap on her head. She waved to Jewell, car keys jingling.

"See ya. And don't worry, Jewell. Everything will work out." The SUV's tires sprayed gravel as Beth Anne drove away.

"Duty calls, Bob." Jewell crossed the asphalt and climbed into her Civic.

"What did she mean, it'll work out?" Bob watched the SUV disappear around the corner.

"Just the battle zone I call my life. I'm about ready to tell Carolyn to choose between me and her new boyfriend," Jewell said grimly.

"Whoa, tread lightly, girl. You could end up on the street sharing a tent with toothless Joe the homeless guy." Bob smiled at the thought. "I was you I'd just find my own place. You got no control over your daughter's love life."

Jewell put her car in gear. "You know I don't like unsolicited advice. However, your sweet wife just said the same thing. There's a room for rent at your family home?"

Bob frowned. "You hear that from Beth Anne? Yeah. Want me to check with Uncle Leo? He's the one who deals with Aunt Doris; she's his sister-in-law."

Jewell pulled a business card from her wallet. "Give him this, would you?" She smiled. "You Stones are the oldest family in town, right? Must be nice, belonging somewhere."

"Yep, We've been in Miwok a long time." Bob put Jewell's card into his jeans pocket. "My dad's brothers raised me after he died. Uncle Leo's the only one left, now." He gave Jewell a friendly smile. "I'll find out if the room's still available. You can use me as a reference."

"Thanks." Jewell nodded. "Well, hasta la vista!"

* * *

In Mr. and Mrs. Nicholas Ploughers' cool, stuffy living room later that day, Jewell and Mr. Plougher sat at a card table working a jigsaw puzzle. As she handed him a puzzle piece, Jewell thought about the Ploughers' many happy years in their modest tract house.

It's no Victorian, but it has a lot of heart.

"Oh, look, Mr. P. This might be part of Goldilocks' eyeball."

Mr. Plougher's eighty-five-year-old head of white hair had been nodding slightly. Now, he snapped to attention and snatched the cardboard piece. When his fumbling fingers couldn't get it to lock on, he grunted, "Nope. Not a fit."

Jewell brushed her hand across the puzzle, covertly rotating the piece. "There; try it now."

"This is hopeless. I wanna go for a walk." Mr. Plougher pushed back his chair and struggled to his feet.

"It's pretty hot out there." Jewell stood, too, and slipped a hand under the old man's elbow.

Ding! From within the folds of her work smock, Jewell's phone chirped. She squinted at the name on the screen. "G.I.s Joe."

"Bob! Howzit goin'?"

"Hey, Jewell. Uncle Leo'll be here at G.I.'s Joe around four-thirty. You want to drop by?"

Jewell groaned. "I'm not sure. Was that him in the red Corvette I almost hit?"

"Matter of fact, it was. Be prepared for his rant about women drivers." Bob sounded like he was laughing.

"O-o-kay. Humility's not my usual go-to, but I'll do my best."

Jewell glanced at the clock: four-fifteen. "Wanna go for a ride, Mr. P.?"

A few minutes later Jewell's Civic pulled into the Baptist Church parking lot. Bob and an older man stood next to the red Corvette, talking.

"Hey, there's Leo Stone!" Mr. Plougher unsnapped his seat belt and struggled free of the Civic's passenger seat, stabbing the ground with his cane as he stepped eagerly out. "Leo, how ya doin'?"

The man turned, a smile creasing his face. "Nicholas Plougher! Good to see you." He quickly closed the distance between himself and Plougher, hand extended. "How are you, old buddy? And Eve? On the mend, I hope."

Jewell climbed from the car. "Mr. Stone? Jewell McDunn. We almost met earlier today." Her mouth turned up in a wry smile.

Uncle Leo scanned Jewell from head to toe, then nodded. "You're the gal who gave me a few more gray hairs this morning. You look better than you drive, that's for sure." He glanced at Bob, then back to Jewell. "So, you want to rent from my sister-in-law? Not a bad idea. I heard she plans to make a few bucks off the upstairs bedrooms." He pulled a tissue from his pocket and mopped his forehead. "You want her number?"

Bob stepped forward and shook Mr. Plougher's hand. "Doris isn't the easiest person to get along with, Jewell, but the house is really nice."

From inside the truck Beth Anne called, "If you want my two cents, it's a great idea. Jewell can keep an eye on things for us."

"What do you mean, keep an eye on things?" Jewell frowned. "I'm not agreeing to spy on anyone."

Uncle Leo cleared his throat. "No need to get excited. It's just, there's bad blood between us and that woman, from years ago. Hell, the property's been tied up in court since God knows when." His attempt at a smile looked more like a grimace. "Your last name isn't Stone, so you got nothin' to worry about." He pulled a card from his pocket and handed it to Jewell. "Here's her number. I wouldn't wait too long to call; the room will rent fast—that house is a very special place."

Jewell studied Uncle Leo's face as she took the slip of paper. "At least you're honest. Oh, by the way, sorry for the near-miss this morning. I should've been looking where I was going." As she guided Mr. Plougher toward the Civic, she added, "Nice meeting you."

* * *

"This is Doris Stone, returning your call. You're interested in my rental?"

Jewell winced at the smoker's voice coming through her phone. "Well, yes, I ...."

"Do you want to come by and see it?"

Jewell sat up and turned away from Mr. Plougher's inquisitive stare. "I only need a place for weekends—I do in-home care Monday through Friday—but of course, I'd rent the room full-time."

"I repeat, would you like to come by?"

"I do need to get out of Carolyn's—I mean, sure." Jewell nodded to the phone.

"I'm limiting the applicants to single people, preferably over forty. And no overnight guests. I'm not sharing my house with strangers."

"Works for me," Jewell said. "And I don't usually admit it, but forty is in my rearview mirror."

A casual tone entered the woman's voice. "I tolerate a little alcohol in the house—the occasional glass of wine—but I won't abide drunkards. You aren't a heavy drinker, are you?"

"Absolutely not. One of my husbands was an alcoholic; I hardly touch the stuff." Jewell paused. "One thing: I have my own furniture. Some of it's in storage, some is with me. How big is the room?"

"You can see for yourself. I'm at 811 Radish, on Victorian row. Rudolph's family built this house when the town was nothing more than a shipping point for poultry farmers."

Jewell glanced at her reflection in the Ploughers' hall mirror. *This lady sounds eccentric, at best.* "How about this afternoon, at 6:00? That's my dinner break."

"Well, my grandson will be here—I suppose he can help me screen you. Yes, that will be fine."

* * *

An aging Volvo sedan sat at the curb in front of 811 Radish Street. The property boasted a three-story Victorian with Southern-style posts flanking a front porch, stained-glass windows, and a widow's walk below a sharply pitched roof. Tall cedar bushes stood sentry at the front steps, screening the porch from the street. Jewell had passed the house many times, always impressed with its regal bearing in this historic neighborhood.

Inside the sedan, she and Mr. Plougher surveyed the place while their driver, a petite, pretty, blond woman in her twenties, finger combed her hair.

"I don't know, Mom. It looks spooky. And God help the dog who lifts his leg on that lawn."

"Spooky? For heaven's sake, Carolyn, the place is amazing. If I could live here, I would think I'd died and gone to heaven."

"I wish you didn't feel like you have to move," Carolyn said, glancing at her watch. "You promise this won't take long? Hank's making pizza tonight. I'll set my timer for thirty minutes. When it rings, we leave."

Jewell sighed. "Thirty minutes should do it."

Carolyn checked her reflection in the rear-view mirror. Okay. Let's get this over with." She leaned back, smiling at Mr. Plougher. "She wants your opinion, too."

Mr. Plougher grunted and climbed stiffly from the car. He held the door for Jewell, then marched up the house's front steps. Jewell pushed past him. "She should see me first—I'm the prospective tenant."

With her finger on the doorbell, she paused. She could hear people talking from inside the house.

"Keep your opinions to yourself, young man. I'm going to have a tenant. End of story." A woman's voice, throaty and tense. Then a male voice, sounding irritated. "It's a stupid idea, Gram. Benny'll kill you when he finds out."

"Not another word, Marco."

The door opened and a woman in her fifties looked out, her dyed brown hair and garish make-up accentuating the lines in her face. Jewell stared.

"You must be Jewell McDunn." The woman looked suspiciously at Carolyn. "And you are...?"

Mr. Plougher took a step toward the woman. "Hi, Cutie!"

"Uh," the woman stammered, "You brought your father and your sister, Mrs. McDunn?"

"Wrong on both counts," Jewell frowned at Mr. Plougher. "He's my employer, and Carolyn's my daughter. I hope you don't mind." She gave the woman a guarded smile. "You're Doris Stone, right?"

At that moment a handsome, dark-haired teenager, tall and loose-limbed, appeared in the doorway. "We definitely don't mind. I mean, uh, I'm Marco Perez, Doris's grandson."

He put a hand out to Jewell, but his smile was directed at Carolyn.

"Come on in, everyone." Mrs. Stone stepped back and led the way to a living room filled with antiques and uncomfortable-looking furniture. Bookcases on either side of a marble fireplace displayed porcelain figurines, Hummel statues, and an ornate cremation urn. One corner was devoted to a large, flat-screen TV.

"Can I get you something to drink?" Doris sounded ill-at-ease; Jewell figured she was new at interviewing people.

"Maybe a glass of water. Have you lived here long, Mrs. Stone?"

"I'll take a screwdriver." Mr. Plougher smirked.

"Water for him, too," Jewell said quickly. "He's not allowed alcohol."

"It was worth a try. Hand me one of those mints, will ya?" Mr. Plougher pointed to a crystal candy dish on a spindly-legged table. "Somethin' sure smells good. We could be talked into stayin' for dinner." He wiggled his eyebrows suggestively.

Mrs. Stone turned so she wasn't looking at Mr. Plougher. "I've been here almost ten years. My husband's—late husband's—family has been in this house for generations." Then, dropping her voice slightly, "You work for this man? What is it you do for him?" Her face took on an expression of distaste.

"I'm a companion to both of the Ploughers." Jewell smiled at Mr. P. "They're my friends AND my employers. I value his input on any big decision."

The words had a curious effect on Mr. Plougher. He sat back, frowning, and stared hard at the room, Doris Stone, and her grandson.

Carolyn glanced at her watch. "Are the bedrooms all upstairs?"

"They are. The house has five of them; bedrooms, that is." Marco blushed. He jumped to his feet. "Gram, show them the room." He turned to Jewell. "It has a great view of the street."

Mr. Plougher leaned forward, preparing to hitch himself up from the couch cushions. "You want me to come along?"

Jewell looked across to the foyer's steeply-curving staircase. "I don't think so. We'll make it quick; I'll take pictures with my phone."

The old man sank back onto the couch, looking relieved. As she followed Carolyn up the stairs Jewell heard him mutter: "Not sure I want to see those pictures. If my memory serves me, this house is cursed."

A shiver traveled down Jewell's spine. *I hope he's wrong. This place is amazing.*

At the top of the stairs Carolyn ran a finger along the banister's polished wood. "You have a lovely home, Mrs. Stone."

"And I intend to hold onto it." Doris Stone led them along a wide, Persian-carpeted hallway. With the doors closed, a wall sconce and one small, leaded-glass window provided the only light. Jewell squinted into the gloom. *Feels like we're suspended in twilight.*

"You'll notice how wonderfully cool it is up here," Mrs. Stone said over her shoulder.

"No need for air conditioning, that's for sure." Carolyn pulled up the hood of her sweatshirt.

They stopped at the last door on the left. "This is it, the house's master suite. I'm sure you'll be impressed." The face Mrs. Stone turned to Jewell was stern, almost somber.

She's giving up the master suite? She must really need the money. That reminds me: I have to ask about the rent.

Mrs. Stone swung the door open into a room whose focal point was a large bay window, heavily draped. Wide-planked wood floors, brass wall sconces, and a small corner fireplace offset the spare furnishings—an iron-framed cot, a bedside table, and a small three-drawer dresser. A braided rug, the likes of which Jewell had last seen in her grandmother's house when she was eight years old, added the only touch of color.

"I imagine there's a lot of natural light when those curtains are open. Do you mind?" Jewell walked to the window and pulled back the curtains. "Wow! Your grandson wasn't kidding about the view."

Carolyn, staring at the window, clapped one hand over her mouth. "O.M.G."

"Get a grip!" Jewell put a warning hand on her daughter's shoulder. "This must be the closet." She stepped across the room and opened the door to a small, fairly deep space that exuded musty air.

Mrs. Stone nodded. "People didn't have so many clothes a hundred years ago." She quickly closed the door. "If you want more storage space, there are always wardrobes."

Much later Jewell thought about the closet and the way the woman rushed them from the bedroom.

They walked across the hall and Mrs. Stone opened a door into a large, old-fashioned bathroom. "You'll be the only person using this."

A claw-footed tub stood in the middle of the subway-tiled room, flanked by a pedestal-footed sink and a toilet with a chain-pull flusher. As Jewell looked around, she wondered if she'd been transported back in time to her great-grandmother's Illinois bungalow.

She returned to reality when Carolyn whispered, "Can we leave now? I've got to get out of here!" Jewell saw terror in her daughter's eyes. *What in the world?*

"Okay. Sorry, Mrs. Stone. We'll have to cut this short. We haven't talked money yet, but believe me, I'm interested. And you couldn't hope for a better tenant. I'm clean, quiet, and responsible."

Glancing at Carolyn, Mrs. Stone frowned. "I'll give you an application. There are other applicants, so get it back to me quickly." She moved briskly along the hall and down the stairs.

Chapter Two

"Let's go." Jewell leaned across the front seat of the car and tapped Carolyn's shoulder. "It doesn't look right, us sitting out front like this. Someone's peeking around the drapes, see?"

Carolyn stared out the front windshield as if in a trance.

"What's with you?" Jewell couldn't keep the irritation out of her voice. "I hope you didn't ruin the deal for me; I want that room."

Carolyn shook her head and mutely started the car. Her phone chirped and she glanced at the screen. "That's my thirty-minute timer." She keyed in a number. "Hi, Hank. Yeah, We're through. Home in a few." To her mother, she mouthed, "I don't want to talk about it." She pulled away from the curb and, eyes on the road, murmured, "Uh, Mom, why don't I ask Hank to try harder to get along with you? Then you won't have to move." She suddenly thumped the steering wheel. "Can you believe that woman, acting all high and mighty with her damned haunted house?"

"Wow! Where's that coming from? She was nervous, that's all. Probably never rented out a room before." Jewell folded her arms across her chest. "For what it's worth, I don't appreciate you saying the house is haunted. It's old, sure, but I like that. Gives it personality." Then, "Hank's not going to change. The room is perfect for me—I've already figured out where my furniture should go."

From the back seat, Mr. Plougher snorted. "You want my opinion? Never trust a woman who serves stale mints." He thumped the seat with his fist. "That Doris—she's a witch, and that kid—I wouldn't trust him with yesterday's trash. Couldn't keep his eyes off Carolyn." His chin drooped, his eyes closed, and he began to snore.

Jewell poked an elbow at her now-giggling daughter. "Cut that out. This is serious!" Then, in a whisper, "Trust Mr. P. to focus on all the wrong stuff; I could care less about the grandson." She looked intently at Carolyn. "Care to explain your behavior in that bathroom?"

Carolyn slid a glance toward her mother. "Um, well, those icy cold patches in the hall gave me the creeps. I remembered a news story from ten years ago—some burglars robbed a house in that neighborhood and killed a woman—garbage collectors saw her body the next morning, hanging in an upstairs window: a bay window."

Jewell groaned. "Good God, Carolyn, the house is old; that's why it was cold. And, give me a break—half the houses on that side of town have bay windows." She turned to stare out at the darkening sky. "I'm not 'sensitive,' like you, but I have pretty good perceptions. I didn't feel a thing."

The car pulled to the curb in front of the Ploughers' home: a wood-frame cottage which, except for its' bright blue trim and rose-bush hedge, was identical to every other house on the street.

"Just do me a favor," Carolyn said as Jewell helped Mr. Plougher from the car. "Look at a couple other places before you decide."

"No promises," Jewell said, tight-lipped.

* * *

"Hey, is Bob around? I want to thank him for putting me in touch with his aunt. I got the room! I'm moving in next weekend." Jewell's excitement was contagious. Beth Anne smiled as she took Jewell's coffee money.

"That's great. You'll have your own place again!"

"Carolyn's the only downside. You'd think she'd be delighted to have me out from underfoot, right? But, oh, no." Jewell groaned. "She got all weird when we looked at the room. It was old-fashioned, but very nice."

Beth Anne's smile faded. "I haven't been to the family mansion in ages. It used to be really elegant."

"Still is. I have no idea why Carolyn freaked out. She kept talking about bad vibes."

"Huh." Beth Anne looked everywhere but at Jewell.

From the rear of G.I.'s Joe, Bob warbled, "Morning, Jewell. I just took some scones out of the oven. You want one?"

"I can smell 'em! What the hell—I'll skip lunch. Who can resist warm cinnamon and sugar?" Jewell put her coffee on the truck's wood plank counter and opened her wallet.

When Bob appeared with the pastry tray she crooned, "Oh, yes. Give me three—I'll take some back to the Ploughers."

Bob smiled. "Did I hear you say you struck a deal with my aunt?"

"Yes. Moving in Sunday. I'll finally have a home—well, a room—all to myself; no tripping over dumbbells, no more waiting forever to use the bathroom."

"Good for you." Bob and Beth Anne exchanged a quick, uneasy glance. "Aunt Doris came by the other day while you were on your break, babe. Asked me about the mortgage payment. Bitch. It's not due 'til day after tomorrow."

Beth Anne's warning gaze rested on Bob for a second before she turned to Jewell. "811 Radish looks old-fashioned because it's a heritage house. It has to stay exactly like it was built. After the first Mrs. Stone died, Bob's Uncle Rudolph tried to update a few things but the town wouldn't let him."

"So, there was a first Mrs. Stone? Interesting. Say, when I'm moved in—I'm on the left side as you're looking at the house from the street, a front room with a bay window—I want you to come by."

"You won't see me in there while Doris is still around. No offense, Jewell." Bob disappeared into the truck's interior.

"What's with him?"

"Aunt Doris grabbed all of Rudolph's assets, including the house, when the old guy died." Beth Anne frowned. "We were going to use Bob's share to start G.I.s Joe. Doris did give us a loan, but she hounds us constantly about it."

"No wonder Bob's pissed at her. I'll be sure and pay my rent on time." Jewell picked up her car keys. "I love the room. I'll just walk softly around

Bob's Aunt Doris." She glanced at her watch. "Time to roll. Take it easy."

* * *

"Are you sure you need a coat, Mrs. Plougher?" Jewell fussed over the old lady as they prepared for the Ploughers' afternoon drive.

"Eve, it's August, for God's sake! You'll sweat off what little fat you still have." Mr. Plougher stepped around his wife and reached for her walker. "How 'bout I carry the coat and you wear your cardigan? That way we'll have it in case of a sudden blizzard, but you won't get all sweaty."

"Jewell and I will decide what I wear, Nicholas. You just worry about yourself." Eve Plougher, a frail, slightly bent-over woman with fluffy white hair and abundant smile wrinkles, flapped a dismissive hand at her husband.

"Humpf!" Mr. Plougher, standing a good half-inch taller and probably five pounds heavier than his wife, glowered at her. "I worry about myself plenty, thank you very much." The frown dissolved into a smile. "Worrying about you keeps me young."

Jewell herded the two octogenarians, one sporting a cane and the other stomping along in a walker, out the front door and to her car. When both were buckled into the back seat she climbed behind the wheel.

"First stop, the pharmacy for those prescriptions. Next, we tour my new neighborhood, then we're off to the Red Rooster for a late lunch. When I get moved in, I'll take pictures—I'd show you in person, but my room is up a long, curving staircase."

"A picture will do just fine." Mr. Plougher covered his wife's hand with his own. "We don't do stairs worth a damn. Lucky it's flat ground at the Red Rooster. Right, sweetheart?"

Eve Plougher nodded vigorously. "Right, dear. What would I do without my weekly chicken salad sandwich?" She gave her husband a shy smile.

Forty-five minutes later, after a successful trip to the pharmacy (no line at the check-out counter, no heated discussion with the clerk about refills on Mrs. Plougher's meds) the Civic turned onto Radish Street.

Mrs. Plougher sat up to peer out the side window. "You're in this part of town? Impressive, Jewell. This is one of the first blocks developed when the town was young. The first mayor's mansion is just a few blocks down the street."

"Right as usual, Eve." Mr. Plougher pointed out his own window. "See the balcony way up on the top floor of that white house? It's called a widow's walk. From there, a hundred years ago, you could see all the way to the bay. A ship captain's wife would scan the horizon in the hope of spotting her husband's ship."

The residential area of Miwok had no traffic in the early afternoon, so when they reached Radish Street Jewell slowed her car to a crawl.

"It's sure pretty, isn't it, with all these old trees on either side? I love the way their branches join hands over the street." Jewell felt a rush of gratitude for her new home, even if it was just a room in somebody else's house.

"There it is, that dark shingled one; my room is the upstairs left bay window." Jewell raised her voice above an awed whisper. "See?"

"Oh, my," Mrs. Plougher gulped. "It doesn't much look like a place where you'd live, Jewell. I mean, it looks all stuffy and severe."

Jewell laughed. "You got that right. I'm more the trailer park type, aren't I?" She was quiet for a moment. "Before I moved in with Carolyn, I had a run-down mobile home. Before that, my second ex and I had a motel room near his fishing boat." She shook her head, dismissing bad memories. "I'll take stuffy and severe, hands down."

"I went inside with her when she looked at it, Eve," Mr. Plougher's voice was quiet. "I wasn't impressed. Damn woman served stale mints."

"Nicholas, for shame! If Jewell likes the house, it's not for us to criticize." Mrs. Plougher gave their caregiver an apologetic smile. "You'll have to excuse him, dear. He used to know some of the people living in these mansions. He thinks every brass door knocker hides a dark secret."

"I got my memories, sure, but I also got a damn good sense of when someone's not the real McCoy." Mr. Plougher frowned. "Gotta say, though, Jewell, if anyone can make lemonade outa lemons, it's you."

The Civic picked up speed as they left Radish Street behind.

"Let's hope nobody grabs your favorite booth at the Red Rooster." Jewell smiled into the rearview mirror at her employer friends.

* * *

"Be careful. Don't let the recliner scratch my banister. I had no idea you had so much furniture, Jewell." Doris Stone flitted back and forth in the downstairs foyer, getting in the way of Hank and his buddy, Chaz, and raising everyone's blood pressure.

"They **are** being careful, Gram. Go unpack boxes or something. Let us work." Marco stood at the top of the stairs in plaid shorts and a spotlessly white tee shirt, holding a lamp and leading the procession.

"Yes, Doris, Carolyn could use some help." Jewell took her eyes off the movers to give her new landlady an apologetic smile.

"I'm not sure my stairs can handle this weight," Doris moaned, moving toward the kitchen.

Hank and Chaz, both young, tall, and buffed, ignored the women and hoisted a recliner chair onto the upstairs landing.

"Take five, Chaz," Hank scanned the hall and the entryway below. "Not bad, Jewell," he called down. "You'll be able to turn around without runnin' into yourself in this place." He chuckled. "And I'll be able to turn around at home without runnin' into you."

Jewell nodded. "Neither of us will miss those tender moments, Hank." She climbed the stairs with an armful of clothing and eased past the recliner.

"Put it in this corner, facing the TV—so I can watch my shows from the bed or the chair." Jewell grinned as Hank and Chaz eased the recliner through the doorway of the mansion's master bedroom.

When the chair was in place, Hank dropped into it and stretched his legs. "Yeah, this'll work."

"Cool room. Check out this window bench. You scored!" Chaz knelt on the window seat and pulled back the curtain. "Great view of the street."

"It's the nicest room in the house." Marco sounded proud, like he was personally responsible for the view. "Nobody's used this room for years, not my grandmother or even old man Stone—when he was alive." His face

16

reddened; the expansive expression faded. "I better check on Carolyn and Gram." He bolted from the room.

"How does that kid know my girlfriend's name?" Hank glared at Marco's disappearing figure.

"Can it, Hank. Are we almost done? I'm due at the gym in ten minutes." Chaz frowned.

After two more trips, the U-Haul truck was empty and Jewell's belongings formed a disorganized jumble in her room.

"Ten-four, Jewell," Hank rumbled. "The rest is on you. Have fun."

"Oh, I will." She sounded tired. "Thanks for the help, Chaz. And you, too, Hank. Let's get the truck back."

Jewell, Hank and Chaz trooped downstairs. At the sound of tense voices in the kitchen, Hank pushed through the swinging door and stopped short. Jewell and Chaz bumped him from behind.

"Oof! What the hell?" Hank snorted.

Looking out from beneath Hank's arm, Jewell saw Carolyn and Doris snarling at one another over a cardboard box. Marco leaned nervously against the sink, juggling apples.

"These things are so chipped—and there's no two alike. I don't have room in my cupboard for this, this STUFF!" Doris sounded whiny.

"Look at it this way." Carolyn's voice dripped sarcasm. "If she doesn't use her own things, she'll be using, AND CHIPPING, yours."

"Time out, you two," Jewell snapped.

"Oh, there you are. Your daughter is just impossible! And, about these kitchen things…"

Jewell sighed. "I'll deal with all this later. How about you empty a shelf for my stuff while we're returning the U-Haul? I'll unpack the box when I come back."

Doris got awkwardly to her feet; when Marco attempted to help Carolyn up he got a cold stare from Hank.

"Okay, Mom, I'm ready to go." Carolyn's gaze slid past Doris to Jewell. "You two will be quite the couple."

* * *

That night Jewell stepped into the shower at 811 Radish Street and moaned with pleasure. She turned slowly, letting the cascade of steamy water caress her aching shoulders. Then, remembering Doris's request to conserve water—Every drop represents a penny, and those pennies add up—she shut off the shower tap.

A few minutes later, wrapped in a towel in front of the sink's ancient mirror, she studied her rosy-cheeked reflection. "Not bad, considering." She crossed the hall, slipped into sleep shorts and a tee, and climbed into bed. *Finally, my own, beautiful place.*

An hour later, startled out of a deep sleep by a piercing shaft of light across her face, Jewell sat up. "What...?" She looked all around the dark room, seeing nothing but the shapes of the furniture and the drapes' black rectangle.

I could've sworn someone shined a flashlight in my face. Must've been dreaming.

Pushing back against the pillow, she lay stiff and watchful under the covers. Night sounds—the hoot of an owl and the creaking of the old house's walls, sent a shiver up her spine. When Carolyn's words about a long-ago murder came floating back, Jewell switched on the bedside lamp and climbed from the bed. Tiptoeing to the window, she pulled back the curtains. Expecting to see a streetlight aimed at her window, she saw only dark, silent houses beneath the night sky.

Jewell returned to her bed and crawled deep beneath the covers, keeping one tiny spot open for breathing. She dredged in her memory for a childhood prayer, found it, and whispered it over and over until sleep finally came.

The next morning the heavenly aroma of brewing coffee woke Jewell. Her bedside clock read 6:45 a.m. She was due at the Ploughers at 7:30.

My landlady's an early riser.

She hopped from bed and hurried across the hall, calling, "Good morning, Doris," as she went. Fifteen minutes later, dressed and ready to leave, she ran down the stairs to the kitchen.

"Good morning." Doris turned from watching the news. "I thought you'd be gone by now. I hope you slept well?"

Jewell frowned, remembering the mysterious light. "So-so. Gotta get used to the new place—different sounds, different smells, you know…say, I hope you didn't think I'd be eating breakfast here. I eat at work."

"I didn't. I'll see you on Friday?"

"Yes. I'll be coming and going during the week, getting settled in, but I won't sleep here again until Friday night."

"Well then, have a good week." Doris turned her attention to the news.

Jewell felt dismissed. She left the kitchen, her happy mood deflated, and trudged down the sidewalk to her car.

Chapter Three

"How was the weekend in Horror House?" Carolyn's tone was teasing.

"I'm in no mood for your remarks, young lady." Jewell held the phone at an angle so she could keep an eye on Mr. Plougher clumsily buttering his wife's toast.

"What's up, Mom? Has something happened? Oh, my God!"

"Calm down. I didn't sleep well, that's all; I'm not used to the place. I'd appreciate you not calling it Horror House."

"Sorry. I gotta say, it's quiet here without you. Hank snored through Sports Center and I had no one to talk to."

"You'll get used to it." Jewell paused. "I'm just across town, you know. You can drop by whenever you miss me. In fact, how about coming over Friday night? We can make spaghetti together in that big kitchen."

"Are you kidding? I don't see myself stirring a pot of pasta in that woman's—I mean your—kitchen any time soon. Oh, gotta go. My phone's dying. I'll call you tonight."

"Okay, but I plan to live there for a long time. It'll break my heart if you never come to see me." Jewell let out a tired sigh. She was talking to dead air.

* * *

Later that week, at the grocery store, Mr. Plougher pointed his cane toward the produce aisle. "Say, isn't that the kid we met at your new place?"

Jewell peered past veggies to the fruit section, where Doris Stone's grandson stood talking to an attractive blonde. When the woman turned to take something off a shelf, she saw the woman's face. It was Carolyn.

"You're right. And that's my daughter. What are they doing together? They barely know each other." Jewell frowned.

"I'll find out," Mr. Plougher chortled. He grabbed his wife's walker and pulled her toward Marco and Carolyn. "Hey, you two! Wait for us!"

Marco's head snapped up; oranges slipped from his hands and rolled across the floor. "Shit!"

"Whoa, Marco!" Carolyn squealed.

As she steered the Ploughers clear of the spill, Jewell giggled. "This is a surprise, Carolyn. I didn't know you two were shopping buddies."

"Hardly, Mom. We just happened to be here at the same time." Carolyn smiled encouragingly at Marco.

"Yeah. Now that you and Gram are roomies, seeing Carolyn here is like bumping into family." Marco flashed a brilliant smile.

Mrs. Plougher spoke up. "You make a lovely couple."

"Eve, honey, he's just a kid. He's not old enough for a hottie like her." Mr. Plougher jerked his chin toward Carolyn.

As Marco and Carolyn blushed, Jewell said, "Okay, I think that's enough chit-chat. We need to finish our shopping. See you two later. Separately."

When the shopping was done and they were back in the Civic, Jewell looked in the rearview mirror at the Ploughers. "Do you mind if I swing by and drop my stuff off at the new place? I'll just be a minute."

Mr. and Mrs. Plougher exchanged glances. "We don't mind," he said. "But park in the shade. Old people, like dogs, shouldn't be left alone in cars."

"Sounds good." Jewell grinned.

From two blocks away it was obvious something was going on at 811 Radish. A green panel truck was parked at the curb, a wooden crate lay on the lawn, and two men were hauling a mattress out of the truck.

Jewell parked a few doors down and turned to the Ploughers: "My landlady said she was bringing in more tenants, but so soon? I haven't even spent my first weekend here."

"My goodness," Eve Plougher spoke up in her chirpy voice, "What will the neighbors think?"

Doris Stone's austere figure appeared in the doorway. She waved to Jewell and walked quickly to the car. "You can't come in right now. There's too much going on."

From the back seat, in a thin, wavery voice, Eve Plougher said, "Do I know you?"

"I don't think so." Doris looked in through the car window.

"Do you, Mrs. Plougher?" Jewell turned to the old woman. "This is Mrs. Stone. She owns the house. See that room up there, on the left side? That's mine. It has a window seat. Nice, hmm?"

"Yes, dear. Very nice." Mrs. Plougher fixed a sharp gaze on Doris. "You aren't Mrs. Stone. I knew her. Lovely woman. She's dead. Someone came in there and murdered the poor thing while her husband was out philandering with a hussy." She gave Mr. Plougher a stern look. "That's why I keep such close tabs on you, Nicholas. Men are such tomcats!"

Doris's eyebrows traveled so far up, they almost disappeared in her hennaed hairline. She gasped.

Jewell grabbed her grocery bag, jamming it through the open car window at Doris. "Here. Put these in the kitchen for me, would you? Sorry about the comments. You're probably used to small-town gossip, though. Anyone who marries into an old family is bound to be talked about."

The Civic pulled away from the curb, made a U-turn and roared away with the white-haired couple giggling in the back seat.

At the Ploughers' home that evening, Jewell sat down for a chat with Mrs. Plougher. "Eve, honey, do you really remember the first Mrs. Stone, like you said today? I heard stories about a death in that neighborhood a few years ago. Was it Mrs. Stone who died? In that house?"

Eve looked at Jewell, her faded, cornflower-blue eyes sparkling. "What's that, dear? Of course I remember Maris Stone. She was at Miss Barton's Finishing School with my daughter. They tied for first place in the final exams. Oh, they had so much fun. Those girls loved to laugh. They pulled some very funny pranks on the teachers. And that boy she married—tall and skinny and with the deepest voice I ever did hear. Rudolph Stone, his name was." Eve turned away, gazing out the window. "The Stone family had the worst luck. Just one tragedy after another. And now they don't even have their home. Life is so sad, sometimes."

* * *

Later that evening Jewell found an opportunity to ask Mr. Plougher about his younger days in Miwok. "Did you know the original Stone family? Bob's grandparents?"

Mr. Plougher's forehead wrinkled. He shook his head. "Nope. Never met Stone, Senior. I came here and opened my shoe store after WWII; if memory serves, the oldest boy took care of his dad in the family home, then stayed there after Stone, Senior passed. No idea where everyone else was." He yawned. "Been a busy day. I'll be turnin' in now." He stepped into the bedroom and closed the door.

Jewell looked over the notes left by Mrs. Plougher's nurse, set out the meds for the next morning, and then settled on the couch. As she flipped through channels, a thought occurred.

I didn't get a chance to ask about the new person at Doris's. Will I have to share the bathroom? I'll go by tomorrow and lock my door.

When the television guide highlighted *The Ghost Whisperer.* Jewell shuddered.

Damn Carolyn and her sixth sense. Now I have to find out the truth about the first Mrs. Stone.

The next morning Jewell climbed out of bed in the Ploughers' guest room and picked up her phone, keying in Doris Stone's number. Doris wasn't answering so Jewell left a message. "Hi, this is Jewell, your new tenant. I didn't know you were moving new people in quite so soon. I'm not sure I locked my bedroom door. Would you check? I can't get away from work today, or I'd do it myself."

I should've asked her to call me back. I'll have to find time today to get over there.

After assisting the Ploughers with their morning routine—meds, toilet, dressing, breakfast, toilet, and, finally settling in their recliners to enjoy the morning newspaper—Jewell took ten minutes for a computer search of the history of Miwok, California. She found a Prominent Families subcategory, typed in 'Stone family,' and a picture of the 811 Radish Street mansion immediately appeared.

Bingo!

"Oh, Jewell, I spilled my water. It's all over my lap!" Mrs. Plougher sounded panicky.

"I'm coming!" Jewell pushed 'print' and ran to help.

It was afternoon before she had a minute to look at the print-out, three pages of pictures interspersed with small-print text. She stared at sepia-toned photos of men who were mustachioed versions of Bob and his uncle, standing stiffly beside solemn-faced women seated on hard-backed chairs. There was an earlier, ragged photo of a farming family lined up before a cabin and, at the bottom of the second page, a picture of the Radish Street mansion.

The third page, titled Current Events, contained a news clipping with a picture of a lovely, smiling woman. "Tragic Death of Prominent Miwok Matron," headed a paragraph which began, "An apparent home invasion early Tuesday morning took the life of Maris Stone, wife of Rudolph Stone and one of Miwok's most beloved benefactors."

Oh, my God—Carolyn's ESP was right!

Jewell read on: "According to Deputy Sheriff Sorenson, the robbery and murder were unnoticed until dawn when Miwok Disposal workers collecting trash spotted the woman's body in an upstairs window. Mr. Rudolph Stone told reporters he was asleep at the other end of the house and heard nothing. The incident is under investigation by the Sheriff's Department."

Jewell put the page down, stunned. She reread the article. It told in lurid detail how the woman's body was hung in a bay window, seemingly on display to anyone on the street. With a shudder, Jewell's thoughts went to Doris.

It was her husband, that man Rudolph, who slept through his first wife's murder. And in that very house. Crap! And Doris married the guy. She's either a saint or a heartless bitch.

Jewell tucked the printouts in her bag, shut down the computer, and went to check on the Ploughers. "Mr. P., would it be okay if I make a quick run across town while the cleaning lady's still here?"

Mr. Plougher looked up from the stamp collection laid out on the dining room table. "Sure, Jewell. Take your time." He turned back to his stamps.

* * *

As the Civic motored through Miwok's streets Jewell put in a call to Carolyn. It went to voicemail.

"Hi, it's me. Call me tonight, please." Jewell clicked the phone off and glanced out at the dignified, proper-looking homes in the Radish Street neighborhood.

The outsides of these charmers don't give a clue to the lives of the people inside—well, maybe at night, when they're full of shadows. She shivered.

At 811 Radish Jewell pulled into the driveway, then drove around to the back of the house. The garage—originally a barn—still had a wooden, sliding door hanging from a metal track. The door was open. Doris's dark blue Buick was parked inside, next to another vehicle.

She's home. Good. So is the new tenant, maybe.

Jewell sprinted up the back steps and stopped on the threshold. Doris was at the kitchen table, studying some legal-looking paperwork.

"Hi, Doris. Did you get my message this morning?"

"Yes, of course." Doris looked up, her hands quickly covering the papers. "Did you make a trip over here just for that? The new tenant doesn't have access to the main house. He's in the basement apartment." She quickly added, "He's here now, getting settled."

"I need to talk to you about something else, too." Jewell squared her shoulders; this wouldn't be easy. "Why didn't you tell me, going in, that someone died here? I think it's against the law to withhold information like that."

The color faded from Doris's face. She looked away, then met Jewell's stare.

25

"Do you mean my husband, Rudolph? He died at the hospital. I had no idea you were so fussy."

"No, I don't mean Rudolph. I mean his first wife, the one who was murdered." Jewell's muscles tensed as anger swept over her. "For God's sake, I have to sleep in that room!"

"That happened so long ago," Doris sniffed, "I'd forgotten all about it." Her mouth went slowly from a straight, tight line to the semblance of a smile. "Let's not get upset. I don't want a little thing like that to hurt our new friendship."

Jewell shuffled her feet, feeling unaccountably guilty. "Well, I wish you would've told me. Does this house have any other ugly secrets? It's not exactly fun, finding things out third hand."

"I apologize. There are certainly no other secrets. Shall we hug and put this to rest?" Doris reached clumsily toward Jewell.

Instinctively Jewell edged away from the outstretched arms. "That's okay. I'll run upstairs and check my door. I have to get back to work."

Doris looked relieved, as if the invitation to hug had not been her idea. "By the way, the new tenant's name is Perez. You won't see much of him."

Perez? Sounds familiar.

* * *

Jewell unlocked her bedroom door and stepped inside. She'd left the drapes open and sunlight washed over the room, creating a bright, expansive feeling. Beyond the window's beveled glass, a huge, flowering Magnolia tree spread its' branches. The blossoms' heavy fragrance embraced the room.

So beautiful, Jewell breathed. *Maybe I **am** too sensitive.*

Her cell phone buzzed. The screen read, 'Carolyn.'

"Hi! I only have a minute, Mom. Hank and I can come over for spaghetti Friday night. Maybe Doris and Marco can join us? It could be like a housewarming for you. What do you think?"

"Uh, Sure. I'll let Doris know. Hey, I found out some stuff about the mansion—can't talk right now. I'll fill you in after dinner tonight."

Jewell stepped into the hall, closed and carefully locked her room, and hurried downstairs and out to her car.

Chapter Four

"Thanks for giving me the run of the kitchen tonight. I'm excited about cooking—this spaghetti recipe comes from my mom. She wasn't Italian, but she worked at a North Beach restaurant in San Francisco for years." While Jewell stirred, chatting happily, Doris watched from the doorway.

"It does smell heavenly. Let's eat in the dining room, though. I never serve guests in the kitchen—that would make the dining room superfluous." Doris gave a small, involuntary sniff.

"No. For me and my family, the kitchen is best. It's my domain." Jewell looked over at Doris. "For tonight, you and your grandson are part of my family. He's coming, isn't he?"

"Oh, yes. He'd never turn down a free meal."

Ding, dong!

"Maybe that's him." Doris hurried to the front door.

Minutes later Carolyn and Hank bustled into the kitchen. "Something smells great, Jewell." Hank leaned in to catch a whiff of spaghetti sauce and give Jewell a scratchy kiss.

Jewell shrugged, feeling a slow smile brighten her face. "Miss my cooking, did you?"

Carolyn gave her mother a half-hug. "Oh, yeah. You know I'm severely limited in the kitchen."

The back kitchen door opened and Marco breezed in, a long narrow paper bag under his arm. "The French bread's here—the party can start! Let me know when to slice this bad boy." He winked at Carolyn, who responded by slipping a hand under Hank's arm.

"You remember my boyfriend Hank, Marco? From when mom moved in?"

Hank looked over his shoulder at Marco. "I'll slice the bread, kid." He turned to the cutting board and swung the knife down, hard.

From the dining room doorway, Doris raised an eyebrow. "Such intensity! That bread requires a light touch, young man." She picked up the jug of red wine Jewell had set out and studied the label. "Pit Bull Winery? Never heard of it. Oh; a screw-top." She sighed. "Well, beggars can't be choosers."

Jewell looked up from pouring rich, meaty sauce over mounds of stringy yellow pasta. "Let's all sit down. Get the salad out of the refrigerator, would you, Carolyn?"

"Sure, mom." Carolyn peeled herself away from Hank's muscular form. "Save me the seat next to you, babycakes."

Marco's head turned. He murmured, "Babycakes?"

A few minutes later Jewell set the spaghetti platter on the kitchen table and untied her apron. "Let's eat!"

With everyone seated, Jewell raised her glass. "Here's to the food, the company, and my new home."

And then it happened.

Carolyn took one sip and began coughing. Suddenly she was spitting dark red liquid, unable to breathe. Her face flushed; her eyes widened in mute fear.

"Holy shit!" Hank jumped from his chair, pulled her to her feet, and raised her arms.

She managed a breath, still coughing, and leaned shakily against Hank. Her eyes filled with tears.

"My God, honey, did you swallow wrong?" Jewell's voice trembled.

Carolyn shook her head. "No. My throat closed up like I was being choked."

Marco, looking shaken, muttered, "Not exactly a first in this house." He stared at his grandmother—Doris was frowning at the ruined tablecloth. "I'm sure that'll wash out, Gram."

Jewell, looking at the wine spatters on the cloth, winced. "Looks like we'll have to eat in the dining room after all, Doris."

Hiding a smile, Doris began gathering plates.

"You got your wish, thanks to Carolyn." Jewell hoisted the spaghetti platter and marched from the kitchen.

When everyone was seated again—in the dining room—Jewell raised her wine glass. "Let's not risk another toast. Dig in, everyone."

For a few minutes, the room was quiet, the soft clank of forks on porcelain the only sound. Jewell looked across the table at Carolyn, picking at her food; Hank, shoveling spaghetti into his mouth while watching Carolyn; and Marco, face over plate with the occasional distressed glance at Carolyn.

"Let's start over, shall we?" Jewell rapped the table with her knuckles. "This is our first meal together; let's introduce ourselves. To make it fun, everyone tell one secret wish. I'll go first." She paused. "I'm Jewell McDunn. I just moved in here and I love to cook. Also, I take care of old folks for a living, but my secret wish is to be a pilot and fly over the Australian Outback."

Carolyn's head lifted. "Okay, Mom, if we HAVE to." She dabbed at her eyes with a napkin and smiled at her mother. "I'm Carolyn Jones. I'm a florist's assistant, but my secret wish is to someday have my own shop."

"I wanna go next," Hank grinned. "I'm Hank Halverson. I—"

Ding Dong!

The doorbell rang. Before anyone could leave the table, the front door opened and a man wearing jeans and a windbreaker stepped inside. "Got room for one more? I'm starving!"

Jewell, Carolyn, and Hank stared at this stranger. He appeared quite at home in the dining room at 811 Radish Street.

"Who—?" Jewell began. Before she could finish, Doris jumped from her chair and gave the newcomer a hug.

"Of course, there's room! I'm so glad you made it!" She turned to the table, her face beaming. "Everyone, Benny Perez is the new tenant in the basement apartment." She waved a hand toward Jewell. "Benny, this my upstairs boarder, Jewell McDunn. That's her daughter," she pointed to Carolyn, "and their friend."

Jewell and Carolyn muttered welcomes and Hank pouted, obviously not thrilled with being dismissed as an anonymous friend. Doris patted the seat of the chair next to hers, cooing, "Sit here, Benny."

Suddenly, Marco pushed away from the table. "I'm outa here." He rushed from the room, slamming the front door as he left. The entire party stared, forks in mid-air.

"That kid needs to learn some manners," Perez said into the silence. He reached for the spaghetti platter, smiling at Doris. "Did you make this? It looks fantastic."

Doris shook her head. "Young people can be so rude." Then, "No, Jewell was our chef tonight." She smirked at Benny. "You know cooking isn't one of my talents."

Jewell saw Carolyn fumbling with something in her lap, then heard the chirp of a cell phone in the kitchen.

"Excuse me. I'd better see who that is." She stood, careful not to look at her daughter as she hurried from the room.

When she located her phone, the screen showed a text from Carolyn: *Who's this guy? Long-lost lover? EEWW! We're leaving in 10.*

Jewell put the phone away and returned to the dinner table, where Hank and Carolyn had their heads together, talking, and Doris watched Perez eat.

"Pass me that bread, dude." Perez glanced at Hank.

Hank ignored him and looked at Jewell. "If there's dessert, serve it now. We're gonna take off. Carolyn's not feeling good."

Doris turned a dour face to Hank and Carolyn. "Surely you're not leaving simply because she swallowed wrong? You'll ruin your mother's party."

"There is dessert, Hank. I'll drop some by to you tomorrow." Jewell swiveled her glance to Doris. "She didn't just swallow wrong. She almost choked to death." In a voice shaking with anger, she added, "My party? How is it my party when you invite people I don't even know and your grandson walks out mad?" She turned to Perez. "I gather you and Doris are old friends?"

Perez reluctantly put down his fork. "You could say that." He darted a quick glance at Doris. "This fine-looking broad is my mother."

Jewell, Carolyn, and Hank all stared, first at Perez and then at Doris. Carolyn, who had put a water glass to her lips, returned it to the table with a thunk. Hank, slouching in his chair, sat up straight. Jewell shook her head in disbelief.

"He's been living out of town," Doris said quickly. "He needed a place to stay when he got back. It's just good fortune I have a basement apartment." She looked fondly at Perez. "I hoped he'd come this evening, but I wasn't sure. What difference does it make, Jewell? There's more than enough food."

Jewell studied Doris for a moment, then turned to Perez. "So, Benny, are you Marco's uncle? He wasn't thrilled to see you."

"No, not his uncle," Doris put in. "Benny is Marco's father. Our family has had, uh, problems in the past few years. Some foolish people took sides." She looked smugly at Jewell. "You must have experienced something similar with all your marriages and divorces." She turned to Carolyn. "I bet you could tell a few stories."

"I beg your pardon?" Jewell felt like she'd been slapped. "I'll thank you not to bring my marital history into this conversation!"

Carolyn pushed back her chair and stood. "That's about all I can take, Mom. The food was wonderful. Sorry about the choking thing. Good night, one and all."

Hank jumped to his feet. "Yeah, Jewell. Your cooking rocked." He grabbed Carolyn's arm as she moved toward the door. "Take it slow, babe."

Jewell followed Hank and Carolyn to the porch. "I'll bring the bread pudding by tomorrow." She gave Carolyn a hug, then stretched to plant a kiss on Hank's cheek. With her mouth close to his ear she whispered, "Thanks for coming to the party."

"Are you sure you want to stay here, Mom? I don't trust those two AT ALL." Carolyn's face was pale.

"This is my home now. I'll deal with them." Jewell looked exhausted, stressed from all the cooking and then the ruined dinner party. "It's just going to take some fine-tuning—I have to get to know Doris and adjust to her personality. Feel better, honey."

Doris and Perez stood at the living room window, talking quietly, as Jewell stepped back inside. They didn't acknowledge her presence, so she ignored them and began clearing the table. After her second trip to the kitchen with an armload of dirty dishes, they'd vanished.

Great. I do all the cooking and she doesn't even help with the clean-up. This better not be the new norm.

Later, when the kitchen was clean and she was ready to head up to her room, Jewell left a note stuck prominently on the kitchen door: **The bread pudding is off limits!!!**

Climbing into her smooth, cool sheets a bit later, Jewell thought about her landlady and Benny Perez. *Are they mother and son? Maybe, if she was a teenager when she had him. She's not Hispanic, but they have the same blue eyes.*

Her next thought was, *I didn't get a chance to tell Carolyn what I found out about this place.*

She climbed from the bed, checked to be sure her door was locked and dropped to her knees in prayer.

* * *

During the night, even though the windows were closed, the curtains moved as if in a slight breeze. The hardwood floors creaked first in one spot, then another. Jewell, exhausted, slept unaware of any intrusion.

A shadow lingered on the window seat. It took the form of a woman in a long cotton nightgown, long black hair flowing around her shoulders and bare feet showing below the gown's hem. An angry red bruise circled her neck, almost like a choker necklace.

She moved away from the window seat and drifted over to the bed. Her wispy form leaned over and inhaled Jewell's breath.

Jewell twitched, then sat up in bed. "Help! Help me!" she mumbled. The sound woke her and she stared into the darkness, panicked. Her fingers fumbled for the bedside lamp switch. When it clicked on, she saw only the quiet room she'd fallen asleep in hours earlier. She took a calming breath.

Nightmare. That's all it was. Tomorrow, I'm going to the Animal Shelter and getting a cat—or a dog—to keep me company at night.

Leaving the light on, she lay back against the pillow. Within a few minutes, sleep claimed her. Across the room a floorboard creaked, then all was quiet.

Chapter Five

When a ray of sunlight angled through a gap in the curtains and touched Jewell's face. one eye squinted open. She twisted to sit up and winced. *Yikes! Why am I so sore? Oh, yeah. That nightmare. And last night's dinner party from Hell.* She thought of Doris and her shoulders tensed. *That interaction with her son—so strange. And when Carolyn choked, Doris acted like it was a bid for attention. The woman is a piece of work.*

After a quick shower, Jewell pulled on her sweats and crept silently down the wide staircase. At the front door, remembering the bread pudding, she turned and tiptoed into the kitchen. Outside a few minutes later, she took a deep breath of the early morning coolness. *Fresh air and freedom—great combination.*

She jogged to her car and was soon queued up in the G.I.s Joe coffee line. When Beth Anne appeared at the car window, Jewell couldn't help smiling; this open, friendly face was so welcome. "You are a sight for sore eyes, girl."

Beth Anne laughed. "If you have time, park across the way. I'll take a break and join you at the picnic table."

"Perfect." The tension in Jewell's shoulders eased a little.

When Beth Anne slid onto the bench a few minutes later, Jewell wiped croissant crumbs from her lips and raised her cardboard cup in a toast.

Beth Anne took a sip of coffee. "You have a date last night? You're lookin' a little weary."

"First night in the new place. I made spaghetti for the kids and Doris."

"Really? On your first night? Sounds like you're off to a good start."

Jewell frowned. "Not exactly."

"Don't tell me," Beth Anne groaned. "Was Doris a bitch? She was, wasn't she? I told Bob we shouldn't have sent you there!"

"She wasn't that bad." Jewell shook her head. "Just kind of ... sneaky. I expected her to be more like Bob: upfront about everything. With his aunt, you never know what's really going on."

Beth Anne nodded and bit into a piece of scone. "They're not actually related. She married Uncle Rudolph right after Aunt Maris died."

"Aunt Maris—she's the one who was murdered?"

"Yeah." Beth Anne looked embarrassed. "You know about that?"

Jewell shrugged.

"The family had a fit when Uncle Rudolph and Doris got married—one week, to the day, after Maris's death. After that, he never spoke to us again. We didn't even know he'd died until the mortician called."

"Wow. That's harsh." Jewell looked around the parking lot, not really seeing the cracked pavement, the dusty oleander bushes, or the elm trees. "Things are okay now, though, right? I mean, Bob's uncle talks to Doris—he recommended me for the room." Jewell crumpled the croissant paper. "I hope you won't quit talking to me 'cuz I live there now."

Beth Anne giggled. "No, silly. That bad juju was ages ago. Doris even loaned us money to start our business."

"Good." Jewell nodded. "Cuz I really like the house, even if it is kind of spooky. My fear of the dark is back, from when I was a kid. Maybe I'll get a dog."

"Good idea." Beth Anne glanced at her watch. "A word of advice—even though the feud's on the back burner, there's still some bad feeling. Try to stay neutral. "

Jewell raised an eyebrow. "Like Switzerland?"

Beth Anne didn't smile. In fact, her tone was serious when she said, "Doris ran through most of Uncle Rudolph's fortune before he died, then tried to sell 811 Radish the minute he was gone. We don't feel sorry for her; her money problems are her own doing."

"I feel sorry for the house. It's been through a lot." Jewell sighed.

"Yup." Beth Anne nodded. "Would you believe that woman invited realtors to Uncle Rudolph's funeral? Thank God for Stone, Senior's will. She can live in the house, but she can't sell it. Renting out rooms is her only option."

"Speaking of which," Jewell mused, "Another tenant showed up last night. Guy named Benny Perez. He's in the basement apartment. Doris says he's her son. You know him?"

"Benny's back?" Beth Anne, startled, got to her feet. "Bob needs to hear about this."

Jewell crumpled her empty cup and watched Beth Anne hurry back to the coffee truck. *I guess that's a yes. They know him.*

Fortified by coffee, Jewell drove through Miwok's quiet streets to Carolyn and Hank's apartment. At their front door, knuckles poised to knock, she realized how early it was. *They might be asleep. Or, worse, they might be awake and enjoying being in bed together without me in the next room. Maybe I should call them, give them a heads-up I'm here.*

To Hank's sleepy, "H'lo," she said, "You want some bread pudding with your coffee?"

"Sure." As he disconnected Jewell heard him yell, "Babe! Your mom's here!"

Five minutes later Hank opened the front door, bare-chested and buttoning his jeans. "Bread pudding for breakfast—I think I love you, Jewell!"

"Hi, Mom," Carolyn called from the bedroom. "Good news: I lived through the night."

Hank took the pudding and went into the kitchen, calling, "Should I start the coffee, Carolyn?"

"Not for me." Jewell smiled at Hank's attempt at manners. "I just came from G.I.'s Joe." *I should have moved out a long time ago. I sure hope my new place works out.* "How's your throat, Carolyn?"

"Fine—just a little sore." Carolyn came into the living room, tying a silky robe around herself. She looked sleepy, but healthy; her cheeks were becomingly flushed. "I have no idea what caused that choking. It wasn't the wine; no one ever choked on a sip of Pit Bull. Funny thing, though. See this red mark?" She pushed back her hair and ran a finger lightly along a narrow, red stripe circling her neck.

Hank glanced at it and rubbed his stubbled chin. "That's not whisker burn, is it? Wouldn't be the first time." He grinned.

Carolyn giggled. "Your chin was nowhere near my neck last night." She glanced at her mother. "This came up right after I choked. It's really sore."

Jewell leaned across the table and touched the red mark with her fingertips. "An allergic reaction?"

Carolyn shook her head.

Hank scraped the bottom of his pudding dish. "How'd last night go?"

"Could have been better. I didn't get much sleep. I kept thinking about that mansion's sad history."

Hank nodded and turned to Carolyn. "I'm thinking you should stay away from that place, at least for now." He flashed Jewell an apologetic smile.

Carolyn frowned but stayed quiet.

"I hate to say it," Jewell whispered, "but he's right. The Stone mansion has been through a lot, and you know how sensitive you are." She turned to Hank. "I'm thinking of getting a dog or a cat—I'm not as sensitive as Carolyn, but that place is spooky."

"A dog?" Hank pushed out his chair and stood. "A guy where I work has one needs a home. She's the last of their dog's litter. She's about six months old, past the worst of the puppy stage. Want me to give him a call?"

"Okay. Sure." Jewell tingled with excitement. She jumped to her feet. "I have to check with the Ploughers; I'll call you after lunch." To herself she whispered, "My own dog!"

As the door closed behind her Jewell heard Hank's quiet, "Whatever it takes to make you happy in your new digs, Jewell."

* * *

Doris: I'm getting a dog. A small one.

I'll keep it in my room. It will be with me at work during the week.

/s/ Your tenant, Jewell.

"That ought to do it." Jewell propped the note against the salt shaker on the kitchen counter and stood back to make sure it was prominently displayed.

I wouldn't put it past Doris to say she never got this.

In her pocket, Jewell's phone warbled—the screen read, 'Hank.'

"Hi. You got dog-related news?"

"Better than that," Hank chuckled. "The cutest girl in town, not counting Carolyn, is trying to lick me to death. You want me to bring her over?"

"No!" Jewell blurted. "I mean, I'll come and get her, if it's okay. First, I'll swing by Petsmart. Do you know what she eats? What about shots?"

Hank switched from laughter to a soothing tone. "Chill, Jewell. Everything's under control. Ray gave me a bag of dog food. I have the papers saying she's had shots, been wormed, the whole deal. There's even a squeaky toy and an old blanket—you may want to burn the blanket. Come on over and we'll introduce you to Lois Lane."

Jewell sighed. "In for a pound, I guess. I talked to the Ploughers—they love the idea of a dog. Haven't seen my landlady, but I left a note on her table. So, all right. Lois Lane, huh? Superman's girlfriend. Perfect. I'll be right over."

After a quick detour to Petsmart for a hundred dollars' worth of supplies, Jewell hurried across town to meet her new dog. Traffic was dense for a Saturday afternoon; she stifled the impulse to flip off clueless drivers.

What if the dog doesn't like me? Does it make sense to get an animal just for a decent night's sleep? What if she can't sleep in that room, either? Shit! Mustn't think about that. When did I last have a dog? I had Fluffy for ten years. But Fluffy was a cat. She liked me. At least I think she did. You never know with cats. My friend, Arna has Rolly. He's a dog. He likes me. I think.

She slapped her palm against the steering wheel. "Enough, already," she muttered. "We'll like each other, and we'll be fine in the room. End of subject." As the car rolled through a yellow light she muttered, "This kind of thing is why people drink." With a nervous smile, she parked the car outside Carolyn's apartment.

"Ruff, Ruff, Ruff!"

Jewell swung out of the car and knelt, holding out her hands to the brown, black, and white ball of fur dragging Hank along the sidewalk.

"Heel, Lois Lane! Heel!" The half-grown puppy turned, looked up at Hank, and then plunged into Jewell's lap. The leash brought Hank forward and he came up inches short of landing atop Jewell and the excited dog.

"Whoa! Hello, girl." Jewell wrapped her arms around the dog's neck, letting Lois Lane lick her cheek. Then she gently pushed away and got to her feet. "Looks like she doesn't know, 'Heel.'"

Hank chuckled. "Yeah, but you can't say she ain't friendly!" He handed Jewell the leash. "Come on upstairs. I'll get her gear and Ray's phone number—in case you have any questions."

* * *

"No one's home, puppy. That's good. We can get you settled before you meet the dragon lady."

Jewell parked her car next to 811 Radish's garage/barn and got a firm grip on the leash. When she opened the car door, Lois Lane scrambled out and headed for the shrubbery.

"Good idea. Put down your scent and do your business, too."

They went inside and upstairs. Lois Lane hesitated at the threshold of Jewell's room, sitting back on her haunches with an anxious look. She clearly did not want to go in there.

Jewell half-dragged, half-carried the puppy in and closed the door, then knelt and looked into Lois Lane's eyes. "This is home, girl. It may take a little getting used to."

Lois Lane put her paws over her ears.

"Oh, my God, you are so funny! What am I going to do with you?"

Lois Lane sniffed at the food-and-water station Jewell had set up in the corner, then turned away. She made a slow circle of the room's perimeter, nose to the baseboards. At the window seat she growled, lowering her body and whining submissively. When Jewell stepped across the room, Lois Lane immediately got behind her new mistress's legs.

What in the world? She acts like she's scared.

Jewell knelt, scratching the dog's ears. "Tell you what: Let's go outside—maybe we'll take this room in small doses."

When they left the bedroom, Lois Lane shook herself violently and dashed for the stairs. Jewell grabbed the dog's collar and let herself be pulled forward. "Hold on, Supergirl. We're just going for a walk, not running away from home."

Lois Lane stopped at the top of the stairs, looking back anxiously.

Jewell sat on the top stair, one arm around her new friend. "I wish you could talk, girl. You picked up a scent back there, and it scared the crap out of you." She stroked the silky fur on Lois's back. "We're going to walk down the stairs, through the house, and out to the back yard. Got it? Walk. Not run, not go crazy." She snapped on the leash. "Let's go."

When they stepped out the back door, Jewell dropped the leash. Lois Lane immediately bounded to the center of the fenced yard, looked around, and dashed eagerly from one bush to the next. She bore little resemblance to the terrified pup of a few minutes earlier.

When it looked like Lois Lane had made at least a working acquaintance with every blade of grass in the yard, Jewell snapped her fingers. "Come!" Lois Lane skidded to a stop at Jewell's feet, pink tongue out in a smile. "Let's check out the side yard."

With the dog at her side, Jewell rounded a corner of the house and saw concrete steps leading down. *The basement. Wonder if Doris's son is there.*

Lois Lane stopped at the top step, standing rigid, tail straight out and one front leg pulled up.

"I'll be damned. She's part pointer!" Jewell reached out and gave the door a tentative knock. There was no response. A low growl came from Lois Lane's throat. "You picked up some scent, didn't you, girl? Jewell pulled the dog away and they continued their exploration.

* * *

At 9:30 that evening Jewell and Lois Lane sat in the living room, companionably sharing the recliner and watching the Nature Channel. On their second trip to the bedroom Lois Lane had avoided the window, but did not seem frightened. "I'm glad we got past that, girl. I hope you'll be okay sleeping up there tonight."

There was a scuffling sound in the kitchen, like the opening of the back door. Lois Lane sat up, ears cocked. "Stay," Jewell murmured, gripping the dog's collar firmly. "Is that you, Doris? I have a surprise."

Doris stepped into the living room, elegantly dressed in green taffeta. Her eyes widened. "That's a dog! You didn't say you had a dog."

Jewell sat up, her arm protectively around Lois Lane. "You got my note, right? The one I left on the kitchen table? It was gone when I came back, so you must have gotten it."

Doris nodded and took a step forward, wobbling a bit on green satin heels. *She's been drinking.*

"I just got her today." Jewell managed an ingratiating smile. "She'll be with me on my job all week. When we're here, I'll make sure she stays out of your way. You'll like her; she's very friendly. You're not afraid of dogs, are you?"

Doris giggled. "You kidding? Dogs are afraid of me...or somethin'...we'll talk tomorrow." She turned away, holding tight to the stair rail as she climbed the stairs.

Jewell sighed. "That could've been worse. Let's go out for your pee break, puppy, before we go upstairs."

*   *   *

Well past midnight Jewell opened her eyes, startled awake by a sound outside the window. She became conscious of a warm, firm body cuddled next to her. A glance at the new wicker dog basket showed it to be empty—Lois Lane was stretched out on the bed, breathing softly in her new mistress's ear.

Jewell relaxed. After a few minutes with no suspicious sounds, her eyelids drooped. She mumbled a prayer to the patron saint of dogs and went back to sleep.

Chapter Six

"**D**id you really think you could sneak that—that *mongrel* into the house behind my back?" Doris sputtered, clenching the handle of a teacup.

"There was no sneaking," Jewell protested. "You weren't here. I left you a note. Besides, my lease clearly states a pet is permitted as long as I keep it under control."

"But you didn't have that creature when you signed the lease. I won't stand for covert behavior." Doris glared at Lois Lane, who responded by putting her head behind Jewell's legs.

"I need to walk 'this creature' right now," Jewell snapped. "We can talk when I get back." She took a breath. "By the way, I don't appreciate being called covert. You're the queen of manipulation, far as I can see." She strode to the back door, Lois Lane in tow. "I mean, really, pretending Perez was just another tenant?"

The back door snapped shut on Doris's response. Jewell stopped at the bottom of the steps for a mood adjustment, determined not to let Doris ruin her morning. *When I get back, I'll be nicer but I won't back down. Lois Lane is here to stay.*

After squatting on the lawn, Lois Lane scampered to the gate and looked back at her mistress. "Looks like you're ready to investigate the world beyond 811 Radish."

By the time they'd circled the block twice, eagerly greeting two other dogs and circling around one haughty cat, Jewell was smiling again. "It's time to go back inside, pup. We can't be fighting with the landlady. I'll apologize for not letting her know ahead of time about you."

When they came inside, Doris was at the kitchen sink. "There's no need for us to argue. In the future, clear major changes with me ahead of time." She turned just enough to give Lois Lane the shadow of a smile. "It looks pleasant enough." With that, she pushed through the dining room door and disappeared.

"Interesting," Jewell muttered. She filled a bowl with water for Lois Lane and poured herself some coffee. "She said it before I could."

Jewell stayed at home most of the day. It was Sunday, and she wanted the dog to acclimate. The house was quiet; she saw, from the hall window overlooking the back driveway, that the only car parked there was her own.

Looks like I have the place to myself. She went back to her room, feeling lighthearted. *I think I'll tackle that closet. Time to wade in there and organize.* Throwing open the closet door, she studied the tightly packed hangers. *I could get rid of half this stuff and not miss it.*

Lois Lane lay on her belly, pushing her nose against a shoe. After a minute she began tunneling beneath a stack of boxes and disappeared under the wobbling cardboard.

At the sound of digging Jewell yelled, "Hey! Stop!" She reached into the pile and touched the dog's hindquarters. Lois Lane slowly backed out, giving Jewell a toothy grin. There was a bit of glistening gold between her canine teeth.

"Whatcha got there, girl?" Jewell put a hand under Lois Lane's chin. The dog hesitated, then dropped a ring into her mistress's palm. Jewell held it up to the sunlight.

"Definitely a wedding ring. Wonder how long it's been in there?" She peered at the band's inner side. Although the engraved initials were worn almost smooth, a central **S** was still visible.

Jewell's fingers felt suddenly hot: the ring began to glow. *What the Hell?* A creepy, scared feeling ran through Jewell. She backed out of the closet and put the circle of sparkling gold on the dresser. *I'm giving that to Bob or his uncle first chance I get.*

* * *

"Something smells good! Oh, grilled cheese! Would you mind making a couple more? Benny and I have been out on errands and we're famished." Doris breezed into the kitchen, smiling.

Jewell, at the table eating lunch, swallowed a bite. "It's my day off, Doris; I'm not cooking for anyone but myself. But, hey, help yourself—the griddle's still warm."

Doris's smile vanished. "Oh. Well, we'll just order in. Please clean up after yourself." She scanned the spotless kitchen and went back outside.

Jewell shook her head. *Do I look like free kitchen help?*

* * *

On Lois Lane's evening walk Jewell noticed a familiar figure across the street, leaning against a telephone pole. When she and the dog left the yard, the figure moved out of sight behind the pole.

That looked a little like Marco. Why would he be loitering on the street?

She turned away, enjoying the twilight view of living rooms in houses where the curtains were still open. "Let's cross the street, Lois Lane. We haven't walked down that way yet." She had one foot off the curb when the dog stepped in front of her, blocking her path. "What's up, girl?"

Lois Lane stood rigid, paw up and tail out stiff behind her. She was pointing again—this time at the telephone pole. Jewell squared her shoulders. "Okay. We'll check it out, just to satisfy your protective instinct."

Halfway across the street Jewell's phone chirped. She dug it out of her pocket, saw an unfamiliar number, and put the phone to her ear. Before she could speak, a voice she recognized as Marco's said, "Don't come over here. Walk around the block and I'll meet you halfway."

Jewell stared at the outline of Marco's shoulders behind the pole, then turned and led Lois Lane back to the curb. Her heart was pounding. She realized her fists were clenched.

What's with the cops 'n robbers bit?

Midway through a fast walk around the block, Lois Lane jolted to a stop, pushing hard against Jewell's legs and barking. "Woof, woof!"

"Now what? This is getting old!"

Marco stepped out from behind a parked car. "Didn't know you had a pooch. Make her back off, will you?"

Jewell put a hand on the dog's head. "He's okay." Lois Lane stopped barking and lowered her butt to the ground. "Good girl," Jewell whispered. She turned to Marco. "Why couldn't you talk to us on Radish Street? And how do you know my phone number?"

"I called Carolyn. She gave me her number when we were at the store. I thought you should know—for your, uh, safety's sake—that guy Benny Perez, the one renting Gram's basement? Not to be trusted. He's my father, and he's a real douche. When he's around, Gram doesn't think straight. She's blind to his bullshit." He stopped, wiping a sleeve against his forehead. "If I'd known he was comin' back here after prison, I wouldn't be here. I'm putting some distance between me and that creep as soon as I'm done with college."

Jewell whispered, "I knew he was Doris's son. And your father. He was in prison?" She hoped her face didn't reflect her shock.

Marco nodded. He looked tired and bitter.

"Sounds like bad blood between you two."

"Mom raised me by herself," Marco mumbled. "They weren't married—we hardly ever saw him. When we did, he beat the shit out of her. She died after he went to prison. That's when I hooked up with Gram."

Jewell wondered what to say. She put a tentative hand on the boy's arm. "Maybe he's changed. Rehabilitated, you know?"

Marco turned away. "Yeah, and pigs fly. Just be careful, okay? Benny and Gram bring out the worst in each other."

"That reminds me," Jewell said, glad to change the subject, "Lois Lane found an old wedding ring in my closet. There's an **S** engraved in it—I'm thinking it belongs to the Stones."

"Makes sense," Marco gave a curt nod. "From what I've heard, the room you're in is the one Mr. and Mrs. Stone shared. So, yeah, it's definitely theirs. If it's small, it didn't belong to Rudolph. He was a big guy. Big hands."

"So, the first Mrs. Stone?" Jewell mused. "What kind of person was she? The ring gives off heat—like it's radioactive." She flashed Marco a curious look.

"Don't know; never met her." Marco looked around. "I'd better get going." He walked away.

With a shake of the leash, Jewell followed Marco along the sidewalk. After a minute he turned back, saying, "What's it like, being up there where someone died? Spooky, I bet. When ol' Rudy's wife came up dead, my mom said it was suspicious." He scowled. "If Benny heard that he would've knocked her lights out."

Jewell's stomach clenched. She frowned up at Marco. "You need to stop talking. I'm trying not to be freaked out by the room—the whole house. You're not helping. That's the reason I got a dog, for heaven's sake!"

A defeated scowl crossed Marco's face. "Sorry. Just trying to help."

When they came back around the block to the Stone mansion, Marco walked away from them. "You're a nice lady. And your daughter is smokin' hot. But don't expect to see me while Benny Perez is around." Lois Lane looked after him, whining.

"You feel sorry for him, too, don't you?" Jewell reached down and patted the dog's head. "Poor kid."

Coming up the walk at 811 Radish this time, the place looked shabbier than before. Jewell paused at the top of the steps, fighting an urge to jump in the car and drive back to Carolyn and Hank's.

I paid my rent; I'm staying. I'll just stay out of Doris's way—-and her son's.

She opened the front door, put her head in, and looked around. No one was home. The foyer was dusky, quiet. She and Lois Lane took the stairs two at a time, flipping on the hall light as they raced by. At her bedroom, the door swung open with a touch of the knob.

I'm sure I locked it when I went out.

Her stomach lurched, again. She gripped the dog's leash and stepped inside. The room seemed undisturbed.

While Lois Lane lapped from her water dish, Jewell tiptoed to the closet and yanked the door open. She let out a relieved breath at the sight of nothing more menacing than neatly hung clothing and rows of shoes. *Okay.* She turned and looked under the bed, seeing the boxes she'd put there. No bad guys.

She sank to the floor against the bed frame. Lois Lane took the opportunity to bounce over and give her cheek a lick. *Maybe I didn't lock the door.*

From downstairs came the thump of the front door closing and footsteps on the foyer's wood floor. Doris's voice floated up, words indistinct but the tone happy.

Jewell got to her feet and went along the hall to the stairs. She leaned over the railing and called, "Hi, Doris."

"So, you *are* here," Doris trilled. "I'm in for the evening, if you'd care to join me."

"Uh, sure. We'll be down in a minute."

* * *

"Shall we finish off this wine?" Doris held a half-empty bottle of rose' in one hand, two wine glasses dangling from the fingers of the other. She set the glasses and bottle on the kitchen table before taking a seat, smiling benevolently.

Jewell set a bowl of salad and the pot of leftover spaghetti on the table. "Sure. Help me get the plates and silverware. We'll make it a meal."

"Put it outside while we're eating." Doris looked sternly at Lois Lane.

Jewell stared. "No," she finally said through her teeth. "She stays with me. She'll be no trouble." Then, raising her glass, "A toast to you, me and my new companion."

Doris just rolled her eyes.

When they'd made a dent in the pasta Doris took a sip of wine, murmuring, "Marco's behavior at dinner the other night? Awkward. He's a big disappointment to his father and me."

"What caused it?" Jewell hoped she sounded innocent. "He seemed genuinely upset."

"There was no good reason. He's very immature." Doris took another sip. "His mother spoiled him rotten and then died, leaving us to deal with him. He's nothing more than an overgrown adolescent. He blames poor Benny for everything." Doris smiled vacantly. "I knew from the first time I saw Racine—Marco's mother—she was wrong for my son. She got herself pregnant, claimed the child was his. Benny never knew for sure."

Jewell concentrated on her half-finished dinner, Marco's words echoing in her mind. *He beat the shit out of her.*

"The boy swallowed his mother's lies, hook, line, and sinker." Doris sniffed in exasperation.

"You and he managed to stay close, though."

"He didn't have much choice, did he? With Racine gone, I was the only relative around. It's time that boy faced facts."

* * *

When Jewell climbed into bed that night and patted the foot of the bed, Lois Lane catapulted on and was soon snoring softly.

Jewell turned out the light and put her head on the pillow. Her eyelids refused to close. Her mind spun with the stresses of the day—the oddly glowing ring, the conversation with Marco, Doris's cold remarks. She sat up, punched her pillow, and burrowed deep under the comforter.

I'll do a prone meditation and say some prayers. I've gotta get some sleep.

Hours later something roused her. After a moment she realized Lois Lane lay rigid next to her, growling.

Jewell's senses sharpened. The room was dark, except for an outline of dim light around the window. The flowery scent of her bath powder hung in the air. A door creaked.

Moving her head just a fraction, she looked across the room. The closet door swung open, then closed with a soft snap. When she felt Lois Lane's chin on her shoulder, she realized they were both holding their breath.

The closet's doorknob turned; the door opened. Then, inexplicably, it closed again.

Holy Mother of God.

Scared into action, Jewell climbed from bed and reached atop the dresser. She felt the smoothness of the ring, cold at first and then rapidly heating. *Okay. Here goes nothing.*

She flipped on the bedside lamp, shuffled to the closet, and yanked the door open. She pushed apart the clothes hangers. On the back wall, she saw faded wallpaper, a small cobweb, and a few flyspecks. Nothing more. She stepped back and slammed the closet door shut. She knelt and lay the hot, slightly pulsating ring on the floor. "You're in there," she murmured, "even if I can't see you."

Jewell stumbled back to bed and cuddled Lois Lane close. In the dimly lit room, the ring's glow faded. The tension in the air eased.

Maybe I was dreaming.

* * *

At work the next morning, Jewell could hardly keep her eyes open. When her trembling hand almost spilled oatmeal in his lap Mr. Plougher grumbled, "Are you hungover from too much weekend? Is that darn mansion a party house?"

Jewell dropped into a chair. One hand went to her pocket, where she'd put the ring. "I wish. You know I hardly drink. It's just, I haven't had a decent night's sleep in days. The weird stuff in that room's gettin' worse. I thought the dog would make a difference, but she's as scared as I am."

Mr. Plougher reached down to pat Lois Lane's head under the table. "It's not her fault she isn't a ghostbuster." He chuckled at his joke, then frowned. "Seems like if the house really was haunted, I'd have heard about it long before this. He wiggled his bushy eyebrows. "I doubt that old bat you live with would put up with ghosts."

Eve Plougher looked up from her crossword puzzle. "Nicholas. Language!" She turned to Jewell. "Maybe you need an exterminator, dear. I've heard of mice doing all kinds of eerie things in old houses."

"Mice?" Jewell smiled. "I'll think about that. For now, I'll stay away for a few days, catch up on my sleep, and start over next weekend."

"Well, I'm glad it's not a party house." Mr. Plougher chuckled. "You're a Spring chicken by my standards, Jewell, but you'll never see nineteen again."

"Don't remind me," Jewell laughed.

The Ploughers' phone rang and, when Jewell answered it, Bob's deep voice resonated against her eardrum. "Beth Anne said you called us. I'm running errands this morning. Want me to stop by?"

Jewell looked across the table to Eve and Nicholas Plougher. "Would you mind if Bob from G.I.'s Joe drops by?"

The old couple both sat up, brightening visibly. "How nice. Yes," Eve smiled.

"Company in the morning? Sure," Nicholas grinned.

* * *

"This is definitely Grandma Maris's ring. She never took it off, long as I knew her. Besides the **S** on the inside, it's got this flower pattern, see? Pretty much worn down, but still visible." Bob rubbed the gold band lovingly. "Your dog found it in the closet? That's weird." He stared silently for a minute. "Her jewelry box was cleaned out in the home invasion and she didn't have the ring on when her body was found. We figured the robbers took it."

Jewell stared at the ring, now cold and lifeless in Bob's hand. She whispered, "When I touch it, it gets crazy hot. Clearly, it belongs with you. Now that it's out of my room, maybe your aunt's ghost will settle down." Her laugh sounded hollow.

Bob glanced at Eve and Nicholas. "Time for me to get back to work." He squeezed Mr. Plougher's shoulder. "Go easy on the hired help today. She's obviously stressed out."

Chapter Seven

J ewell stepped out onto the front porch with Bob. As the door closed, she confronted him. "Friends don't let friends move into a house where someone's been killed, Bob. I thought you and Beth Anne were my friends."

"How could we know Doris would put you in the murder room, for God's sake?" Bob let out a long breath. "Sorry, Jewell. Try not to think about it, okay? It's still a helluva nice room. I'm more concerned about that effing Perez showing up on your doorstep; he should've never got early release. He's got a long record."

"A career criminal? I didn't need to hear that." Jewell rubbed the back of her neck. "Could you at least come by, maybe see how the ring acts at the house? If there is a ghost, maybe it'll leave when you show up." Jewell squinted somberly up at Bob. "Please?"

He slowly shook his head. "That's crazy. No one really believes in ghosts." Then, glancing away, he added, "I'll talk to Beth Anne. This 'woo-woo' stuff is more up her alley."

"Thanks." Jewell attempted a smile, failing miserably. "You got any advice on how to survive Perez? Staying completely out of his way will be impossible under the circumstances."

"When you have to be around him, be careful." Bob rubbed his chin thoughtfully. "I'll talk to Uncle Leo. He works for a security company. And he hates Perez."

Jewell jammed her hands in her pockets. "Doris is delighted her son's back. Maybe I'm worrying about nothing. Maybe he won't stay long." She shivered.

"I'm not a fan of maybes."

"No harm thinking positive. From what I remember, basement living wasn't Perez's style. Probably has an exit scheme already percolating." Bob climbed into his truck. "I'll have Beth Anne put you in touch with a ghost whisperer." He grinned.

"That's right," Jewell grinned back. "Have a laugh on me. Watch out I don't sic your ghost-aunt on G.I.'s Joe."

Bob revved the engine and drove away.

As Jewell turned to go back inside, she caught a glimpse of a green paneled van easing in behind Bob's vehicle. The driver looked a lot like Benny Perez.

Her phone beeped.

"Hi, Mom. How was last night at the house?" It was Carolyn. "How's Lois Lane? She getting along with your landlady?"

"I didn't get much sleep, but it wasn't the dog's fault. Or Doris's, now you mention it." Jewell tried to match Carolyn's cheerful tone. "She gave me the all-clear on the dog. Not that it matters; Lois Lane's staying. She's the best thing that's happened to me lately."

Carolyn hesitated. "How's it going with that creepy dude, Benny Something? Maybe Doris will mellow out, now he's there. Women do behave better with male energy around."

"That's a matter of opinion," Jewell sneered. "Say—" she changed her tone, "do you know anyone who does seances?"

"You mean, like a medium?" Carolyn's voice went up a notch. "Holy cow, are things that bad? Maybe you should move back in with me and Hank."

"Oops, time to go. Forget I mentioned it." Jewell disconnected. *I should have kept my mouth shut.*

* * *

Jewell and the Ploughers were gathered around the television that evening, eating chicken salad and watching the news. All three gasped when a well-dressed, artificially-tanned man on the TV news announced, "There was a bit of excitement this morning in the sleepy town of Miwok. Someone tossed a bottle bomb into a coffee truck. Here's Debbie, at the scene."

Suddenly G.I.'s Joe was center-screen, wisps of smoke drifting from its' front window and surrounded by firemen and cops. The camera turned to a young woman standing nearby.

"Debbie Warton here, at the corner of Eighth and Corn Streets. Behind me you see the heartbreak of vandalism. According to witnesses, an incendiary device was tossed from a passing van at Miwok's own G.I.'s Joe coffee truck mid-morning today. The barista, Beth Anne Stone, was taken to the hospital with serious burns. The incident is under investigation."

Mr. and Mrs. Plougher, arms reaching wildly for walker and cane, struggled to their feet. "We have to do something—that poor girl!"

Jewell took a deep breath. *Stay calm. Don't let them see you panic.*

"Mid-morning? Bob was here. That's why Beth Anne was running the truck by herself."

Mr. Plougher shuffled across the room, knuckles white on the cane handle. He opened the front door. When cold air rushed in, he snapped the door shut, muttering, "Where was I going?"

Jewell crossed the room and put an arm around the old man's shoulders. "To see what happened to the coffee truck. Let's get our coats. We'll all go."

"That's right. I knew that." Mr. Plougher looked at his wife. "Don't cry, dear. Things are okay here."

Jewell sighed. *I feel like crying, myself.* She left a message on Bob's phone and then, clucking like a mother hen, bundled her elderly charges into the back seat of the Civic.

"Slow down. If one of you fell, I'd never forgive myself."

Traffic was light on the short drive to G.I.s Joe. Within minutes the Civic pulled to the curb. When Jewell opened the back door and peered in at the Ploughers, her heart lurched. They sat huddled together, looking frightened. *They're so vulnerable. How do I reassure them?*

The church parking lot lay eerily quiet and empty: no G.I.'s Joe, no vehicles of any kind. Where the coffee truck was usually parked, an occasional wisp of smoke drifted from small mounds of wet, black garbage. The oleander bushes ringing the lot showed grey and ashy in the twilight.

"Truck's been taken away." Mr. Plougher sounded disappointed.

"Looks like the fire department did a thorough job drowning everything flammable. That burned stuff must be what's left of the truck's inventory." Bits of smoke still in the air scratched Jewell's throat.

"Looks like World War II," Mrs. Plougher rasped.

"Is it my fault?" Jewell stuttered. "I joked with Bob about setting a ghost on them."

"Don't go blaming yourself." Mr. Plougher's tone was brisk. "You had nothing to do with this. Whoever's responsible—destroying a war veteran's family business, for God's sake—I'd like to punch their lights out!"

Jewell climbed back in the Civic and drove slowly back to the Ploughers' home. "Probably no point in going to the hospital. We don't know if they kept Beth Anne overnight. You want me to call Mr. Stone?"

Mr. and Mrs. Plougher both nodded.

* * *

After settling her charges in front of the TV again, Jewell dug in her purse and found Leo Stone's business card. There was a gruff, "Stone here," as soon as she keyed in the number.

"It's Jewell McDunn, Mr. Stone. The Ploughers and I saw the news about G.I.'s Joe. How is Beth Anne? How can we help?"

There was no response for a split second. Then, softly, "Probably a good time to start calling me by my first name. It's Leo. Beth Anne's arms are burned—her apron caught fire—but it could've been worse. The guy didn't have a clear shot—a group of customers walked up just as he launched the bottle. It hit the metal flashing behind the stove. A window shattered; glass missed Beth Anne, thank God." Stone took a breath. "Truck's gonna need a thorough cleaning before they can open for business; Bob's worried—got no cash cushion whatsoever."

"I feel so guilty," Jewell whispered. "Bob was here at the Ploughers around the time it happened."

"Don't even go there. Whoever tossed the bottle, that's who's to blame."

Stone bit off the words.

"Has anyone been arrested?" Jewell paused. "Doesn't sound like kids, middle of the morning like that."

"The cops have no leads. One customer said he saw a van, but he couldn't give any details." Stone swore softly.

"A van? I saw one on the road behind Bob's truck today." Jewell heard the fear in her voice.

"Yeah? When?" Stone inhaled noisily.

"This morning. Around ten. Bob came by here, stayed maybe fifteen minutes. I gave him something I found in my closet."

"G.I.'s Joe was hit at 10:45. You see the driver?"

The question dropped like a pebble in a quiet pond. Jewell tried to focus. "Well, kind of. He had on a hoodie. Reminded me of someone I met recently. Probably not the same guy."

"Hold on while I write this down." Jewell heard paper rustling. "Okay. I got it. I'll mention this to Bob, see if he noticed anything. He's a compulsive periphery scanner—picked up that skill in Iraq."

"Tell him we want to help any way we can. In fact, Mr. Stone—Leo—tell him we expect to hear back from him on this."

Leo chuckled. "You're a force to be reckoned with, aren't you? I'm sure they'll appreciate your offer." Then, "One question: you said the driver looked like someone you met recently. Care to elaborate?"

Jewell held the phone away from her ear. *Here goes nothing.*

"It's my landlady's son," Jewell spat out. "I'm a little irritated because one, she didn't tell me he'd be living at the house, and two, she didn't tell me he was fresh out of prison."

"Sheesh," Leo muttered. "Are you talking about Benny Perez? Is that loser out of the joint already?" There was a moment's silence. "That's who you saw following Bob?"

"I think so. I didn't see his face. He doesn't drive a van, though, far as I know." She paused. "What'd he do, anyway? To get locked up, I mean."

"He was a three-time loser. Guy's been butting heads with the law since he was a kid—he's a sociopath—thinks the rules don't apply to him." Leo's voice was somber. "Listen, keep this conversation to yourself. Understand?"

"Uh, sure." Jewell stared at the phone. *What's going on here?* "By the way, what's with you guys talking me into renting a room where someone died? I thought Bob and Beth Anne were my friends."

"You heard about Maris? Sorry. We didn't know Doris would put you in that room. No one's used it since...." Leo cleared his throat. "Just stay out of Perez's way, Ms. McDunn. Don't go picking any fights with him. He's way out of your league."

A chill moved down Jewell's spine. "Thanks for the advice. Bob said Benny never stays in one place very long. I hope he's right."

"Let's all hope so. Say, how'd you learn about Maris Stone? No one's talked about that in years."

"I stumbled across it. You could say, 'a little ghost told me.'"

"Huh. Ghosts. Right." Leo chuckled. "When we get G.I.'s Joe back in business, how about I buy you a coffee? You can tell me your ghost story."

"It's not a story." Jewell rolled her eyes. "I appreciate the offer, but I'm still in gut-wrenching terror mode."

Through the phone, Leo's laugh sounded like a witch's cackle. "All right, girl. I like your honesty." He disconnected.

Jewell stared at the phone. *First guy to flirt with me in a month and it has to be Bob's uncle. Go figure.*

"Who was that?" Mr. Plougher looked guiltily away from the television. He'd obviously been listening throughout the phone conversation.

"Leo Stone, as if you didn't know," Jewell snapped. Then, "Sorry. My nerves are on overtime. Is Mrs. P.'s show finished?"

Mr. Plougher nodded. "Not that it matters. She dozed off twenty minutes ago." He looked expectantly at Jewell. "How's Beth Anne?"

Jewell sighed. "Her arms were burned, but she's going to be okay. And the truck's not too badly damaged. The inside got the worst of it—I didn't get the details. Bob's worried their insurance won't keep them afloat 'til they can reopen."

"Did they catch the scumbag that did it?"

Jewell shook her head. "Not yet.

"Tell you what." Mr. Plougher frowned. "Tomorrow, make me an appointment with my lawyer. And call Chief Jorgensen. He worked at my store when he was in high school. I'll make sure he puts his best men on this."

Jewell patted Mr. Plougher's arm. "Okay, boss. Right now, let's get you and Mrs. P. to bed."

At ten o'clock, with both Ploughers' snores audible on the baby monitor, Jewell sat down on the couch and prayed.

You haven't heard from me in a long time, God, but here I am. Things are getting really messy down here in Miwok. Any chance you could lend us a hand? You, of all people, must believe me about the ghost, and I bet you're hurting right along with Beth Anne and G.I.'s Joe. Oh, about that creep, Perez: is he worth a second chance? Maybe I should chill and let you handle him. Please give me strength for all this, God. And courage. Amen.

The prayer still echoed in Jewell's thoughts when the phone in her pocket vibrated.

Probably Carolyn. Jewell checked the readout. 'Beth Anne.' *Oh, my God!* She squawked, 'Hello?"

"Jewell, you still awake? I can't sleep—can we talk a minute? I didn't want to call my mom—she's such a worrier."

"Absolutely." Jewell's voice came out in a strangled squeak. "Mr. Stone told me about the fire. I'm so sorry you were hurt. Are you home?"

"No, still in the hospital." Beth Anne's voice rose. "Someone tossed a bottle bomb at our truck, Jewell." She gulped. "Docs say maybe I can go home tomorrow. Bob really needs me; his PTSD got triggered, bad." Her voice faded to a whisper. "My arms hurt like hell. You ever been burned?"

Jewell ran a hand across her eyes. *Shit!* She cleared her throat. "Not like that, I haven't. Don't be in a rush to leave the hospital, hon. Bob wouldn't want you coming home before you're ready. Want to talk about what happened?"

"It's kind of a blur, you know? I handed a lady her latte and turned away to answer my phone. There was a thud, a flash, and," Beth Anne's voice trailed off, "next thing I know, I'm on a gurney, screaming my head off."

"I can't even imagine. Listen," Jewell controlled her shaky voice, "Maybe you should ring for the nurse—have them give you something for the pain."

"They're way ahead of you. I'm hooked up to a drip. They iced my arms for a while, too. It was mostly my arms, you know, took the hit." Beth Anne's voice began to fade. "Mom's driving up from San Jose tomorrow." She made an odd, chuckling sound. "You'll have to drink Starbucks lattes for a couple of days."

"I'm so glad you called, honey. So glad you're alive. I'll check on Bob tomorrow, okay?" Tears made tiny rivers down Jewell's cheeks.

"Gotta go. Nurse … here." Beth Anne's voice trailed off to a whisper.

Jewell heard, brisk and low-pitched, "Off the phone, now. Time to rest."

Just before disconnecting, Beth Anne whispered, "That woman who does seances, Cara Os…she'll call you."

Beth Anne got in touch with a medium for me, and remembered to tell me about it.

Fresh tears fell.

*   *   *

After letting Lois Lane out for a final pee Jewell wandered from room to room, locking up. Then, with the dog curled up and snoring, she sat in the dark at the foot of the bed in the Ploughers' spare room, rubbing her forehead. The attack on G.I.'s Joe played over and over in her brain.

Beth Anne's at the counter, in full view of the street. She finishes serving customers, she turns away. That's when the bottle comes—from the street—from a van—thrown by the driver? Does he stop to aim? Or wait at the corner and then drive fast and throw. Is it Perez? If it is, why? To settle some old score now that he's out of prison?

Jewell's phone chirped and showed an unfamiliar number but a local area code. "Hello?"

"Jewell? It's Doris. I hope I'm not calling too late."

"I'm not asleep yet. What's up?"

"I've decided to move you to a different room. Benny was upset you're in the master suite. You don't mind, do you?" Doris words were clipped, as if she was in a hurry.

Jewell stared at the phone incredulously. When she spoke, it was all she could do to sound civil. "Yes, I do mind. Why does he care which room I'm in? I specifically rented **that** room. I'm not changing." Then, mentally grinding her teeth, she forced a softer tone. "Listen, can we talk about this tomorrow? I'll come by in the morning."

Doris was silent so long, Jewell wondered if she'd disconnected. Finally, "You can come by tomorrow, but the decision is out of your hands." The line went dead.

What does she mean, It's out of my hands? I have a contract!

Jewell climbed into bed, falling back against the pillows with a thump.

Tomorrow's going to be hell.

Chapter Eight

"Please let me help any way I can. I consider you and Beth Anne family."

Jewell put her phone on speaker and rested it on the table near Mr. Plougher, who pulled his chair closer and shouted, "Is Chief Jorgensen taking good care of you? I told him to put his best men on this case. And you should hear from Steinberg, my lawyer, today or tomorrow. He'll get the ball rolling with your insurance company." Mr. Plougher sat back, looking satisfied.

"Thanks for your help, Mr. Plougher." A tinny version of Bob's voice came through the phone. "I'm still not thinking straight. Every time I think of Beth Anne laying in that hospital bed, I go crazy."

Leo Stone's voice broke in, "Jorgensen will be here in a few minutes, Nicholas. I'll pass his report on to Bob's insurance carrier and your lawyer." Then, softer, "Jewell, I've decided to tell Jorgensen what you saw. Expect an official visit."

Jewell scowled at the phone. "Is that really necessary? I don't do well with authority figures—their interests don't usually jibe with mine—can't I just help out when Beth Anne comes home?"

"Her mother's here now. We're covered." Bob spoke up. "Listen, Jewell: The cops need any leads you can give them."

Jewell groaned.

* * *

After breakfast, Lois Lane's morning walk was combined with a quick visit to Radish Street. They were half a block from the Stone mansion when Jewell's phone rang. It was Doris.

"Hi, I'm almost at your front door." Jewell looked down the street. "If you came outside, you'd see me."

"When you get here," Doris said, "come straight into the kitchen." She disconnected.

"That was weird." Jewell frowned at the phone.

She walked faster, forcing Lois Lane, tongue out and smiling, into a trot. "Beat you to the gate," Jewell laughed. "Like that's going to happen!"

As they stepped into the kitchen Jewell paused, pulling Lois Lane close. The curtains were tightly drawn and it took a minute to adjust to the dim light.

Doris was seated at the table, wearing sunglasses and with a lock of hair awkwardly draped over one side of her face. She glanced at Jewell, then quickly looked away.

"That was fast. You **were** close by." The greeting was hard to understand: Doris opened her mouth just slightly to let the words out, and her lips seemed bruised.

Jewell slid into the chair. *What in the world is going on?* "I only have a few minutes. I have to get back. About me changing rooms: my lease clearly states I have that bedroom. And it's signed by you, not your son."

Doris's puffy lips formed a straight, frowning line. "We want you downstairs, in the room that used to be the library. It will be much more convenient for," she glanced at Lois Lane, "that animal. You have no reason to object." Her voice faded, as if she'd used every bit of energy to speak.

Jewell looked away for a second to hide her confusion. She'd been terrified in the master bedroom, but moving from it? That wasn't up to Doris. "No. I don't want a different room. What's with your son? Why does he have a say in this? What's going on here?"

Doris made an odd, whimpering sound. "That room has sentimental value for him." Almost inaudibly she said, "He wanted me to kick you out of the house, altogether." She lowered her glasses to look at Jewell with the one eye not covered by her hair. "Believe me, you'll be more comfortable in the library."

Outside the kitchen, tires crunched on gravel. A car door squeaked open and then snapped shut.

Doris pushed back from the table and carefully got to her feet. The lock of hair fell back, exposing an ugly, half-moon bruise under one eye. She quickly covered it. "We'll make the final decision this weekend. It's time for you to go." She turned and strode through the living room and to the front door, gesturing for Jewell and Lois Lane to follow.

"Okay. Sure. I'll see you Friday night." Jewell and Lois Lane let themselves be hustled out onto the porch.

Jewell glanced at the driveway. The back end of a green van stuck out beyond the corner of the house. She whispered, "Pick up the pace, Lois Lane," and they jog-trotted away from 811 Radish Street.

Two blocks down the street, out of breath and with a stitch in her side, Jewell slowed to a walk.

I knew the woman was strange, but a shiner? Where'd that come from? A week ago, if she'd said she was putting me in a different room, I wouldn't have cared. I shouldn't care now, but something's fishy here: what's it to Perez what room I'm in? Does he know I found that ring? How could he? I haven't told anyone but Leo and Bob.

Lois Lane turned to look quizzically at Jewell. At that moment the phone beeped.

"What?" Jewell snapped. "I mean, hello?"

A heavy Eastern European accent resonated through the phone: "I vant to speak to Jewell. I am Cara Oslavka, friend to Beth Anne Stone."

"Beth Anne?" Jewell squeaked. "You must be the medium. Hey, sorry for snapping at you."

"Is okay. Since the attack on G.I.'s Joe, everyone is snapping." The woman's tone was soothing. "You vish to contact a loved one from the Beyond? I am not a medium, but I have much experience in this field. I vould like to help a friend of Beth Anne."

Jewell felt herself relaxing for the first time in days. "You vould? You do? I mean, uh, thank you. I need a séance—that's what you call it, right? As soon as possible."

Oslavka uttered a delightful chuckle. "Some people use that vord. I'm not that formal. Ve gather vhere the spirit vas last seen alive, and invite it to join us."

"That would be my room in the Stone mansion. Do you know where it is, on Radish Street in Miwok?"

"Oh, yes. I live many years in Miwok. I know of that house."

"Then you know about the murder of Bob's aunt. She's the ghost in my room, far as I can tell."

"That vould make sense," Oslavka said softly.

Jewell hesitated, then blurted out, "What do you charge? I need your help but I'm not exactly wealthy."

"As I said, I am not licensed as a medium—I simply help friends and acquaintances in need. However, if you vant to make a donation, I vill accept it." Oslavka's tone was confidential.

"Thanks. I can't tell you how much I appreciate this. I'm usually only in my room on weekends, but I'll arrange to be there whenever you say."

"I live in vest Miwok, not far from Radish Street," Oslavka said. "Vould you like to meet at the mansion early this evening?"

"Vould I?" Jewell fairly chortled. "Absolutely! Can I bring my daughter for moral support?"

"Of course. It's a shame Bob can't join us, too, since he's blood kin." Oslavka paused. "Could you get some small item containing the dear departed's energy—a hairbrush, or a handkerchief? Some spirits need coaxing."

Jewell hesitated. "Well, there is the wedding ring I found in my closet. It definitely has energy—it spooked me so much, I turned it over to Bob. I'll ask him if we can borrow it." She added, "That ring is scary."

"Really." Oslavka's tone changed, became authoritative. "Definitely bring the ring. If it belongs to the spirit, she may be angry that you removed it. Perhaps ve vill apologize. Shall we meet at the mansion at 7:00?"

Jewell sighed with relief. "Perfect, Ms. Oslavka. I'll meet you at the front gate. We'll go in together."

As soon as Ms. Oslavka disconnected, Jewell texted Carolyn: *Can you come to my room tonight at 7? I'm having a séance there with a friend of Beth Anne's. Hank can come, if he wants to.*

To Doris, she texted: *I'll be in my room this evening with friends. Not staying the night.*

Then, shaking Lois Lane's leash, "Let's get back to work, girl. I can't wait for that seance!"

* * *

It wasn't until she was serving the Ploughers their dinner—beet juice ran into the mashed potatoes and created a bruised look—that Jewell thought of Doris's battered face.

I should have asked her about it. What if it wasn't an accident? She's not the type to let herself be hit. Huh. Even I know there's no type. Hold on—am I starting to feel sorry for her?

"Earth to Jewell," Mr. Plougher said. "You gave me all the chicken and Eve got both dishes of pears. You worried about Bob and Beth Anne? If it'll ease your mind, my lawyer called not ten minutes ago—he's already talked to the insurance company."

"Oops! Sorry, folks. I must have been daydreaming." Jewell made the food switch with an embarrassed grin.

"That's okay, dear. With everything that's going on, it's a wonder any of us can think straight." Eve Plougher patted Jewell's hand.

Jewell checked her watch. "Time for me to go. Remember, just leave everything on the table. I'll be back before your bedtime."

* * *

When she pulled into the driveway at 811 Radish, street lights twinkled in the dusky air. Although neighboring properties were brightly lit, the Stone mansion was dark.

Looks like no one's home. I wonder if Doris got my text. Maybe I'm in luck and we can get this whole weird process finished without interference.

Jewell was out of the car and halfway to the gate when a blue Prius glided to the curb, followed closely by Carolyn's Volvo. Jewell reached the gate before turning to greet the woman climbing gracefully from the Prius. Cara Oslavka was a slim, attractive older woman, dressed smartly in a designer business suit.

I thought she'd look more like the fortunetellers I've seen in movies—flowing, colorful clothes and lots of makeup. She could be an office executive, or a bank manager. Hmm. Hope she knows her stuff.

Carolyn, wearing her trademark shorts and carrying a shoulder bag, hopped out of her car and started toward the gate. When she saw the well-dressed woman, her face reddened. She sidled over to stand next to Jewell.

"Madam Oslavka, this is my daughter, Carolyn. Carolyn, this is the person I told you about, Cara Oslavka."

"Pleased to meet you." Carolyn threw Jewell a sharp glance. "You certainly aren't what I expected, Madam Oslavka."

"I hear that all the time, dear. People picture me arriving in a gypsy wagon." Oslavka laughed. She turned to study the front of 811 Radish. "This house has many secrets."

"You think so?" Jewell turned to Carolyn. "Ms. Oslavka—am I pronouncing that right? Is not a professional medium, but she knows how to communicate with people who have, uh, passed."

Carolyn, gawking at Oslavka, shrugged. "I'm impressed, no matter what your business card says."

"Let's go inside. It looks like my landlady isn't home. Maybe we can get this done before she comes back." Jewell looked apologetically at Oslavka. "You think I'm a skeptic? Compared to my landlady, I'm a foaming-at-the-mouth believer."

Jewell turned on the foyer light and shook off a tingle of fear. Something about the house's sense of anticipation—brought on by the dark wood paneling, high ceilings, and pristine quiet, jarred her. While she and Carolyn hurried upstairs, Oslavka followed slowly. The woman nodded from time to time, as if in silent conversation with the Stone family portraits lining the stairway.

Carolyn stayed close behind her mother, clutching her shoulder bag nervously. When Jewell unlocked and opened the bedroom door, Carolyn hurried inside and immediately tossed her bag on the bed. "Bob gave me the ring. It's in my bag, Mom."

"Thanks for getting it. How'd Bob look?"

"Not good." Carolyn frowned. "Like he hasn't slept in days. He said Beth Anne's coming home tomorrow; maybe then he can relax." She glanced at her shoulder bag. "Did you know that ring glows? It is so creepy!"

Jewell frowned, feeling a little defensive about asking Carolyn to get the ring.

I should have realized she'd pick up on that weird energy.

She opened the bag and peered inside, digging past Carolyn's wallet, makeup kit, and car keys to a small black jewelry box. Ignoring her stomach's sudden spasm, she lifted the box out by two fingers and turned to Madame Oslavka. "Will this do the job?"

Oslavka had been examining the bay window, her face grave. "That is the ring you found here? Excellent." She turned to Carolyn. "Thank you for coming. Your mother told me about your unfortunate experience last time you vere here. I vill make tonight as easy for you as possible." She touched Jewell's shoulder. "Let's get started. I sense an anxious spirit in this place." She pointed across the room to Jewell's coffee table. "Ve'll sit around that."

A deep feeling of dread swept over Jewell; she closed her eyes. *Oslavka senses the presence, too. It's real, not just me being crazy. What if it's not happy we're barging into its' world?*

She shook off the feeling and got busy arranging the furniture, placing two chairs across the coffee table from the recliner. Meanwhile, Madam Oslavka produced a candle and a bright, multicolored scarf which she draped on the table. She lit the candle, saying, "Carolyn, you'll feel safest if you aren't close to the window."

As Jewell set the ring box down, she felt heat coming through the cloth-covered cardboard. When she opened the hinged lid, the ring sparkled and glowed in the candlelight.

"Perfect," Oslavka murmured. "The spirit is definitely present."

"Do we need a chair for the ghost?" Jewell whispered.

Oslavka shook her head. "They don't usually sit."

With the three women seated around the table, Madame Oslavka intoned, "Let us join hands, close our eyes, and bring our hearts and minds to this circle." She grasped Jewell's hand, then Carolyn's. "Ve offer our support to the spirit in this room. Come, you who are troubled. How can ve help?"

Carolyn's hand, now icy cold, held Jewell's in a death grip.

A slight breeze circled the table. When Jewell heard a soft THUNK, she opened her eyes. The jewelry box had tipped over and the ring teetered at the table edge. Jewell gasped. Her chest felt suddenly tight.

Oslavka squeezed her hand. Jewell turned and stared at the Medium's serene face until the panic ebbed. She glanced at Carolyn, sitting rigid with her teeth clenched, and had a comforting word formed when the floor creaked.

In a soft, soothing monotone Oslavka spoke. "Velcome, troubled spirit. Ve come in peace." As her mellow voice filled the room. Jewell felt Carolyn's hand relaxing.

Suddenly the closet door banged open, the window's heavy drapes clattered back on their brass rings and a high-pitched wail filled the room. The ring, now glowing furiously, lifted and hovered a few inches above the table.

As Jewell and Carolyn sat frozen with fear, Madame Oslavka raised her voice above the wailing. "How can ve help you?"

Like a light switch turning off, the shrieking and the air turbulence stopped; the room was utterly silent. Then, without warning, a low, breathy voice came from within Oslavka.

"The love this ring holds was ripped from me when my life was taken. Corruption took the love, but not my spirit. Now, corruption has been joined by evil. Cleanse this house!"

Oslavka shuddered; she seemed to cast off all muscle tension in a rolling wave, from the top of her head to the soles of her feet. She stretched her neck, as if finishing a rigorous workout, and spoke—in her own voice.

"God grant you peace, dear spirit. Thank you for reaching out to us."

Oslavka opened her eyes, stared vacantly for a moment, then focused on Jewell.

"I'm afraid you have vork to do before Mrs. Stone is free to go. Vhat she said about corruption being joined by evil? You'll need to find out who those terms represent." Oslavka looked around. "Do you have any vater? My mouth is parched."

Jewell blinked and gave herself a good shake. "Uh, yes. I'll get some." She turned to Carolyn who, pale and shaking, was almost doubled over. "You okay, baby?"

Carolyn shook her head. When she spoke, her voice was barely a whisper. "No. This whole séance thing was a terrible idea. All it did was prove what I already knew, Mom." She pushed away from the table and stood. "I think I'm gonna hurl." She dashed from the room and across the hall to the bathroom.

Jewell jumped up to hurry after her daughter, returning a few minutes later with a glass of water for Oslavka.

"She'll be okay. Maybe I shouldn't have included her in this tea party." Jewell looked intently at Oslavka, who sat quietly, eyes closed and lips moving silently.

"I'm still in shock," Jewell whispered. "I had no idea you could really summon a ghost. Sorry I doubted your talents." With a quick glance at the ring, now lifeless on the table, she said, "Corruption replaced by evil—you think she means people?"

Oslavka opened her eyes and, without looking at Jewell, put the cloth and candle in her bag. Then, very gently, she returned the ring to its box. "The depth of the departed's pain has drained me." She was silent so long, Jewell wondered if she should say something. Then, "Evil and corruption both flow from the same source: the human heart. Now that you know the departed one's pain, the action for healing vill come to you." She handed Jewell the ring box, started toward the bedroom door, and turned. "This is the most intense contact I've ever had. I may have to document this with my organization, Spiritualists Worldwide."

As they crossed the hall to wait for Carolyn, Oslavka looked intently at Jewell. "Protect that ring. The evil spoken of by the late Mrs. Stone is real and present."

* * *

An hour later, after pressing two twenty-dollar bills into Madam Oslavka's hand and escorting the still-terrified Carolyn home, Jewell pulled up to the curb outside the Ploughers' house. She turned off the engine and stared blindly through the windshield, the reality of the past hour finally sinking in.

Had to be a trick. There's no such thing as ghosts. Oslavka did some smoke-and-mirrors thing. Only, she didn't. And the ring. It was weird before I even called her. No denying that. Oh, God, what am I going to do?

The enormity of the situation—a real, live ghost in the room she'd chosen as her home—overwhelmed Jewell. She rested her face on the steering wheel and began to cry large, gulping sobs that deteriorated into moaning, face-rubbing, and wet fingers through her hair. After a little while—ten minutes, maybe twenty—a light blinked at the edge of her vision. Using a shirttail to mop her face, she looked around. Someone had turned on the Ploughers' porch light.

The area beyond the hood of the car came into focus; a pick-up truck, the 'Stone Cold Security' logo on its door, stood in the Ploughers' driveway.

Leo Stone? What's he doing here?

She jumped from the car and ran through deep shadows to the porch's welcoming, 60-watt safety.

Jewell leaned against the front door in the living room for a minute, lost in absorbing the sense of safety she felt in the Ploughers' modest cottage. Gradually, the sound of loud conversation in the kitchen got her attention. Mr. Plougher was excited—*that's not good for his heart*—and Mrs. Plougher was chirping like a distressed bird—*or her blood pressure*. Leo Stone's calm baritone filled the sound gaps.

Woof! Woof! Whine!

Lois Lane rushed at Jewell with a noisy, insistent greeting, licked her mistress's tear-stained face, and backed off with her head cocked in puzzlement.

Jewell hugged the dog's ruff for a minute, then hurried into the kitchen. "Hi, everyone! What's up?"

"Thank goodness you're back." Mrs. Plougher's walker stomped double-time across the room to reach Jewell. "The police want to arrest your landlady."

Chapter Nine

"Whoa, there, Eve," Mr. Plougher protested. "Let the woman get her coat off before you slam her with bad news."

"It's okay, Mrs. P." Jewell put a calming hand on Eve Plougher's shoulder. "What do you mean, the cops want to arrest Doris?" She looked across the table at the haggard and curiously embarrassed face of Leo Stone. "She's joking, right? I've had enough shocks for one night."

"Wish she was." Stone's tone was solemn. "Fact is, the cops are looking at good old Doris for the G.I.'s Joe drive-by. Seems the bomber used a rented van, and guess whose credit card came up on the rental?"

"Oh, God." Jewell dropped into a chair. "Did they arrest her? I just came from 811 Radish; No one was there—at least, no one living."

Stone gave her a puzzled frown. "That I don't know. I just swung by here to warn you to stay away from there, for now." He locked eyes with Jewell. "What do you mean, no one living? What were you doing over there? You're supposed to be here during the week."

Jewell, bristling at being interrogated, growled, "Hold on there, buddy. Where I go and why is none of your damn business." She flicked an apologetic glance at Eve Plougher for the swear word. "For your information, I spent an hour in my room—where I have a right to be at any time, weekday or not—with my daughter and a friend. I didn't see Doris or her son. No cops came by while we were there, either."

Stone reared back in his chair, looking startled. "True, it's not my business, but—"

"Leo didn't mean to put you on the spot, dear," Eve Plougher cut in. "He's worried about you." She rested a hand on her husband's arm. "Don't you think so, Nicholas?"

Mr. Plougher, whose head had been swiveling from Jewell to Leo Stone and back, grinned widely. "I'll never tell. Isn't it bedtime?" He looked confused. "You don't live here, do you, Leo?"

"Nicholas," Eve Plougher snapped, "You know perfectly well who lives here." She turned to Leo Stone. "Thank you for coming by to warn Jewell. The news is distressing, but at least she didn't have to hear it on television. Do the police think Doris threw that bottle? She doesn't look like the athletic type." She sighed. "I hope this information doesn't upset Bob. He's been through so much already."

"That reminds me, I have to return the ring." Jewell glanced at Leo. "The ring I found in my closet—the closet of the room you suggested I rent." She rolled her shoulders in a tired stretch. "Shall we call it a night, everyone?"

Leo got to his feet. "I doubt Doris will be arrested, Eve. Interviewed, for sure. And Jewell, I came by tonight because Bob asked me to. He's the protective one. I'm just the grumpy old uncle."

Jewell turned away, busying herself with helping Mrs. Plougher. She murmured, "Leo, can I have a word with you before you leave?" She didn't catch the smile creasing his lined face.

A few minutes later, as Leo stood on the front porch gazing down the dark street, Jewell slipped outside to join him. She put a hand lightly on his arm, whispering, "I might have been a bit sharp in there. Sorry. I'm worried about Beth Anne, Bob, even Doris." She sighed. "With Doris, it's not just this arrest thing—when I saw her today, she had a black eye."

Leo said nothing for a minute. He turned slightly and snapped his fingers at Lois Lane, who had finished her business and was meandering toward the sidewalk. Lois Lane stopped, looked at Leo, and reversed course. She bounded up the steps and stood quietly next to Jewell. Leo stooped and rubbed her ears, saying, "The way Doris treats people, she doesn't deserve your concern."

Jewell nodded. "I know that. Unfortunately, my feelings aren't attached to my brain."

Leo shrugged. "How'd the séance go?"

Jewell frowned. "I didn't hold much hope for it." She followed his gaze toward the street. "The woman was genuine, though. Your brother's first wife showed up like clockwork; said she's not leaving 811 Radish until her killer is caught."

"That's crazy," Leo muttered. "That Medium-person conjured up a ghost? And you bought it? I gotta hand it to the woman, she did her homework—she must've known all about the home invasion ten years ago."

"Madam Oslavka—that's her name—had no way of knowing. The spirit of Mrs. Stone really appeared. It wasn't fake," Jewell stuttered.

"Let me get this straight: If you want any peace in that room, you have to solve a crime that happened years ago, that hardly anybody believes even happened? Not to mention, Doris wants you out of your room, ASAP?"

"Yeah." Jewell shook her head. "I'm sure there's no connection. It's weird, though, isn't it?" A shiver ran down her spine.

Leo folded his arms across his chest. "Do me a favor, will you? Stay away from Radish Street for a few days. Hang out over here, take care of Eve and Nicholas. Try to forget all that ghost stuff, and make yourself scarce until Doris's son takes off. She's not a threat to anyone, but that son of hers? He's a different story. I don't want you getting hurt before I get to know you."

Jewell, blushing, started to fold her arms across her chest, realized she was mimicking Leo, and put them awkwardly at her sides. "You know, don't you, I hate being told what to do? And truthfully, I can't just do nothing. That spirit is so miserable. Not to mention, I have to stand up for my rights. For crying out loud, I have a lease!"

"There we are," Leo murmured. "You pretend to be tough—hell, it's not pretense—but your heart gets in the way." He put a tentative hand on Jewell's shoulder. "If I can't stop you, how about I join your team?"

Leo's face was very close to Jewell's, and his eyes shone with ... compassion? Jewell felt herself trembling. She brushed her cheek against his shoulder. His arm went around her in the briefest of hugs. She pulled away, looking up at him.

"I could use an assistant," Jewell smiled. "As long as you don't get the idea that you're in charge."

"You got it, kid. Go get some rest, and let's talk tomorrow." Leo jogged jauntily down the steps to his truck.

Jewell stepped back inside, enjoying the warmth of that gentle hug. When was the last time a man had this effect on her? She didn't bother to think back; she wanted to concentrate on the feeling.

* * *

At barely eight o'clock the next morning Jewell's cell phone buzzed. The screen read, 'Carolyn,' so she answered. "Hi, early bird. You at work yet?"

"Oh, yeah." Carolyn sounded sleepy. "Our guy comes back from the flower mart at oh-dark-thirty and it's my job to sort flowers for the day's orders." She sighed. "We need to talk about last night, Mom, but not right this minute. I wanted to let you know I got a call from that guy, Marco. Your landlady's grandson, remember? He woke us up out of a sound sleep—he's worried about his grandmother. I think he was high. Said he tried your phone but got no answer, so he called us."

"Sorry about that. I left my phone in the kitchen last night." She took a breath. "He's worried about Doris? I am, too. Last time I saw Marco he talked about leaving the area. I wonder if that's changed."

"No clue. Hank grabbed the phone, told Marco to lose my number." Carolyn's voice dropped to a half-whisper. "Marco started crying—that cooled Hank's heels. He told the kid to come by the job site this morning if he sobers up and still wants help."

"The way Marco's been flirting with you? Hank's a better person than I thought."

"Mom!" Then, quietly, "Yeah. We figure he's desperate. Was Doris at the house last night? I didn't see her."

"No." Jewell began whispering, too, then raised her voice to its' normal level. "Listen, you should get back to work. If Marco and Hank actually make contact, have one of them give me a call. And, call me tonight. We need to talk about the seance."

"Will do, Mom. Love you." Carolyn disconnected.

Jewell filled Lois Lane's food dish with kibble and gave her a good morning pat. "What do you think, girl? Should we worry about Doris? She doesn't give two hoots about us." Lois Lane, nose-deep in the bowl of kibble, ignored Jewell.

Maybe Marco saw that shiner. If Perez hit her, that's just the beginning. She doesn't stand up to him at all.

Hours later, on a walk around the block with Lois Lane, Jewell's phone beeped. "G.I.'s Joe," according to the screen readout. When Jewell answered she heard Beth Anne's voice, tired but cheerful.

"Hi, Jewell!"

"Beth Anne? Honey! I heard you were home; I figured I should wait a few days to call. How you doin'?"

Beth Anne's tone was guarded. "A little better. It's good to be home. I'm making phone calls for Bob—I can't do much else." She sighed. "He's decided to get G.I.'s Joe repaired and open again, thank God. At first, he wanted to cut and run, desert the business and this whole town. With me home and the cops closing in on the bad guy, though ...." Her voice became muffled. "Right, babe?"

Jewell heard Bob's baritone in the background, then Beth Anne said, "Did you hear they've linked Doris Stone to the attack? Can you believe it?"

"I did hear that. And, no, I can't believe it. She's shifty and irritating, but violent? I don't think so." Jewell softened her tone. "Can I come by for a few minutes tonight? You can show me your battle wounds and I can return that ring."

"Sure." Beth Anne's voice faded. "See you tonight."

Jewell disconnected and shook the leash—Lois Lane was sniffing a nearby tree trunk—and scanned the sidewalk ahead. Long afternoon shadows made the Stone mansion, halfway down the block, dark and forlorn. Shuttered windows across the front accentuated a somber message: Misery lies within. "It wouldn't hurt to do a quick pass-by." Lois Lane gave Jewell's hand a lick and trotted away.

They'd reached the corner when two police patrol units rolled up Radish

Street and stopped in front of the mansion. *Are they going to arrest Doris? Oh, my God!* Jewell suddenly felt scared for her crusty landlady.

The cops climbed the front steps and knocked on the door, then came back and convened on the sidewalk. Jewell couldn't hear them, but based on their body language—shaking heads, gesturing arms —they weren't happy. One by one they turned their blue-uniformed backs on 811 Radish, got into their vehicles, and ... sat there, parked.

Guess she's not home. How long will they wait?

Jewell's phone beeped. "That's the reminder for Mrs. Plougher's meds, Lois Lane. Let's go."

As they jogged along the sidewalk the two police units cruised past. *Hmm. They didn't wait long. Maybe they know something I don't.* Jewell picked up the pace, laughing when Lois Lane lunged forward to maintain the lead.

* * *

The Ploughers were settled in the living room, watching the local news, when Leo called Jewell. His voice was smooth, intimate as he said, "For my first official act as part of the Miwok Ghost Busters, I called in a favor—got access to the file on Aunt Maris's death. You interested?"

"Are you kidding me? Of course!" Jewell stepped away from the blaring television—Miwok High School's football team was in the news—and said, "Can I have a look at them, or are they classified?"

"Hardly." Leo paused. "It's just a couple of pages. If you want, I'll make prints and bring them by."

"I have a couple of hours off tonight; I'm heading over to Bob and Beth Anne's. You could meet me there, if you want."

Leo's voice came up a notch. "What time we talkin' about?"

"Seven-thirty, eight o'clock?"

"Roger. Uh, don't be surprised if you get a call from Miwok PD. They're still looking for Doris and I told them you're her tenant."

"They were waiting for her out in front of 811 earlier today. She hasn't come home yet? Where is that woman?" Jewell let out a breath. "See you later."

* * *

When she pulled into the last available parking space at a shabby, two-story apartment building flanked by a tire store and vacant lot, Jewell double-checked her GPS for accuracy.

"Yep. Lancelot Arms, 62 Main Street. This is it. Somehow, I thought Bob and Beth Anne would have their own little cottage with a white picket fence. There I go again, transferring my unfulfilled dreams to the rest of the world."

She snapped the leash on Lois Lane's collar and stepped from the car. The dog led the way to a ground-floor unit. At the first rap of Jewell's knuckles, Leo Stone opened the door.

"Come on in, beautiful."

Jewell laughed, blushing a little. "Hello to you, too."

From somewhere within the apartment Beth Anne called, "Hi, Jewell."

Bob hurried into the living room and wrapped Jewell in a bear hug. Lois Lane stiffened, a low growl sounding in her throat. Bob immediately dropped his arms, stepping away from Jewell while eyeing the dog. "Okay, pooch. I get it. No touching."

Jewell, embarrassed, rested a reassuring hand on Lois Lane's head and murmured, "Sit." The dog immediately sat. Jewell bent down, whispering in Lois Lane's ear, "It's okay. He's one of the good guys."

Leo, watching, smiled. "You've trained her well."

Jewell shook her head. "I've only had her a few days. I'm discovering she has some interesting talents."

"Beth Anne's in here." Bob ushered them through the living room and across a tiny hall to the bedroom.

"Hi, everyone!" Beth Anne, a sadly diminished version of the perky, freckle-faced woman Jewell shared coffee with days earlier, stretched her left arm out in welcome.

Jewell stepped carefully into the hug—Beth Anne's right side was heavily bandaged and wisps of singed hair lay flat against an unnaturally red ear.

When Beth Anne gasped, Jewell jumped away.

"It's not you. My whole body's super sensitive."

Jewell shivered. A prayer rippled through her. *Thank You, God, for saving her. Please heal her fast.*

"The Ploughers sent chocolates. They think chocolate is good medicine. And, the ring is in the bag, Bob. Keep it in a safe place. It's special."

"I noticed." Bob frowned. "In fact, I'm thinking maybe you should take it back to the house. It's creepy." He looked sheepishly at his uncle. "Not like I was scared or anything—just weirded out."

"That's why I gave it to you," Jewell whispered. "But I guess you have enough goin' on here without adding a haunted ring."

Impatience crossed Leo's face; he quickly stifled it. "That reminds me. Jewell and I are trying to figure out how that ring got in the closet. From what I remember, Maris never took it off." He glanced at Beth Anne's pale face and switched gears. "But, first things first. Let's dive into that candy. Do you feel like sharing?"

"Absolutely!" Beth Anne handed the bag to Bob. "Open it, would you, hon?"

Half an hour later Beth Anne had drifted off to sleep and the others were studying the official-looking photocopies spread out on the coffee table.

"Thanks for getting these." Jewell cocked her head. "It'll take a while to go through them all."

She lifted a photo by one corner and peered at a blurry, poorly lighted shot of her bedroom ten years ago. The photographer must have been standing in the doorway, because bulky furniture sat across the room on either side of the bay window. The drapes were open and a long, narrow form hung suspended from the valence.

As Jewell's eyes adjusted to the blurriness, the form became a human torso with its profiled face turned to the ceiling. The hand at the end of the left arm was closed in a fist. One finger of the fist wore a ring.

Jewell's stomach lurched. She dropped the photo to the table. *God in Heaven. How did it get in the closet?* she gulped. "That definitely tells a story. Where's the fingerprints, DNA, all that stuff?"

Leo frowned. "You gotta remember, this was ten years ago. The department's resources weren't exactly state-of-the-art back then."

"That's right," Bob added. "The crime rate was close to zero—on high school graduation night, a stoned teenager might pee in the courthouse fountain. The town fathers relied on the sheriff's office for anything serious."

"According to this report," Jewell mused, "They interviewed Rudolph and ruled him out as a suspect. Says here he was immobilized from a cast on his foot, didn't know anything was going on at the other end of the house." She looked up at Leo. "Any idea why they discounted your brother as a suspect? Not to mention a neighbor, or a friend?"

"Based on this file," Bob said, "the cops saw it from the beginning as a robbery gone bad. They didn't explore anything else. Right, Uncle Leo? I was still in high school—my memory's like swiss-cheese." He frowned. "Back then, I was stoned most of the time."

Leo put the papers together in a neat stack, his face grave. "There was a home invasion down the road in Ignacio a couple weeks before this happened. No one was hurt, but the community was shaken up. No suspects were ever caught. It was natural our cops would consider this a repeat crime, or at least a copy-cat situation." He looked down at his hands. "I never bought that theory. For one thing, the house wasn't ransacked. And they took Maris's jewelry, but didn't take other valuables in the house. Her murder didn't fit the first case, either. Even if she caught the burglars in the act, murder was too extreme. Two and two never made four, in my mind."

"I agree with you," Jewell whispered. "Especially since the séance." She turned to Bob. "That's what I borrowed the ring for. I got a medium to come to the room and communicate with your aunt's ghost." Bob looked stunned. Jewell blushed. "Crazy, I know. But the ghost really showed up. And, she said the evil and corruption that caused her death are still in the house."

Bob leaned back, his eyes closed. "I'm not sure I can help with this. Not right now, anyway. I'm barely keeping it together since the fire-bombing." He pulled himself up from the couch. "I understand you need to go through it all; just leave me out, and be careful."

"You got it, son," Leo said. Jewell nodded. Leo slipped the documents back into their folder.

"One last thing." Jewell leaned in to kiss Bob's cheek. "My dog will just have to get used to me hugging you."

When the apartment door closed behind them, Leo took Jewell's arm. Lois Lane stared at him for a second, her lip curled back, and then scampered along the cobblestone walkway to re-mark the bush she'd visited earlier.

Leo looked down at Jewell. "What do you think? Did we learn anything tonight?"

"I did," Jewell nodded. "A lot of questions went unanswered back when your sister-in-law died. I'm going to research the old news reports."

"I'm glad I'm on your team, girl," Leo smiled gently. "Maris's death has been an unhealed wound in our family for too long. We need some answers."

Chapter Ten

Driving back to the Ploughers with Lois Lane curled up asleep on the passenger seat, Jewell had trouble keeping her mind on the road ahead. Her thoughts kept slipping back to 811 Radish and the horror it accommodated ten years ago.

With a deep breath, she switched to the present. Immediately, Doris's discolored, swollen face floated to the forefront of her mind.

Her eyes were red, too, come to think of it. Both eyes. She'd been crying.

Jewell pulled to the curb, dug the phone out of her purse, and called the Ploughers' nurse. "Hi, Ashley. Will you be okay staying another half hour? I need to swing by my new home."

At the sound of Jewell's voice, Lois Lane lifted her head and opened her mouth in a toothy yawn.

"I know it's your bedtime, girl." Jewell put the car in gear and pulled back on the road. "Okay if we make one quick stop?"

Lois Lane put her muzzle between her paws and closed her eyes.

"Looks like that's a yes."

At this hour Radish Street was quiet. Although street lights were spaced too far apart to be of any real use, slivers of light around the edges of curtained windows provided a reassuring, occupied sense. Jewell figured most of these houses had sheltered the same families for generations. That comforting idea disappeared when 811 came into view; the old Victorian was dark except for feeble amber rays from somewhere in the back yard.

"Looks like Perez is home," Jewell whispered. "And I don't see any cop cars. Did they arrest Doris? Maybe they just questioned her, and she's in the basement with her son. I'll check there before I put the ring back."

She pulled into the driveway and around to the rear parking area. The Nova's headlights reflected off two sets of taillights. "Doris's car, and Benny's. They're both here."

Jewell and Lois Lane climbed out onto the graveled driveway. Jewell took a minute to summon her courage, then followed resolutely as Lois Lane bounded across the grass. At the basement apartment Jewell's knuckles were raised, ready to knock, when the door opened.

"What the hell? Where'd you come from?" Perez jumped back; he evidently hadn't expected to see Jewell at his door.

"I—uh—what do you mean, where'd I come from? I live here, as you well know. I'm looking for Doris. Your mother. Is she here? I'm worried about her—last time I saw her, she didn't look so good." Jewell snapped her mouth shut. *Maybe the wrong person to talk to about that.*

"Don't worry about Mom. She bruises easy. Always has." Perez studied Jewell's breasts. "You're the boarder, right? How you doin'?" Perez gave Jewell a toothy leer.

"Fine." Jewell pasted on a phony, good-neighbor smile and attempted to look beyond Perez into the apartment. "Is she in there with you?"

"No." Perez stepped forward, pulling the door shut behind him. "She went somewhere. Haven't seen her since yesterday. That reminds me: you got notice to move downstairs. You doin' that now? Or are you moving out altogether? I was you, I'd take that option, pronto. You by yourself?"

Lois Lane had been standing obediently by. When Perez stepped forward, she moved in front of Jewell. Perez stiffened. His hand went inside his jacket. "Tell your bitch to back off."

Gun?!! Jewell backed away, pulling Lois Lane with her. "I don't know that command. Tell Doris to call me." She turned and walked stiffly across the grass. At the driveway, she risked a quick glance back. Perez was still watching her. The ingratiating leer had become a cold, hooded stare.

Jewell looked straight ahead, forcing herself to ignore the fear she felt. She was dimly aware of Lois Lane herding her toward the Nova.

When her car's bulky form loomed in the shadows, Jewell expelled a cold, shivering breath. She pulled the car door open and plunged in, feeling like she'd run the bases and got to home plate barely ahead of the ball.

Lois Lane made a flying leap over Jewell's lap to the passenger seat. As Jewell slammed the door and started the engine she muttered, "Glad you agree. It's time to get the hell out." Nosing the car onto the street, she tapped the brakes for a second look along Radish. *Like there'd be traffic at this time of night.* A hysterical giggle escaped her.

In fact, the street was completely empty of vehicles, moving or otherwise. Jewell glanced in the rearview mirror in time to see, one after another, two sets of headlights ease around a far corner and onto Radish. She tensed again and fought off panic.

Who is that? The cops? Maybe. Be cool.

Jewell pulled to the curb, motor running and lights on. She watched in her rearview mirror as the vehicles approached, came alongside, and passed her by. It was not the cops. It was Hank, driving his truck, and Marco Perez in an old van.

Once again fear ebbed from Jewell's muscles, leaving her almost dizzy. She keyed Hank's number into her phone. After two rings she heard, "Yeah, Jewell? What's up?"

"Don't 'what's up' me, Hank Halverson. You and your little comrade can just pull to the curb. I want to have a word with you. Together."

"Hey. was that you parked back there?" Hank snorted, something Jewell knew he did when he was nervous.

"It sure as hell wasn't Santa Claus."

Both vehicles pulled to the curb halfway down the block. Jewell eased in behind them and rested her hand on Lois Lane's head. "At ease, soldier. These guys are not the enemy."

Lois Lane sat up, pushed her wet nose against Jewell's cheek, and turned to stare out the side window.

The truck and van doors opened simultaneously, as if choreographed. Marco and Hank went from their vehicles into the Nova's back seat in a rush of cold air. When Jewell turned to watch them squeeze into the too-small space, her hand grazed a paper sack next to her purse.

Damn. I forgot about the ring.

She stared hard at Hank, then Marco. "Care to fill me in?"

Hank and Marco exchanged glances, trying not to laugh. "Lighten up, Jewell," Hank finally said. "It's not like we're out after curfew or something. I'm trying to help the kid locate his grandmother."

"Yeah, Jewell—I mean, Mrs. McDunn," Marco stuttered, "Hank said we should check out the house—see if she packed a bag, or what. Did you go inside? Is she there?" His voice cracked, reminding Jewell how young he was.

"Okay, relax. You're not in trouble. Not yet, anyway." Jewell kept her voice soft. "I only got as far as your father's door, Marco. He said she went somewhere yesterday, isn't back yet." Jewell paused. "Her car's there, though. Wherever she went, she didn't drive."

"She wouldn't go off without telling me; we don't always get along, but we look out for each other." Marco sounded panicked.

"Think about it." Hank's voice was falsely cheerful. "If she had something to do with the firebombing, she'd make herself scarce for a while."

Marco shook his head. "Gram's selfish to the bone; I'll give you that. But firebombing? No way. She's not crazy." He looked out the window, surreptitiously swiping at a tear.

"Maybe," Jewell mused, "she's in there, hiding. She drinks a bit, right? Could she be keeping company with a bottle of JD, hoping the cops will give up and go away?"

"I can't sit folded up like a pocket knife much longer," Hank grumbled. "Let's make a decision. How about you create a diversion, Jewell, while we slip in and check the place out?"

"Create a diversion? Are you out of your mind? I barely got away alive as it is!" Jewell felt her pulse rise. "Listen: I need to get into my room, anyway. Why don't we all, QUIETLY, walk back to the house, go in the front door QUIETLY, go upstairs without turning on any lights, and you can look in her room while I take care of my business. Any chance you can do that? QUIETLY?"

Marco's face lit up. He smiled for the first time since getting into Jewell's

84

car. "Absolutely. Yes. Thank you so much, Mrs. McDunn." He turned to Hank. "Can you move quietly? I can, but I'm not beefed up on 'roids."

Hank stiffened. He lifted a meaty fist and put it very close to Marco's nose. "Little man, ever think about the sound of my fist breaking your face? No? Well, all the sound would be inside your head. That's quiet." He smiled at his own cleverness.

"Hank, dear," Jewell purred, "If you EVER mention hurting anyone in my presence again, you will be very, very sorry. And noise will be the least of your pain."

Shrugging, Hank reached for the door handle. "Yes, ma'am. I know that. And it was a joke." He raised his eyebrows. "Let's go. We're wasting time I could be spending with Carolyn." He grinned and stepped out of the car.

With Hank in the lead and the others trailing single file, they hurried along the narrow, poorly-lighted sidewalk. When Hank stopped suddenly, Jewell bumped into him and Marco, close behind, stepped on her foot.

"Ouch!" Jewell swallowed the cry. Hank looked down at her, a finger to his lips.

Jewell glared back and stomped away into the gloomy mist. Hank and Marco followed, shivering and rubbing their arms in the bone-chilling damp.

The fog had settled to ground level. Jewell strained, looking for landmarks—God forbid they'd wander blindly past the mansion. When an outline of pointed-spear iron fencing appeared, she sighed. They'd reached 811.

Beyond the fence the indistinct hulk of the Stone family mansion took shape. *How sad it looks. If houses have hearts, this one's broken.*

Jewell turned to Hank and Marco, signaled silence, and carefully lifted the gate latch. Hank reached around her, pushing the gate hard. It swung open with a loud squeak. Jewell's glare was returned by Hank's goofy grin. *Saints preserve us. He thinks this is a joke.*

At the front steps, Jewell faced her companions. "When we get inside," she whispered, "we count to twenty so our eyes can adjust to the dark. No talking. Remember, we're walking around on Benny's ceiling. Going upstairs, I'll lead: I know which stairs squeak. Walk in my footsteps. At the top, we split and you go to the right. Doris's room is the first door. Got it?"

Hank rolled his eyes, muttering, "Yeah, yeah. Let's go before I catch pneumonia."

"Shouldn't we search the downstairs, too?" Marco's voice was shaking. *Poor kid's really scared.*

"We'll check the kitchen on the way out." Jewell gave him what she hoped was a reassuring smile.

The moment the lock clicked Lois Lane's nose was at the door. When Jewell turned the knob, the dog shouldered past and looked back at Jewell. *I guess her eyes don't need to adjust.*

Jewell, Hank, and Marco slipped inside and stood, shoulders touching, in palpable darkness. An ancient wall sconce provided the only light in the cavernous hallway.

The sound of music came from below the floorboards: Benny's TV. Jewell mouthed, "Perez," and signaled Lois Lane to start up the stairs.

Marco stayed directly behind Jewell, stepping on her heels. Hank, though, took the steps two at a time and thumped to the hall landing before Jewell. She glared at him, waved both of them toward the right wing, and followed Lois Lane along the left hallway. At her bedroom door, she turned to watch the two men fade into the darkness. *This is like an episode of Scooby-Doo.* She frowned. *It won't be funny if we bump into Perez.*

"Step back, puppy." Lois Lane had her nose to Jewell's door and was softly growling.

Juggling the leash, the ring bag, and her purse, Jewell felt with one finger for the keyhole. It was unusually scratchy. When she attempted to insert the key, it slipped to one side. *Damn. Gonna need the phone light.* She pointed her phone at the knob and quickly flicked the light on and off. The keyhole was not just scratched—a nail was stuck in it. *For crying out loud.*

Jewell pushed back a flash of anger: Someone had tried to pick the lock. *Must have been Perez; Doris has a key.* She dug into her cosmetics kit and pulled out the tiny, mostly-for-looks pocket knife Carolyn had given her ages ago. Using the knife's tweezers, she grasped the nail and pulled. The tweezers slipped off the nail head.

Okay. Let's rethink.

Next time, rather than pulling, she twisted. The knob turned and the door's latch gave way. With a sigh of relief, Jewell opened the door. Lois Lane stepped across the threshold, then stopped. She lifted one paw and pointed.

Jewell leaned into the shadowy room, eyes wide, and scanned the entire space. It looked benignly comfortable—everything was exactly as she'd left it after the séance. She nudged Lois Lane aside and stepped in, shutting the door.

A faint, keening hum came from behind the closet door. With Lois Lane pressed against her leg, Jewell reached into the paper sack and pulled out the ring box. The humming stopped. *O-kay. Here goes nothing.*

Lois Lane, stiff-legged, moved slowly to the closet, ears cocked. Jewell made the sign of the cross, Catholic-style, and pulled the closet door open. Two shadowy figures took shape in a gloomy back corner. When she realized who they were, her heart stopped. She crumpled slowly to the floor.

* * *

Something scratchy and wet pressed against Jewell's cheek. She tried to move her head. Her face collided with...cloth. Her eyelids flickered open: blue denim and Lois Lane's tongue were right there, close.

"She's not dead." Hank, whispering.

Jewell's eyes snapped shut. *Is this Hank's lap? Oh, God. I fainted.*

"I saw...I mean..." Jewell struggled to sit up. She looked around the room dazedly and locked eyes with Marco. He was ashy white and had the ring box between two fingers.

I must have dropped it.

"Give me that," Jewell whispered hoarsely.

Marco handed her the box, then put a finger to his lips signaling quiet. From the hallway came the soft thump of footsteps. Then, a ray of light flowed under the door. The thumping stopped. The doorknob rattled; a low, masculine voice said, "Fuckin' jammed lock! No way anyone's getting in there." Lois Lane's ears went forward; Hank rested a hand on her head.

Marco gripped Jewell's arm.

The light disappeared; the footsteps receded. A minute later, from the downstairs hall, the front door snapped closed.

"I'm okay now," Jewell whispered.

"We heard you fall. What happened?" Marco's voice trembled.

"I opened the closet and saw…"

"We can talk later," Hank hissed. "Let's get the hell out of here." He pulled Jewell to her feet.

"Can't leave yet," Jewell mumbled. "Have to put the ring back." She turned to the half-open closet, forcing herself to look inside. There she saw clothes on their hangers, shoes neatly lined up on the floor, and plastic bins tucked on the overhead shelf; nothing but this prosaic display.

Hank cleared his throat. "Was it the over-the-top neatness that scared you, Jewell? 'Cuz it's enough to make me want to keel over." He beamed angelically.

"That's not funny, Hank," Marco whispered.

Jewell ignored them. "You saw it, didn't you, Lois Lane?"

The dog looked up, whining soulfully.

"I wish she could talk." Jewell's voice took on a defiant tone. " I fainted for a reason—I'm stone-cold sober, and I'm not the fainting type. I saw ghosts, two of them. Whether anyone believes me or not."

Hank shrugged. "No big deal, Jewell. This place is so old, It's probably crawling with ghosts."

Marco shook his head. "I don't give a shit about ghosts. Where's my grandmother? She wasn't in her room; where is she?" His chin wobbled, like he was trying not to cry.

"Look at it this way, bud," Hank said. "Maybe she doesn't want to be found. Maybe she just got the hell out of Dodge for a couple days."

Jewell wrenched her thoughts away from the closet with its unwelcome visitors and patted Marco's shoulder reassuringly. "That makes sense, even if it did come from Hank. Let's check the kitchen on our way out, in case she left you a note."

They crept silently from the room and down the stairs. After a quick survey of the kitchen—no Doris, no notes, no sign of anyone—they slipped out the front door.

On the dark front porch, Jewell whispered, "If you're really worried, Marco, talk to Miwok PD. They specialize in finding people."

"Yeah," Hank put in, "But first let's get out of here."

Marco nodded, his face desolate. They hurried through the gate and down the block.

At the corner, Hank laid a meaty paw on Jewell's shoulder, "Maybe you should have your blood sugar checked. Carolyn gets dizzy when hers gets low."

Jewell tried to keep the snarl out of her voice. "It wasn't low blood sugar. I saw a ghost. Believe it or not."

Marco's eyes flitted to Jewell and away, barely aware she was talking. Hank, though, exhaled noisily and blurted, "For cryin' out loud, Jewell. Haven't you about beat that ghost business to death?"

"Absolutely." This time, Jewell's snarl came out full bore. "I'd be delighted to drop the whole thing and get on with my life. You got any idea how?" She sighed. "For your information, smarty pants, the nonexistent ghosts are multiplying. There were two of them in there tonight." Jewell yanked at Lois Lane's leash and marched the remaining few yards to her car without looking back. "Go home, you two," she called. "And, no more playing detective!"

As she climbed into her car Jewell realized she still had the ring. She sighed.

Chapter Eleven

"What took you so long? Ashley gets crabby when she has to work overtime." Mr. Plougher focused his faded blue eyes on Jewell. "I know, I know," Jewell soothed. "I ran into a couple of friends and we had to take care of something. I'm sorry. It won't happen again."

"Now, Nicholas," Eve Plougher chimed in. "don't exaggerate. Ashley said she was glad for the extra hour." Her frail body sagged. "Can I go to bed now? I was just staying up until you got back, Jewell."

All-to-familiar shame coursed through Jewell. Her face turned bright pink. *Damn. I've let them down. Can't I do anything right?*

* * *

Later, punching her pillow one more time and resting her head in a futile quest for sleep, Jewell glanced across the room to the student desk. The sack containing the ring glowed dimly.

Did I really see two ghosts huddled in my closet? Two ghosts who weren't there the next time I looked?

She sat straight up in bed.

Did I imagine it? Am I having a nervous breakdown? If I'm not, 811 Radish is home to two murdered women, not just one.

She climbed out of bed and tiptoed to the desk.

I'm not imagining the ring's weirdness: Bob noticed that, too.

Jewell stared into the darkness, reviewing the earlier experience.

There was an odd, metallic smell near the closet. When I touched the door handle, I got a shock. When I opened the door I saw an older woman—grey hair, flannel nightgown—holding a second woman against her shoulder. When I looked again with Hank and Marco, the closet was empty. Who were those women? Where'd they go? Did they escape down the hall while I was unconscious? No. Hank and Marco would have seen them. She groaned. *Is it possible I'm imagining all of this?*

Jewell had done a good job of scaring herself with her thoughts. She twisted her face in a silent scream, then switched on a lamp. Immediately reassured by the Ploughers' bland, musty guest room, she looked around. Seeing her image in the dressing table mirror, she gasped at the haggard, wild-eyed face staring back at her. *God, help me.*

She tiptoed to the bathroom in search of Ibuprofen for what had become a splitting headache. On the way back to bed, her foot bumped Lois Lane. The dog opened one eye and thumped the floor with her tail.

"Sorry, girl. Go back to sleep."

Lois Lane. Hmm. She reacted to the ghosts, too. So, I'm not crazy—those ghosts are real.

Jewell climbed between the sheets, stretched out, and stared at the ceiling. *Now would be a good time for some heavenly reassurance, God.*

* * *

Mr. and Mrs. Plougher glanced at Jewell as they sipped their coffee and pushed scrambled eggs around on their plates.

"You should have slept in, dear. We don't mind doing for ourselves once in a while." Eve Plougher's voice was full of concern.

Jewell shook her head. "Absolutely not. I'll pick up steam as the day goes by." *Note to self: get a grip. These people shouldn't be worrying about me.*

Halfway to the table with a plate of toast, Jewell heard a soft knock at the patio slider. She put the plate down, stepped to the door, and pulled back the drape.

"For crying out loud."

Carolyn, Hank, and Bob stood there, looking like they'd slept in their clothes and hadn't bothered to change. Carolyn gave her mother a tentative finger-wave; Hank and Bob stared vacantly at their feet.

"It's family," Jewell groaned. *Whatever brought them to the Ploughers' back door at 8:00 in the morning must be serious.*

Mr. Plougher leveraged his hands against the table and pushed to a standing position. "What're you waiting for," he crowed, still slightly bent over. "Let 'em in!" He grabbed his cane and thumped across the tiled floor to the slider, elbowing Jewell aside in his enthusiasm for breakfast company.

"How delightful," Mrs. Plougher chirped. "Can you make another pan of eggs, Jewell? I'm sure your young people brought their appetites."

When Nicholas Plougher had fumbled the door open, Carolyn, Hank, and Bob sidled in. They stood shoulder-to-shoulder, nervous.

"To what do we owe this pleasure?" Jewell snapped.

"They don't need a reason, Jewell," Mrs. Plougher's tone was crisp. "It's delightful to have friends drop by. It brightens our morning." She smiled at the tousled trio. "Please pull those side chairs up to the table. Will you have some eggs and toast? The jam is delicious."

Carolyn took a step forward. "We didn't come to eat. Thank you, though." She gave the egg platter a quick, yearning glance, then turned to the Ploughers. "We're hoping you can help us convince Mom to cooperate."

At that, Jewell's head came up; her lower lip pushed out. "Convince? Cooperate? What is this, an intervention? Now I've heard everything!"

Bob stepped from behind Carolyn and pulled a chair up to the table, smiling at Mr. Plougher. "I'll have some coffee, Nicholas, since you're offering." He looked back at Hank, who had eased over to the table and was eyeing the eggs. "What we have to say might be easier on a full stomach, dude."

With a sigh of relief, Hank lowered his bulk into a chair. "Amen. Strawberry jam's my favorite."

Jewell sagged against the counter and looked imploringly at Carolyn. "What's going on?" Bob cleared his throat. "Hank called me last night when he got home. From what he said, the Stone family mansion isn't good for you." He stared intently at Jewell. "I got you into this mess; it's up to me to get you out." He turned to Nicholas Plougher. "Can she stay here until we find other digs?"

Without warning, Jewell's temper erupted. She shouted, "Hold on a darn minute!"

Everyone at the table froze. Nicholas Plougher's mouth dropped open; his fork clattered to his plate. Mrs. Plougher paled, clutching her chest.

"Oh, God," Jewell gasped. She ran across the room and held a glass of water to the old woman's lips. "Take a sip. And breathe. Everything's okay. That's right. Have another sip." She leveled a gaze at Carolyn and her crew. "I don't believe you guys, coming here and trying to throw your weight around!"

Carolyn leaned across and slipped an arm around Mr. Plougher's shoulders. "We didn't mean to upset anyone, Mom. We just thought if we got them on our side, maybe you'd listen."

"I'm all right now, Jewell," Eve Plougher rasped. "And I agree with Bob. You need to move out of that place." She turned to her husband. "We'd love to have her stay here until she finds a better spot, wouldn't we?"

Nicholas Plougher smiled weakly, his face still reflecting shock.

Jewell willed herself to relax. "Let's start over. I appreciate everyone's support. You're worried about me; I get it. But, your way of expressing it? Not cool."

Five heads nodded. No one spoke. Jewell stepped to the patio door. "Bob, will you be kind enough to stay in here with the Ploughers while I talk to Hank and Carolyn outside?"

As the door slid shut behind them, Jewell smiled through the glass at the Ploughers before turning to Hank and Carolyn. "Are you out of your effing minds? Where do you get off, coming here and telling me what to do?"

Carolyn stepped protectively in front of Hank, a move which at another time would have been ludicrous. Now, though, Hank huddled gratefully behind his petite girlfriend.

"Get a grip, Mom," Carolyn's tone was soothing. "You're in over your head and too stubborn to admit it. That old house isn't worth dying for."

"Yeah, Jewell," Hank muttered from within Carolyn's hair. "I'm sorry I was such an ass when you lived with us. I wanted you to move out, but not to a

93

freak show." He peered at Jewell's stony frown from above Carolyn's head.

"I don't blame you, Hank," Jewell said. "I was glad to find a place of my own." She reached around Carolyn and pulled Hank into view. "You must know that if I really thought I wasn't safe there, I'd be first out the door." She studied her chipped fingernails. "I've been bouncing from place to place all my life—you know that, Carolyn—you've been there with me for most of it. Run-down trailer parks, seedy apartment houses, even a seaport motel room served as home for me. When I saw 811 Radish, well, it was a dream come true—my childhood dream. I can't give up on it."

Carolyn and Hank exchanged glances; Hank frowned. "We tried, babe." To Jewell, he said, "We'll keep the spare bed made up, just in case."

"I understand, Mom," Carolyn murmured. "Just remember, if the dream falls apart on you, we're still around."

Jewell turned away from her daughter's gaze, blinking back tears. Assuming a cocky grin, she pulled the slider open and whispered, "Smile. For the Ploughers."

A few minutes later Jewell stood with her back to the kitchen counter and rapped a spoon against the coffee pot. "Here's the deal. I admit the last few days have been hard—for all of us. Even so, I'm not ready to give up on 811 Radish."

"I'm not ready to bail on the family home, either." Bob nodded. "But a lot has changed since my grandparents moved me in there and raised me. Back then, that house represented shelter and," he cleared his throat, "even love."

"Right," Jewell said quietly. "I'm assuming you spell change D-O-R-I-S. I need to figure out how to get on her good side—if she has one."

Bob's phone chirped. "Gotta take that. It might be Beth Anne." He pulled it from his pocket and looked at the screen. "Uncle Leo."

Jewell's eyes widened. "Have him call me, would you?" She turned to the rest of the group. "I know you're trying to help. Sorry I lost my temper—you know how I am with bossy people." She sighed. "Tell you what: I promise to be careful. Will that do, for now?"

As she stared into their somber faces, Jewell felt tears trickling down her cheeks. These five people were the closest she had to a caring family.

"Don't you all have someplace you need to be? Except you two." Jewell grinned at Nicholas and Eve Plougher.

"Just a second, everyone." Carolyn raised her voice against the sound of chairs scraping linoleum. "For the record, I don't agree with Mom. I don't think she's safe at that mansion." She stared solemnly at Jewell. "How're you going to be careful around Doris and stand up to her demands, too? Be reasonable, Mom."

Jewell sighed. "When I think of something, you'll be the first to know." She walked quickly through the living room and opened the front door, avoiding eye contact as Hank, Bob, and Carolyn filed out. When the door closed, she leaned against it, exhausted.

If only they'd asked me how they could help, instead of trying to tell me what to do.

"Your phone's beeping, Jewell," Mr. Plougher's raspy voice called.

"Let it go. We need to get our morning back on schedule. "Did you take all your meds, Mrs. Plougher?"

* * *

Leo Stone, handsome in fresh-pressed jeans and a Hawaiian shirt, waved to Jewell as she and Lois Lane entered the Miwok Pie Company's open-air dining area. Jewell, suddenly awkward and glad her earrings matched her new magenta sundress, nodded in recognition. She crossed the tree-shaded space to Leo's table and paused, a little unnerved by his solemn stare. When his face broke into a smile; she relaxed and they both laughed.

"Thanks for getting a table outside; I debated about bringing my dog along. Now, I'm glad I did." As Jewell slipped into a spindly, wrought-iron chair, Lois Lane crawled under the table. She was completely hidden except for her tail.

"Not every day," Leo deadpanned, "I have a lunch date with a beautiful woman and her canine companion."

A smile lit up Jewell's face. "I like your attitude. Silly me, I was afraid this lunch was just for crime-solving."

"Yeah, well," Leo chuckled. "I've always been one to grab opportunities as they show up." He handed her a menu. "You ready to order? This place is famous for its shepherd's pie. I suggest we eat first, save crime-solving for dessert."

"Definitely." Jewell turned her attention to the menu. "Shepherd's pie sounds good." Then, "Hey, they have Murderously Good Mud Pie!"

Leo stared at the menu, then broke out in a loud guffaw. Jewell felt herself relax. *Gotta love a guy who gets my sense of humor.*

A bit later, when both plates were cleared of everything but flaky pastry crumbs, some gravy, and a few salad greens, Leo leaned back in his chair. "You know, don't you, your kids and my nephew are damn worried about you?" He looked at Jewell from over his coffee.

Jewell pushed her plate away. *Don't get defensive. This guy is not the enemy.* She lifted her chin to look squarely at the good-looking, sharp-eyed man across the table. "Of course, I know. I'm worried, too. That's why I'm here with you, now." She glanced out at the street, then met his eyes with a shy smile. "One of the reasons."

"I understand something strange happened to you at 811 Radish last night. Care to tell me about that?" Leo's voice was so low, she barely heard him above the restaurant chatter.

"I would." Jewell reached into her bag and brought out the cardboard jewelry box. "Actually, I was at the house twice. Once by myself, once with my daughter's boyfriend and Doris Stone's grandson."

"Marco, right? Marco Perez? Benny Perez's son?"

"Yes. On the first visit, the plan was to put the ring back in my closet and talk to Doris. The house was dark, so I went around back—where Perez lives. He was there." She gave an involuntary shiver. "He said Doris wasn't home. Said if I knew what was good for me, I'd do what Doris requested and move out. Pronto."

Leo's eyes locked on Jewell's face. "He threatened you?"

"Yeah. Scared the beans out of me. Lois Lane growled at him and, swear to God, he almost pulled a gun on her."

The toothpick Leo had been playing with snapped between his fingers. He rubbed a hand across his face and leaned down to pet Lois Lane under the table. "Good girl," he whispered.

"When I left," Jewell continued, "I ran into Hank and Marco." She laughed softly. "Actually, I flagged them down. Couldn't figure out what they were doing together—and in that neighborhood, for God's sake. The first time the two of them met—we all had dinner my first weekend at the mansion—Marco flirted with Carolyn and Hank almost flattened him." She smiled at Leo. "Turns out Marco was so worried about his grandmother, he called Carolyn and Hank."

Leo signaled for the check, then drummed his fingers on the table. His casually interested expression had become a worried frown. "Fast forward a little, will you? Perez's behavior toward you has me worried. If I don't understand something, I'll ask."

Fast forward? Huh. He has some nerve criticizing someone he hardly knows.

Jewell was quiet for a second. Then, coldly, "Okay. We went in the house, they checked Doris's room, I went to my room—someone tried to break in, unsuccessfully—the guys didn't find Doris, I saw two ghosts in the closet, I passed out." She exhaled, her mouth a straight, hard line. "Is that fast enough for you?"

Chapter Twelve

As Leo stared at Jewell, looking puzzled. He dropped some money on the table and pushed back his chair. "Let's finish this conversation outside. And, I changed my mind. I want a lot more detail." He paused. "Especially the part about Perez."

Jewell grabbed Lois Lane's leash and followed Leo from the restaurant, catching up with him on the sidewalk. "In case you didn't notice, I don't allow myself to be treated like a Chatty Kathy doll; I'm not a toy you can be rude to and get away with it."

Leo looked straight ahead, silent. They walked up the street and around the corner, Jewell getting angrier by the moment. She stopped, pulled away from him, and swiped at a frustrated tear.

"This lunch date, or whatever it was," Jewell whispered, "is dead in the water."

Surprise flooded Leo's face. "Hey, I'm sorry, okay? I'm no good at polite conversation. When your feminine personality starts showing through whatever you're saying, I get ... diverted, you could say. Hell, if I had any social skills whatsoever, I wouldn't have two ex-wives laughing their way to the bank every month." He gently touched her arm. "Could we go sit down over there and you give me another chance?"

Jewell's anger dropped a notch.

He sounds scared. Good.

She moved to a bench outside Cones 'n Scones, Lois Lane in tow, and sat. "I'm not promising anything."

Leo dropped down next to her. "Look, no one intended to put one over on you. Moving you into the mansion seemed like a great way to infiltrate hostile territory." He frowned. "It's not like it's actually dangerous. Bob and Beth Anne know how good you are at getting along with people—we figured you could handle Doris."

Jewell nodded. *Makes sense, so far.*

"I guess you've heard she took my brother for everything he was worth. His lawyer was getting divorce papers together when Rudy had a heart attack and died. Ownership of the place has been bogged down in court ever since." His face took on a sorrowful expression. "Besides the property, there's all the valuable antiques my parents and grandparents collected. Those things belong to the Stones, dammit! They're practically part of our DNA. An insider to keep an eye on things? You bet we liked that idea."

Jewell scooted to the far end of the bench before facing Leo. "You put me in there to snitch for you? Why wasn't I filled in on this little detail? Oh, I get it. You thought I'd say no."

At Jewell's sharp tone Lois Lane stood, ears cocked, and rested her chin on her mistress's lap.

Leo's face reddened. "Don't think of it that way. it's a beautiful place; we thought you'd like being there." He paused. "We just didn't figure on Perez showing up."

Jewell focused on the clock above the door of the bank across the street. "And yet, he did. Can we talk about the haunting? I'm due back at work in a few minutes."

"Sure." Leo sounded relieved. "Again, I am sorry." He leaned toward Jewell and gently brushed her cheek with his hand. Pedestrians strolled by unnoticed by Leo, Jewell, or, to a lesser degree, Lois Lane.

Jewell smiled, a little hesitantly. *Apology accepted.*

"When I opened my closet door yesterday," she began, "the clothes were pushed to the side and two women were pressed up against the back wall. I could see right through them." She waited for a snort of disbelief, but there was none.

Leo nodded, unsmiling. "Go on."

"I fainted. Woke up with my head on Hank's leg. I told the guys what I saw;

99

they didn't believe me. When we looked in the closet again, zilch. Nothing was there."

"Damn, girl, I don't know what to say." Leo sounded impressed. "I believe you—one of the things men who've seen combat don't talk about is the ghosts they see." He scratched his chin. "The mansion wasn't always haunted. If it is now, Doris hasn't said anything. I'm wondering what's stirred things up?"

"Actually," Jewell stood and picked up Lois Lane's leash. "I'm the first person to sleep in that room in years, according to Marco. Maybe my presence is what did it. Not to mention, Benny Perez has been gone for years, hasn't he? And now he's back."

Leo took the leash and they began walking.

"I've been assuming one of the ghosts was Maris, your sister-in-law," Jewell continued. "Tell me, did she have red hair, kind of long and fluffy, as a young woman? Did she wear skirts and short-sleeved blouses?"

"Oh, yeah. That was Maris around the time she married Rudy. She was a pretty girl; worked as a typist here in town. Wore clothes like that all the time." Leo's voice was barely audible above the street noise.

"I didn't get a good look at the other ghost," Jewell mused. "She had her back to me. Have any other women died in the house?"

Leo swiped a hand across his forehead, swearing softly. "Nope." He frowned. "You sure the other ghost wasn't a man? Like, maybe, Rudy?"

"Positive," Jewell murmured. "It was a woman, hair in curlers and wearing a silky bathrobe."

She checked her watch again. "I have to get back to work. You think I should give the ring to the cops?"

"No. They don't need it unless they're looking into Maris's death. If you want, I'll put it in my safe deposit box." Leo took Jewell's arm and steered her toward the Civic parked nearby. "I hope we'll try this again, without the fireworks. I promise to leave my attitude at home." He smiled ruefully.

Jewell returned his smile. "I might've had a smidge of attitude, too." She handed him the ring box. "Maybe when this is with the rest of your family valuables, the ghost will disappear."

Leo leaned against the doorframe while Jewell and Lois Lane got into the car. "I'll swing by and have a little chat with Perez. He needs to find himself a new address." After rubbing a knuckle tenderly against Jewell's cheek, Leo stepped back and watched her drive away.

* * *

"Your phone's buzzing." Mr. Plougher's raspy voice echoed along the hallway.

Jewell dashed from the bathroom. "Thanks!" She grabbed her phone and tapped the screen. "Hello?"

"I'd like to speak with Jewell McDunn," a brisk, low-pitched female voice said.

"Who is this?" *Another darn sales call.*

"Officer Downey. Miwok PD."

"Oh." Jewell's tone softened. "Hi. I'm Jewell. How can I help you?"

"Your residence address is 811 Radish Street, in Miwok? You live with Mrs. Doris Stone?"

"Uh, yes. That is, we don't 'live' together. I mean, technically, I guess you could say that. I rent a room there. I do in-home care during the week, so I'm only there on weekends." Jewell's voice squeaked.

"We've been trying to locate Mrs. Stone. Do you know how we can contact her?"

"What's going on?"

"Is she away on a trip?" The officer ignored Jewell's question. "Did she mention travel plans to you?"

"No. Last time I saw her was Monday, when I went by the house to get something. She didn't say anything about a trip, but I've only lived there a short while and we're not close. You might want to check with her son. He lives downstairs."

There was a pause. Jewell could hear Officer Downey breathing. "Do you know if Mrs. Stone had access to a van recently?"

So that's what this is about. The van in the G.I.'s Joe bombing.

"I have no idea, but if you want my opinion, I'd say it's unlikely. She has a car, not a van."

"Uh, huh. One last question: Did Mrs. Stone say anything to you about losing a credit card?"

"No. Like I already said, I hardly know the woman. We've had, maybe, two conversations." Jewell hesitated. "I don't know if it's important, but the last time I saw her, she had a black eye."

There was silence on the line for a second. Then Officer Downey cleared her throat. "I'll note that, Mrs. McDunn. Had she been in an accident recently? Anything to explain the injury?"

"Not as far as I know. She wouldn't necessarily confide in me though. It's not like we're close friends."

"Huh." Jewell imagined Officer Downey shaking her head. "Okay. Thanks for your cooperation. If we have any other questions, we'll call back." The line went dead.

It rang again immediately. Jewell answered and smiled at the sound of Leo's soft baritone. "Interesting news, Sugar. I just came from the mansion; there's a For Sale sign in the front yard."

"What?" Jewell dropped into a nearby chair, feeling suddenly weak. She took a deep breath. *I just moved in and my home's being sold out from under me?*

"I'm going over there right now. Can you meet me out front?"

Before Leo could respond, Jewell disconnected and jumped to her feet. She hit the living room running, grabbed her bag and was halfway out the door before she remembered the Ploughers. She hurried back inside.

"Will you be okay on your own for an hour? I need to run over to 811 Radish."

The Ploughers, nestled in their recliners watching television with a neighbor, looked up.

"Sure, sure. Go ahead," Nicholas Plougher said absently. Then, noticing her frantic expression and her bare feet, he added, "You might want to put on some shoes."

"Right," Jewell whispered. She slipped into her sandals and snapped her fingers to Lois Lane, asleep on the cool wood floor. "Let's go, girl."

Driving through the quiet, late-afternoon streets of Miwok, Jewell struggled to calm herself. She noted the stoical, almost smug expressions of the old, well-kept homes and the smooth, dream-like procession of sedans, work vans, and a bicycle along the historic street paralleling Radish. Then her thoughts zoomed back to Leo's call.

Why didn't Doris tell me she was putting the house up for sale? Is she going to kick me out? I have a lease. And, what about the Stone family? How can she sell before the courts decide who the place belongs to?

When her Nova rounded the corner onto Radish, Jewell zeroed in on a red and white sign attached to 811's wrought-iron fence.

OMG, he was right.

The curb was lined with cars; Jewell felt lucky to find a parking spot around the corner. Then she and Lois Lane hurried along the sidewalk to 811 Radish, stopping dead at the FOR SALE BY OWNER sign.

Doris is selling the place on her own.

Lois Lane, sniffing the grass beneath the fenceposts, lifted a paw and looked up at Jewell with a puzzled expression.

Why isn't she using a realtor? A house like this, historic and valuable, a person would go through a realtor. And when was she going to tell me?

Jewell studied the front of the house: lawn, shrubbery, porch, windows—it looked amazingly normal. Curtains were pulled gracefully back to showcase antique windows sparkling in the afternoon sun; the sprinklers had left a bit of dew on the recently mowed lawn.

As she turned to follow Lois Lane around back, Jewell noticed a shade snap up in one of the attic windows. *That's creepy.*

Lois Lane made a beeline to the garage, loping around to the side entrance. "No cars, so no Perez. What about Doris?"

Jewell jogged along the gravel to join Lois Lane, whose nose was pressed into the gap between the side door and the concrete foundation. A shiver ran along Jewell's spine. *Maybe we shouldn't look in there.*

She tried the knob; the door was locked. After a quick rub of the door's grimy half-window, she peered inside. When her eyes adjusted, the shadowy hulk of a sedan took shape.

"Doris's car is still here. Maybe she's home." Relief flooded Jewell. Her quick hug of Lois Lane's neck earned her a slobbery ear lick. "Whoa, girl!"

Jewell stepped away, laughing. "Let's check the basement apartment while we're waiting for Leo."

Lois Lane bounded across the lawn, leash trailing. Jewell followed, stepping carefully on the damp grass. When she noticed a wide swath of crushed lawn between the basement and the back door, she stopped. *What caused that?*

She took a deep breath and pulled in the aroma of bruised grass, then became aware of the yard's quiet—the house blocked noise from the street and an old, overgrown hedge absorbed sounds to the rear of the property. Bees buzzing in a nearby flowerbed made a counterpoint to what now felt like creepy silence.

"Come back, girl," she whispered. Lois Lane responded immediately, turning toward Jewell and then retracing her steps to stand nearby.

With a finger to her lips, Jewell tiptoed around the corner to the basement apartment. The door was slightly open.

"That's odd."

She gave it a push; it swung wide. Lois Lane stepped past Jewell, growling low in her throat. Jewell grabbed the dog's collar and peered around the door.

"Take it easy."

The room's one window was covered by a pull-down blind. In the subterranean gloom dustballs, scuff marks, and a frayed, rolled-up rug along the far side were the only signs anyone had lived there.

"It's empty. Has he moved his furniture into the house? One more thing to get straight from Doris when I catch up with her. That guy in the house, maybe using my bathroom? Not if I can help it."

Jewell pulled Lois Lane back—it wasn't easy; for some reason the dog was extremely agitated, growling and dancing around—and shut the door. As they retreated across the yard she looked around. It felt like someone was watching. At the back door of the main house, she took a minute to breathe.

I hope Doris is in the kitchen; I don't have time to search the whole house.

One hand was on the kitchen doorknob when she heard male voices, muffled, from inside. Through the door's half-window she saw a man in a maroon running suit standing by the table, his back to her—Perez. Across the room, two men in black uniforms shifted their weight. When one walked to the sink, Jewell sighed with relief. Cops. They were both cops.

She opened the door and stepped inside, keeping a tight hold on Lois Lane. The conversation stopped as all eyes swiveled toward her. Perez broke the silence, saying smoothly, "That's the woman I was talking about; my mother's tenant."

One of the officers nodded, looking at a notebook. "Jewell McDunn? You rent a room here?"

Suddenly Jewell felt tongue-tied. Authority figures, especially in uniform, had that effect on her. She looked down at Lois Lane sitting obediently beside her, eying the cops. For some reason, the dog's presence calmed her. "Yes, I do. I moved in a little over a week ago."

"I'm Officer Brahn, Miwok Police," one of the uniforms said. "That's Officer Lynch." He jerked his chin toward the other officer, who nodded to Jewell. "Mr. Perez here just told us his mother is away on a trip. Do you know anything about that? We need to talk to her."

Jewell straightened her shoulders, reminding herself she was not the person in trouble here. "I have no idea where she is. I need to talk to her, too—I've had some problems with my room—what did he tell you?" Jewell moved so one of the cops stood between her and Perez. Marco's face popped into her mind. She added, "Did you check with her grandson, Marco Perez? Or, maybe he filed the Missing Persons report?"

Perez shifted slightly so he could see Jewell. Then, pulling his gaze away, he said smoothly, "This broad doesn't know us very well. Mom gets fed up with that brat, Marco. She needed some breathing room, you know? She wouldn't have a clue about any vandalism—how'd you connect her with that, anyway? She's practically a senior citizen, you know?" He pulled on his ear, frowning. "She took off to Tahoe for a couple days; said she had a sick cousin—probably playin' the slots."

He's lying. I know it. Jewell felt her jaw stiffen.

Officer Brahn turned to Jewell. "Mr. Perez, here, didn't file the Missing Persons, ma'am, but he is next of kin. At the moment, we're here about the vandalism report." He exchanged a glance with Officer Lynch. "We still need to question her. Where's she staying in Tahoe?"

Perez all but laughed out loud, his eyes twinkling. "If she didn't tell me, her son—which she didn't—she sure as hell wouldn't tell this chick." He snickered. "She's practically a stranger."

Both officers looked quickly at Jewell—at Perez's remark her face turned bright red, but she kept her mouth tightly shut—then Officer Lynch said, "We have her cell number, but she hasn't responded to our calls. If we haven't heard from her by the end of the day, we'll have to put out an APB."

Both officers snapped their notebooks shut and turned toward the back door, nodding to Jewell.

"I'm leaving, too," Perez said. "Let's go out the front." He smiled genially and ushered the cops from the kitchen. As the dining room door closed, he looked over his shoulder at Jewell. The smile had been replaced by cold, blank dismissal.

Chapter Thirteen

The kitchen door was still swinging when Jewell's phone beeped. A text from Leo read, "U in there? Why cops?"

She quickly typed in, "Yes. U out front? I'll come to u." Jewell and Lois Lane hurried from the kitchen and down the back steps.

A car engine's roar came from the driveway. Lois Lane stopped short, catapulting Jewell past an ancient, thorny rosebush and onto the gravel.

"Aiiee!" Jewell landed on her hands and knees, gravel and thorns gouging deep. She managed to roll away from Lois Lane, who took off after the disappearing car, barking furiously.

Untangling hair and clothes from thorns with bleeding fingers took a few minutes. Finally, Jewell swallowed a sob and got to her feet. When the dog sidled around the corner of the house, tail between her legs, Jewell grabbed a handful of fur and buried her face in it.

"I have a first-aid kit in my van if you need it."

Jewell pulled her face out of Lois Lane's ruff and saw, first, jeans-encased legs, then the rest of Leo, standing respectfully about three feet away. When she put out a hand, he helped her to her feet.

"We almost got run over!"

"I saw Perez light out of here like his ass was on fire; let's go inside and wash the dirt out of those scrapes." Leo's tone was brusque, but his eyes flashed with anger.

* * *

"So, fill me in." Leo dabbed Liquid Band-Aid on Jewell's scratches. "What did Doris say about the For Sale sign?"

"No idea." Jewell winced at the stinging medicine. "Turns out there's an APB out on her."

"Really?" Leo stepped back, admiring his medical handiwork. "How'd Perez take that?"

"He was cool. Said she went to Tahoe to gamble. Sounded fishy to me but the cops bought it." Jewell limped to the sink, filled a glass with water, and took a long drink. "If she's at Tahoe, who put up that sign?"

"Good question. That reminds me; I just got off the phone with my lawyer. He'll squash this sale nonsense like a slow-moving cockroach."

Jewell's phone beeped; a text from Marco appeared. "Heard from Gram. She's okay!" It ended with three smiley faces.

"For cryin' out loud!" Jewell murmured, shaky with relief. "Perez was telling the truth." She paused. "Do Perez and truth belong in the same sentence?"

Leo read the text and shook his head. "Doesn't add up. Why would she take off for Tahoe when the son she hasn't seen in ten years just got here? And how's she doing a 'For Sale By Owner' long distance?"

"Too bad she's not here so we can ask her." Jewell heard the irritation in her voice and quickly added, "Sorry, Leo. I'm beyond frustrated with everything right now. You know she told me to move downstairs, and I refused? If she had plans to sell the house, wouldn't she just tell me to move out altogether? And why have Perez move out of the basement and into the main house, if it's being sold?" Jewell leaned down and absentmindedly patted Lois Lane's head. "I'm sure glad I have this little lady. No way could I stay here on my own."

"Perez is in the house, now? I don't like the sound of that at all." Leo's voice rose. "You do know the guy's got two strikes?" He held up two fingers. "He did time for armed robbery, got out and went right back in for killing a guy in a bar fight. A third strike'll put him behind bars for life. Stay away from him."

Jewell rolled her eyes. "I know, I know. I got here first, though, and I have a lease. I'm not leaving." She gave Leo a rueful smile. "I know that brands me as stubborn; so be it." Then, "Maybe Doris took off—and put the place up for sale—to get away from Perez. Somebody gave her that black eye." She shrugged and smiled coyly at Leo. "You want a tour of the place? A walk down memory lane?"

"All right," Leo grumbled. "But if Perez gets anywhere near you or your room without permission, I'll see he's back in Q so fast his head'll spin." He held out an arm and Jewell took it gratefully; her knees and palms were throbbing.

"I'm the tour guide," Leo smiled back. "I used to live here, you know."

"Right." Jewell let Lois Lane push past, then she and Leo moved more slowly to the foyer. There, when her senses absorbed the sounds, the smell, the feel of the old house, everything seemed as usual—the clock ticking in the library, dust motes dancing suspended in a side window's sunlight.

Lois Lane trotted to the living room and sat, ears cocked.

"It's been a long time," Leo said quietly. "It feels strange, being here as an outsider. This house was the heart of my family." His smile disappeared. "That reminds me: Since we're here anyway, let's put the ring back upstairs. Every time I think about taking it to the safe deposit box, it starts glowing. I don't think it wants to go there." His face radiated embarrassment.

"I'm not surprised," Jewell whispered. "I thought if I got the ring out of here, the ghost would go, too. It's beginning to look like it's the other way around. When the ghost leaves 811 Radish, the ring will be just a ring again."

She looked across the room to the mantel. "Something's not right. Where are the knick-knacks? The photographs? The place has been cleaned out!"

Every surface in the living room was completely bare.

"Son of a bitch," Leo swore grimly. "Let's do a recon. I have a blueprint of this place in my head. On this floor, besides the kitchen and the living room, there's a library, sewing room, half-bath, and a laundry room. Oh, and a storage space under the stairs."

The ceiling creaked. "That's my bedroom up there," Jewell whispered. "Do ghosts walk heavy?"

"I didn't hear anything. Could have been the wind. Let's finish looking around downstairs, then tackle the second floor."

They opened doors on rooms with a sewing and ironing workspace, a washer, dryer, and drying rack, and a lime-green toilet-and-sink combo surrounded by garish floral wallpaper.

"Library's next, through there," Leo said.

Jewell stepped up to a massive oak door, opened it, and stopped short.

"Shit," Leo whispered.

Four walls of shelving, once filled with books, were bare. Stodgy leather club chairs and a long mahogany table were clustered awkwardly in the middle of the room.

"I can't believe this," Leo whispered. "My dad filled this room with books; first editions, most of them."

"It was full of books last weekend; I saw them." Jewell retreated to the hallway. "Maybe Doris sold them. The statues and things in the living room, too. Some of them looked valuable."

"They were. Maris's hummel collection alone was worth a mint." Leo looked stricken.

"It's time we confronted Doris. Let's track her down." Jewell crossed the foyer and hurried up the stairs.

When they reached the second floor Leo went directly to a pair of white double doors in the right wing. "Back in the day this was our playroom. Probably Doris's bedroom now."

From the doorway the view was benign: The bed was made—a pale blue satin comforter with darker blue pillows flanking a mahogany headboard. Window shades hung at half-mast and a pair of blue satin slippers sat beneath a velvet boudoir chair.

"This room hasn't been stripped," Jewell whispered.

"Not yet, anyway."

"Maybe she's not leaving."

"Oh, she's leaving. She's been wanting to sell this place for years." Leo looked into Jewell's eyes. "Doris had the plan on hold while Perez was in prison. He's out now. The ball's rolling again."

Jewell hugged herself, chilled at Leo's frankness. "I knew from the beginning the woman had a cash register where her heart should be. I was naive to think it wouldn't affect me." She opened the door to an ensuite bathroom and put her head in for a quick look. Cosmetics and brushes littered one end of the sink counter, along with tissues and a cell phone. "Wherever she is, she won't be gone long." Jewell ran her fingers tiredly through her tousled hair. "Let's put the ring back and get out of here."

They hurried along the hall, stopping at Jewell's door.

Can I go in there again? God help me if I see another ghost! "You sure you're ready for this, Leo? I have to go in—it's my home—but you could opt out."

"If you can take it, so can I," Leo's eyebrows went up a notch. "We Stones aren't deserters."

Jewell looked from him to Lois Lane sitting alertly at the door. "I like that. I'm not a Stone, but I know how to walk through fear." She slipped a pocket knife from her purse and used it to release the still-jammed lock. The door swung open. Lois Lane padded in first, nose to the floor. Leo, next to cross the threshold, stopped short. There was an ominous stillness and the air seemed thick, hard to breathe. Leo's face drained of color.

"What?" Jewell peered in past him. The room looked exactly as she, Marco, and Hank had left it—the table and chairs used for the séance were clustered by the bed, the closet door was closed and the drapes were open.

"So," Jewell said. "What's up?"

"For starters," Leo's voice cracked like a nervous teenager, "The place reeks of White Gardenia. That's Maris's cologne." He stumbled to the foot of the bed and sat down. "If I closed my eyes I could see her, maybe perched on the window bench writing in her journal." His mouth turned up in a half-smile. "She was a corker. You remind me of her, Jewell. She had that same stubborn, no-nonsense streak. A great sense of humor, too. We were best friends, Maris and me. She loved Rudy, but she liked me. I never had a sister, but when Maris married Rudy, she filled that space in my heart." Leo froze, then suddenly jumped to his feet. "What was that?"

"What? I didn't hear anything." Jewell quickly crossed the room to stand next to him.

"Someone laughed," Leo whispered. "Maris's laugh. I'm sure of it! And the ring is going nuts." He took the glowing jewelry box from his pocket and put it on the nightstand.

Jewel reached for Lois Lane's collar—the dog stood with her nose to the ring box, whining—and said, "Now will you believe the ghost of your sister-in-law is here?"

Leo turned away, looking as if he was about to cry.

Oh, no—I hurt him. Damn my big mouth!

Before she could put together words for an apology, the air above Jewell's dresser flickered. As she watched, a tube of lipstick rose from the dresser top and began scrawling words across the mirror.

Leo, following Jewell's horrified stare, watched as the lipstick spelled out, "Under closet floor." After forming the R in 'floor' the lipstick fell, rolled off the dresser, and dropped to the rug. As Lois Lane pounced on it, Leo whispered hoarsely, "Maris?"

This time Jewell heard the laugh—a throaty, engaging chuckle. As it faded, the tension in the room dropped several notches and Jewell's eyes opened, wide. It was as if she'd been sleeping soundly. A glance at Leo told her he was in the same process—testing reality.

"Holy shit," Leo stood at the dresser and used a pinky finger to touch the scrawled words. "I'll be a son of a bitch. Maris always did have terrible handwriting."

Jewell managed to whisper, "Let's get out of here." She wondered if her heart would come right up out of her throat. "I can't handle dead people writing on mirrors."

"It's got to be a trick." Leo emitted a high-pitched giggle. "Okay. Whoever you are, the joke worked. We're scared shitless." He knelt by the dresser and looked beneath it. "Nothing down there." He stood, scanned the room, and stepped over to the curtains. "Eeyah!" He gave the curtain a karate chop. "Ouch!" He pulled back his hand. "That's a hard wall."

Jewell moved quickly and wrapped her arms around him. "Steady, big boy. Take a breath. There we go."

"Sorry," Leo muttered from within Jewell's hair. He pulled back enough to be eye to eye with her. "I gotta hand it to you, Mrs. McDunn. You're one strong lady."

Jewell felt her knees shaking. "About that. The ghost is getting stronger fast, and I'm more scared by the minute. The thought of spending another night in here—I don't think I can do it." When she cleared her throat, the sound came out as a whimper. "Why did I ever move into this place?"

Leo sank to the floor, his face between his hands. "I've never lost it that bad before, not even when I was in the Army. His voice dropped to a whisper. "My family should have pushed the cops to find out what really happened the night Maris was killed. If we had, her spirit wouldn't be stuck here, scaring innocent people." He snapped his fingers. "Didn't that fortune teller say the ghost will leave when the evil's cleared out? Am I psychotic, or does that sound like a solution?" He flipped Jewell's pocket knife in the air. "What the hell is the evil?"

Jewell sighed. "I don't know. One thing's for sure: in this room, everything starts with the closet." She stepped over and yanked the door open. Inside, she saw clothes, shoes, and shelved boxes; no dead women.

Leo pulled apart the rack of shirts and dresses and stared at a back wall containing nothing more frightening than faded wallpaper.

Lois Lane pushed her way in, sniffing along the floor. After a minute she turned, bounded from the closet, and jumped onto the window seat. There she stood in the window, growling furiously.

"What's up, girl?" Jewell grabbed Lois Lane's collar and glanced out the window. "Oh, boy. Leo, you need to see this."

In the driveway below, Perez stood leaning against Doris's Buick. As they watched, a truck turned the corner and pulled to the curb. A beefy guy in baggy shorts and a knit cap climbed out, nodded in Perez's direction, and slowly circled the Buick. After a minute Perez handed him something.

"Keys," Leo breathed.

The man climbed into the Buick and drove away down the street.

"Am I seeing what I think I'm seeing?" Leo muttered.

"I have no idea," Jewell breathed. "Why in the world did that man drive off in Doris's car?"

"Only one reason I can think of."

Perez went to the passenger side of the truck and leaned in through the open window, talking with someone.

"Chattin' up the guy's girlfriend," Leo muttered.

Five minutes later the Buick was back. Knit cap got out, walked over to Perez and handed him some bills. At that, a girl with long, impossibly red hair climbed from the truck and scampered delightedly across the sidewalk to the Buick.

"Heads up." Knit Cap tossed something to her. The girl caught it with one hand and got into Doris's car.

"Saw that. Keys." Leo grunted.

Knit cap bumped fists with Perez, got back in the truck, and followed the Buick down the street. Perez looked in both directions along the street, then turned toward the house. Jewell heard the crunch of his footsteps along the gravel driveway.

"Tell me that moron didn't sell his mother's car," Jewell whispered.

"Sure looked that way." Leo gently pulled Jewell back from the window. "One thing's for sure, that was a transaction we weren't supposed to see. He must not know we're here. Where'd you park? I'm down the street, on the other side."

"I'm around the corner. Shouldn't we confront him? Ask him if Doris knows he sold her car?" Jewell's voice rose. "It feels like we just witnessed a car theft."

"Not until we have more answers." Leo looked around the quiet bedroom. "Let's put off the ghostbusters work until I make sure he can't sell the house the same way." He glanced at Lois Lane. "How did she know that slimy maneuver was about to happen?" His mouth turned up in a wry smile. "Don't tell me doggie ESP's at work here."

"I'm learning not to question Lois Lane—her sixth sense is way more developed than mine." Jewell put a finger to her lips. "If we're sneaking out, let's do it quietly."

Leo's eyes twinkled. "Okay, but if we run into Perez, we act embarrassed and tell him you were 'showing me your room.'"

Jewell rolled her eyes and restrained a giggle.

Chapter Fourteen

Halfway down the stairs—moving as quietly as possible for two adults and a dog—Leo's phone vibrated. He waited until they were out the front door before checking the message.

"It's from Chief Jorgensen. New development in the bombing." He took Jewell's hand. "I have to run over to Miwok P.D."

"What's up? Are Bob and Beth Anne okay?" Fear choked Jewell's words.

"It wasn't about them. Don't worry." Leo held the door of Jewell's Civic as she put Lois Lane in the back and climbed behind the wheel. "I'll fill you in as soon as I can."

Feeling unusually submissive—she wondered later what that was about—Jewell murmured, "Sometime today, right?"

'You got it, sweetheart." He leaned in and kissed her cheek through the open window, then stepped back and watched as she drove away.

Jewell speed-dialed the Ploughers' house. "Be there in five minutes, Ashley. Sorry I'm so late."

"That's okay." Ashley sounded a little rushed. "Their attorney is here so I haven't given them dinner yet. Would you mind doing it? I'm due at a meeting in ten minutes."

"Absolutely. Go ahead and leave. I'm rounding the corner as we speak. Thanks for covering. You're the best."

* * *

When she stepped through the front door, relief washed over Jewell. *Made it to home base one more time.*

The Ploughers and their attorney, Mitchell Steinberg, were seated at the dining room table thumbing through a pile of legal-looking papers. All three looked up when Jewell came in.

"Where were you?" Mr. Plougher blustered. "We were just about to order out for pizza with Steinberg, here."

The Ploughers' attorney, a trim, intense-looking man with a shock of unruly black hair, leaned back in his chair. "Nicholas does like to yank your chain, doesn't he? Ashley offered dinner but they wanted to wait for you."

Eve Plougher, cheeks rosy with excitement, said, "Eugene knows a way for us to help Bob get the coffee truck open again. Isn't that wonderful?" At this moment, in the muted dining room light, Mrs. Plougher resembled a slightly wrinkled, happy child.

"Absolutely! You three are Bob and Beth Anne's guardian angels," Jewell grinned. "I'll get dinner together while you finish talking. The menu isn't pizza, Mr. Steinberg, it's Salisbury steak, but there's plenty."

"Can I take a rain check?" Steinberg began stuffing papers in his briefcase. "My wife's joined a cooking club—tonight's experiment is zucchini and clam chowder—she'll have a fit if I'm not home to appreciate it." He turned to Mr. Plougher. "This should do it, Nicholas. I'll tell Bob Stone to expect a call from the insurance company."

The men stood and walked to the door. From the table Eve Plougher warbled, "Give our best to your beautiful wife."

Steinberg looked up from his phone—it beeped right when he was closing his briefcase—and said, "I will, Eve. You know she's your biggest fan." Then, looking across the room to Jewell he continued, "This text should make you happy: A Court Order was issued today preventing anyone from selling 811 Radish. That means your rental agreement's safe."

"Wonderful." Jewell suddenly felt bone-tired. "Not sure I want to be around, though, when Doris gets the news."

A calculating expression crossed Steinberg's face. "Let me know if she tries to pull a fast one. Illegal sale of a property's a felony." He paused at the front door, eyebrows raised. "Court House scuttlebutt has it someone put out a Missing Persons on her."

"That's true." Jewell nodded. "It's inactive, though. Her son told Miwok P.D. she was on a trip to Tahoe."

Steinberg's confident smile slipped. Without it, he looked young and tired. "That guy? Don't believe anything he says without hard proof. My criminal-law attorney friends use him as a worst-case scenario, client-wise." He stepped outside, shutting the door quickly to keep out the chill of early autumn.

One more person who's not a fan of Benny Perez.

Jewell bustled out to the kitchen, back a short time later with plates of food. "Sorry you had to wait for dinner. The quick trip across town got sidetracked."

"Don't mention it, dear," Mrs. Plougher murmured as she dug into her mashed potatoes. "We always enjoy Ashley, and then Mitchell dropped by. We couldn't have eaten earlier, anyway."

Nicholas Plougher forked a bite-sized piece of steak. "You run into Doris's son or the cops while you were there? Is that how your hands got scratched?" He peered somberly at Jewell. "I'm thinking your daughter and those two clowns of hers have the right idea—you ought to move out of the Stone mansion."

Jewell dropped into an empty chair and crumpled a napkin. "The house hasn't exactly welcomed me with open arms, has it?" She leaned forward, resting her elbows on the table. "Can I stay here this weekend—and maybe next weekend, too?"

"Of course. You don't even need to ask." Eve Plougher reached across the table and gently turned Jewell's hand so the bandage showed. She emitted a little gasp. "For goodness sake! And to think we let you cook dinner. Shame on us, Nicholas."

"No, no," Jewell protested, "It's just scratches. I'm fine." She pasted on a bright smile. "If I stay here, it'll be temporary—until I can get in touch with Doris. I'm not giving up my room, just taking a breather." She sighed. "Between the late Mrs. Stone and Doris's loser son ... well, any ideas on how to get rid of a ghost?"

"Oh, dear," Eve murmured, "No. Please reconsider moving out; you must put your safety first, dear." Her shoulders sagged and she suddenly looked very old. "The Stone family was devastated after Maris died; when Rudolph started escorting a new woman and her jailbird son around town, the family like to had a fit. It's no wonder Maris's spirit is restless."

Lois Lane, asleep on the mat by the stove, wagged her tail in canine agreement.

"I'm with you on most things, Eve, but not this," Mr. Plougher grumbled. "The trouble in that house has been a banked fire all these years; it had to burst into flames sooner or later." He put his napkin down and eyed a cherry pie sitting on the sideboard. "Besides, Jewell isn't what ails 811 Radish, it's Doris's no-good son." His face lit up. "Is there ice cream to go with our pie?"

"Thanks for the vote of confidence, Mr. P." A tiny smile crossed Jewell's lips. "I'm a little short on that right now. We're not short on ice cream, though. That, we have oodles of."

Later, the Ploughers ate pie ala mode in front of the television while Jewell tidied up the kitchen. Her rubber gloves were wrist-deep in soapy water when the phone buzzed. The glowing green letters proclaimed, 'Leo Stone.'

Jewell tapped the screen with her elbow. "Hi, Leo."

"Hi yourself, sweetheart. How's it goin'?"

As if on cue Lois Lane stood, shook herself, and trotted across the room to lean against Jewell's leg. Jewell absentmindedly rubbed behind the dog's ears and murmured, "Better than at 811 Radish, that's for sure. It really happened, didn't it? The lipstick message and the ghost sighting?"

"Oh, it happened." Leo paused. "My first, and hopefully my last, ghost sighting. Clearly, Maris is reaching out. Lucky for me, this fits nicely with my determination to get to know you better—a lot better." He chuckled softly. "I'll be helping my sister-in-law and enjoying your company at the same time."

Jewell felt herself blushing. She was glad he couldn't see through the phone. "I think I speak for both Maris and me when I say we're glad you're on board." Then, "Not to change the subject, what were the cops calling you about?"

Leo was silent so long, Jewell wondered if they were still connected. She was about to disconnect when, "Not sure you're ready to hear this," he said. "Someone torched a van early this morning at the rental-car lot north of town—just one truck in a sea of vehicles. You want to guess which one they hit?"

"No," Jewell sighed. "I'm too tired for games."

"It was the van used in the hit on G.I.'s Joe."

Jewell dropped the phone to the table and stared vacantly, her heart pounding.

Oh, my God.

"Jewell? You still there?" Leo's voice rose from the table-top, tinny.

"Yeah." She picked up the phone. "Sorry." Then, in a stronger voice, "How bad was it? Any chance the cops went over it for evidence before it was torched?"

"Nope. It was a total loss. and they hadn't called in forensics yet—you know how understaffed Miwok PD is. Hell, they were barely up to speed on tracing the credit card back to Doris. This clinches it, though. She's linked to the fires."

"That's crazy." Jewell's voice trembled. "She hasn't even been in town the last couple of days."

"Take a breath, baby." The calm in Leo's tone flowed from the phone like honey on warm bread. "Look at it this way: someone's scared and trying to cover their tracks. Jorgensen's crew will give the case their complete attention now."

As Jewell's panic receded, any energy it fueled went, too. She slumped in her chair. "The first fire wasn't vandalism. Someone targeted Bob and Beth Anne. Or coffee trucks. Or...what? And, why?"

"That's the big question. The police might think it was random. but I don't. I'm telling Bob and Beth Anne to stay out of sight for a while, just in case. You live here all your life like Bob has, you're bound to make a few enemies." Exhaustion came through clearly in Leo's voice. "On a happier note, I drove by 811 a few minutes ago. The For Sale sign is gone. Looks like the Court Order did the job."

"Thank God!" Jewell put some perky energy into her tone, hoping it would spread to Leo. "I was about ready to head for Tahoe and beat the bushes for Doris. I'm still steamed she'd put the place up for sale without telling me."

"Doris Stone had no idea who she was dealing with when you showed up on her front porch." Leo sounded a touch more upbeat. "By the way, I told Jorgensen about all the stuff missing from the mansion; he said I should make a list, then canvass the pawn shops. You want to help?"

"Absolutely. Meet me at the mansion in the morning. I'm staying at the Ploughers' this weekend, but I'll be there early tomorrow for another look at my closet floor. I feel guilty it didn't get done today."

"Shit," Leo groaned. "You're right. Maris's ghost is probably steamed about that."

"Just what we need, a pissed-off ghost." Jewell's laugh sounded more like a whimper

"Not an image I'm fond of."

"Uh, Leo?" Jewell's voice purred. "When this mess is all figured out, and Lois Lane and I are spending happy weekends at 811 Radish, I hope you and I'll still be buddies."

Leo's smile flowed through the phone. "Oh, yeah. Glad you're looking beyond all this crap—I knew you were special the first time I set eyes on you. This just proves it. Us together, without ghosts or felons coming out of the woodwork—pardon me if I blush." He chuckled.

Jewell's smile turned into a yawn. "Hold that thought, okay? We're not there yet."

"You got that right. Sleep well, babe. I'll meet you at 811 around 9:00 tomorrow."

"Okay. 'Night."

Half an hour later Jewell stood in the shower, hot, steaming water flowing around her like a lovely, tingly blanket. Without warning the shower door popped open and Lois Lane's black nose appeared through the fog.

"What? You don't want in here, do you? You aren't a water dog!"

As she peered down into brown canine eyes, Jewell heard the buzz of her phone. She turned off the water and stepped from the tub, grabbing a towel on her way across the tiled floor.

The screen readout said: Carolyn. Jewell put the phone to her ear and immediately heard a whispered, "Hi, Mom. Are you in your room at 811 Radish?"

"No." Jewell's breath caught. Carolyn sounded like a scared little girl. "I've decided to stay at the Ploughers' this weekend. Is something wrong? You aren't sick, are you?"

"We're fine. There's a little problem, though; Hank thought I should call you." Carolyn paused. "I told him it was too late to bother you."

"Hold on a sec." Jewell wrapped herself in a towel and crossed the hall to the Ploughers' guest room, where she slipped into sweats and a tee and perched on the edge of the bed. "Okay, honey. You caught me in the shower. I can talk now. A problem, you said?"

"Yeah. Marco Perez showed up on our doorstep a while ago, drunk off his ass and crying about his missing grandmother. We don't want to kick him out—he's in no shape to drive—but he's so loud we're afraid the neighbors'll call the cops."

Jewell heard howling in the background.

Marco.

"Put him on the phone."

The howling subsided to convulsive whimpering. Then a slurred, hiccupping whisper sprayed into the phone. "Gram? 's that you?"

"It's Carolyn's mom, Marco. Jewell. Your grandmother's friend."

"She'sh fresh outa friends. "Where's she? She'sh in trouble. We, I, you gotta find her." The whimpering went up a couple of decibels.

Oh, boy. How do I get through to him?

"Marco." Jewell made her voice slow and calm. "Doris texted you this morning, remember? She's okay. She went to Tahoe. Remember?"

There was silence on the other end of the phone.

At least he's quit whimpering.

"That's just it," Marco suddenly sounded cold sober. "I texted her again this afternoon and her phone's been cut off. I'm scared, Mrs. McDunn. Even if she got a new phone, the service would be switched over. It feels like she's gone."

Jewell held the phone away from her ear and stared at it.

Gone? As in, dead? My God, he's right.

"That's the booze talking, Marco. Sleep it off, on the kids' couch if they'll let you. If you're still worried in the morning, meet me here about 8:30 and we'll drive over to 811 Radish. Your father'll know where she is."

There was a loud, CLANK, like the phone dropping. "Marco? Marco!"

"Mom? It's Carolyn. What'd you say to him? He hit the table with his fist and ran out the front door. Hank went after him."

Jewell groaned, staring at the phone. "I told him to sleep off the booze. I'll help him find Doris tomorrow. If he's freaked out, it's not because of me."

There was a moment's silence on Carolyn's end, then, "I can see the street from our kitchen window. Hank's coming back. Looks like he lost Marco."

"Let's pray he doesn't wreck his car, drunk as he is."

"Oh, yeah. Talk to you tomorrow, Mom."

Jewell disconnected and moved through her bedtime routine vacantly, Marco's anguished voice loud in her thoughts.

He thinks she's dead. Well, her phone service was shut off. Interesting he went nuts when I mentioned his father—I didn't even get a chance to tell him ol' Benny sold Doris's car.

A cold, tight feeling settled in Jewell's stomach—dread—a sense she'd gone to great lengths to avoid most of her life.

If Doris is dead, Benny knows it.

"She can't be dead," Jewell muttered. "She was fine last time I saw her—a little beat up, but generally okay."

The word, *murdered*, surfaced in Jewell's mind. She squeezed her eyes shut, willing it away. *Murder. Not part of my reality. Still, there's Maris's ghost. She was murdered. So it **is** part of the reality at 811 Radish.*

"Oh, God," Jewell whispered. "Someone needs to find Marco. What if he's on his way to 811 Radish to confront his father? He's no match for that guy!"

She looked at the clock: ten-thirty. *Too late to ask anyone to go with me. I'll take Lois Lane and snag Marco out in front. I promise myself I won't go inside.* She pulled on sneakers and a sweatshirt, then rummaged in the nightstand drawer and found a flashlight. *Note to self: buy a gun.*

Lois Lane, stretched out next to the bed, lifted her head and eyed Jewell. At Jewell's command, she got slowly to her feet.

Chapter Fifteen

"Y ou're ready for bed, aren't you, girl? With any luck, this won't take long." Jewell gave the dog's ears an absentminded scratch.

What if Marco didn't head for 811 Radish? Maybe when he rushed out of Carolyn's, he went home—wherever that is. Should I hang out on Radish Street all night, just in case he shows up? Probably not. But I might.

She moved quietly through the house, Lois Lane one step behind, and paused at the sound of someone whistling, off tune, in the kitchen.

Someone's still up?

The kitchen door opened, revealing a bathrobe-clad Nicholas Plougher. He stood backlit, wearing a halo of wispy white hair. "Where are you off to, Missy? Sneaking out for a quickie with your boyfriend? Heh, Heh."

Jewell saw the gleam in the old man's rheumy blue eyes. "I have to check on something—I won't be long."

"Tell the guy I don't approve of this sort of thing."

At Jewell's sweatshirt and jeans, Plougher looked puzzled, then crowed, "You're not meeting a boy—you're going to the Stone place! For crying out loud, do you have a death wish?" Glancing at Lois Lane, he muttered, "You need more than a dog for protection against that Perez guy." He reached for his overcoat. "I'll keep you company."

Jewell tried hard not to scowl as she put a restraining hand on the old man's shoulder. "I'll be careful, I promise. I'm not going inside, just out front. I have to find Doris's grandson." She dropped her voice to a stage whisper. "But, thanks for having my back." She planted a quick kiss on Plougher's cheek and hurried out.

* * *

The streets from one side of Miwok to the other were quiet; tourists and the town's late-night revelers—the twenty-something crowd and a few chronic drunks—were still inside the breweries and corner bars. Jewell drove past the tiny 101 Hot Dog stand, smiling at the sight of bored teenagers wiping down counters while scanning for last customers in the darkness beyond the parking lot.

That's where Marco should be. A stale hot dog might sober him up.

"Wait a sec," Jewell breathed. Tiny, round taillights appeared when an old VW van pulled away from the curb and onto the street directly in Jewell's path.

That's gotta be Marco. He didn't even look when he pulled out.

The two-car procession—Marco's van creeping along the road and weaving badly, Jewell's Civic a safe distance behind—rolled through a stop sign.

Gotta get his attention: do I honk? No. Poor kid's barely conscious. Call him on his phone? Maybe.

As she reached for her phone Jewell noticed another car, headlights off, emerge from the street they'd just crossed. It fell in behind her Civic. From across the intersection a fourth vehicle, lights also out, joined the parade.

What the hell?

The misty rays of a streetlight caught a red lightbar atop the car behind Jewell.

Cops.

The police unit hit its siren as it moved past Jewell. With a sigh of relief, she pulled over and watched it close in on the van. "Marco, a DUI has your name on it."

Lois Lane cocked one ear and lifted her head.

"We'd better stay with them, girl." Jewell put the Civic in gear and moved back on the road, following at a discreet distance. "There's still a chance Marco could tangle with his father."

The van continued its erratic path toward the intersection of Radish and

Grand in spite of the flashing lights and chirping sirens now shattering the residential peace. When a loudspeaker blared, "Pull to the curb and turn off your engine," Lois Lane put her paws on the dashboard and gave Jewell a questioning look.

"That's not for us. We're getting out, though, and you're staying right next to me. Understand?"

The VW lurched to a stop. The driver's side door opened and Marco put his head out, blinking into the lights. With an arm across his eyes, he stumbled from the vehicle and fell to the ground.

Jewell and Lois Lane watched as an officer hoisted Marco to his feet and marched him to the sidewalk. She looked toward the homes lining the street—there should be an audience for this pathetic show—but a flutter of curtains in one dark window was the only sign of life.

As she watched, one officer talked to a slumped-over Marco while another pulled the youth's hands behind his back.

No sobriety test? Maybe this isn't a DUI bust.

Marco suddenly straightened, looked around, and yelled, "You don't get it! I wouldn't hurt her. I'm trying to find her!"

Lois Lane sat quietly next to Jewell, her attention on Marco. When he shouted, Jewell instinctively pushed her driver's side door open, just a crack. Lois Lane evidently took this as her cue, because she lunged across Jewell and out of the car toward Marco—and the armed cops.

"Stop! Come back," Jewell screamed. She threw herself forward, landed on Lois Lane, and dragged her into a nearby hedge.

Oh, my God, twice in one day!

Lois Lane struggled to free herself, but Jewell's sheer weight won out.

"Don't you dare nip me, you bad girl," Jewell growled. With one arm firmly around the dog's neck, she managed to sit up.

"Freeze, lady," one of the cops yelled.

Jewell gasped, turning her head as slowly as possible. The cops casually chatting with Marco had transformed into a weapon-wielding human wall; four lethal-looking guns were pointed ominously at her and her dog. "Don't shoot," Jewell squeaked. "She's just a little frisky."

One of the officers, the one standing closest to Jewell and Lois Lane, slipped his gun into its holster. The others followed suit. The first officer stared intently at Jewell before saying, "Put the dog in your car. Now. And you. Stay in there with her."

From behind the four cops, Marco's wavering voice squeaked, "Mrs. McDunn? 's that you?" A drunk, frightened squeak.

"Yes," Jewell called back. "I'm here." She climbed stiffly to her feet, frowning at Lois Lane. The dog stood quietly now, tail between her legs and head down in humiliation. "What's with you and cops?"

She boosted the unprotesting dog into the Civic, then climbed in and got behind the wheel. *What can I do to help Marco?*

Rap, Rap. A knock on the side window; Jewell turned, saw a blue cop uniform, and rolled the window down.

"I'm really sorry about my dog," she began.

"You're damn lucky one of us didn't shoot her," the officer snapped. Jewell wondered if there was fear behind that sharpness.

Law enforcement as a career—not one I could handle.

"Yes, sir. Thank you for that. Uh, could I ask you a question?"

The officer gave the slightest of nods.

The words came in a breathless rush. "If you're arresting Marco for drunk driving, don't you have to give him a sobriety test? I'm not telling you how to do your job. I was just wondering."

At that moment, wailing sobs came from a few feet away. *Marco. Carolyn was right, he's loud.*

The officer rolled his eyes. "We're taking him in for questioning. The DUI's a sidebar." He looked intently at Jewell. "Are you a relative?"

"No. He's Doris Stone's grandson. She's my landlady. I live down the street." Jewell pointed toward the dark hulk that was 811 Radish at midnight.

"You aware your landlady's gone missing?" The officer looked sternly at Jewell.

"Yes, sir. Are you aware Marco, there, is the person who reported it?" Jewell smiled to soften her tone. "Can I ask what you're questioning him about?"

The officer—Winston, according to his badge—looked past Jewell and into her car to Lois Lane.

"Not unless you're his next of kin. Which you aren't."

"Well, see, that's the problem. His next of kin's his grandmother, the one who was reported missing. He's worried about her."

Officer Winston shook his head. "Yeah, right. Not the way I heard it. You'd best be on your way, ma'am."

Jewell felt the hairs on the back of her neck rise. "What? Wait a sec. Is this about his grandmother? Didn't you get the word she's at Lake Tahoe?"

Officer Winston's thick blond eyebrows went up and his mouth formed a tight-lipped smile. "I'm going to need to see your license, Miss …?"

With a defeated sigh Jewell dug into her bag for her driver's license and silently handed it over. Officer Winston studied it, looking from Jewell to the tiny plastic photo card.

Yes, it's a lousy picture. And I changed my hair color. Is that a crime?

When one of the other cops approached, Winston handed back Jewell's license. "Take my advice, Mrs. McDunn: Keep your nose out of other people's business." He walked away, saying over his shoulder, "And learn how to control that dog."

As she pulled from the curb Jewell caught a bit of the other cop's words to Winston, "… wants to know who made the call …"

What's going on? Someone called the cops on Marco for … what? Being a worried grandson?

* * *

Jewell drove slowly along the street, one eye on Marco and Miwok's finest in the rearview mirror. She pulled into the driveway at 811 Radish, turned off the engine, and pounded the steering wheel in frustrated rage. Lois Lane immediately climbed onto the passenger seat, whining.

"Sorry, girl. Did I scare you?" Jewell used her sleeve as a facecloth and then picked up her phone. "I'm out of control. I need help."

Carolyn was speed-dial number three. Within five rings Hank answered, sounding sleepy. "Yeah?"

"Marco's been arrested. And Lois Lane almost got shot."

"Where are you right now?" Hank was suddenly wide awake.

"At 811 Radish. The cop in charge told me to go home and mind my own business."

Hank emitted a noisy breath. "Shit, Jewell. With you, the fun never stops."

Jewell stared at the phone, finally spitting out, "Focus, Hank! Marco's in trouble. He's been arrested. Remember what he said at your house, about Doris being gone?"

There was scuffling and whispering on Hank's end of the phone. "Mom?" Carolyn, sounding sleepy. "You okay?"

"Yes…" Out of the corner of her eye Jewell saw a shadow move past the Civic. Lois Lane snapped to attention, pressing herself against the side window and growling. "Hold on, Carolyn." Jewell laid the phone on the armrest and stared into the darkness beyond the front of her car.

"You saw it, too, didn't you?" Jewell whispered to Lois Lane. "I don't see anything now. Do you?"

For no reason other than, maybe, synapse-overload, Maris Stone's ring popped into Jewell's head. She blinked, but the ring hovered just beyond her eyelids. It glowed, seeming so real she grabbed at the air in front of her face. When her fist came up empty, she moaned, "I'm losing it."

She buried her face in Lois Lane's neck, then glanced out the side window. In the glow of the Civic's headlights Marco's face—stubbled chin, bloodshot eyes, and pasty white skin—hung above a shadowed body. His mouth opened, but no sound came out. He looked like a fish gulping water.

Chapter Sixteen

Jewell blinked. *Am I imagining this? No. He's still there.* She cringed against the driver's side door.

From the phone on the armrest a tinny version of Carolyn's voice, said, "Mom? Mom!"

Lois Lane gave a delighted yelp and pawed the window frantically.

"You see him too? He's really there?" Jewell climbed from the car, Lois Lane pressed against her leg. Together they squinted into the darkness.

A tall, angular shape emerged from the shadows. "Gotta find my father." It was Marco, sounding scared. "Cops are right behind me."

As if on cue, the wop, wop of a siren sounded nearby.

Jewell reached for his arm. "You resisted arrest? Are you crazy? They'll lock you up for the rest of your life!"

"You don't get it. No one gets it!" Marco turned and faded into the darkness.

Jewell moved cautiously after him, glad for once that Lois Lane wanted to lead the way. *I wish I had her night vision. It's pitch-dark back here.*

She slipped a hand into her pocket, wrapping her fingers around the hard, reassuring metal of the flashlight. Before she could turn it on, a flesh-against-wood thump sounded from the door of Perez's apartment. It was followed by Marco's hoarse scream.

"Open up, Douche bag! I know you're in there!"

The flashlight pinpointed Lois Lane leaping at Marco and knocking him to the ground, then worrying him like a mother dog impatient with her puppy—growling, but without bared fangs.

"Oof," Marco grunted, sounding like he'd had the wind knocked out of him.

"Stop!" Jewell yelled. "Get off him, this minute!"

Lois Lane gave Jewell a quizzical stare and planted both feet firmly on Marco's back.

Maris Stone's ring, glowing ominously, popped into the forefront of Jewell's thoughts. "Go away," she pleaded. "Can't you see I'm busy?" She reached for Lois Lane; the dog twisted away and began sniffing along the bottom of the basement door.

The hairs at the back of Jewell's neck rose; she realized the sirens' chirping had stopped and aggressive, jostling energy was flowing into the dark yard. Someone grabbed her arm.

"Miwok Police! Stop where you are!" Officer Winston appeared and pulled Marco to his feet.

"My father's here somewhere," Marco screamed. "Benny Perez, get the Hell out here!'

"Quit yelling, kid. If your old man's in there, he's not showing his face." Winston grinned

at a younger cop. "You better hope *my* cuffs don't fall open by themselves."

The younger cop impassively stepped over to Marco. "We got you for resisting arrest, now, too. That make you happy?" He began reading Marco his rights as Jewell stood by, fists clenched and helpless.

Who called the cops on Marco? Not Doris, apparently. His father? Where is Benny, in the house? She cleared her throat. "Uh, excuse me, officers ...."

Lois Lane had been digging at the basement door. She stopped, now, and sat back on her haunches, howling.

"What the hell? Lady, control your dog!"

"She really wants to get in there." Jewell looked at Officer Winston. "Can I ...?"

At the officer's nod, Jewell stepped past Lois Lane and inserted her house key in the lock. The door swung open. The space, the main room of a one-bedroom apartment, was low-ceilinged and cold. A sickening odor of mold, dirt, and something else hung heavy in the air. Jewell flipped the light switch.

Nothing happened.

"Probably works off a wall outlet," Winston muttered.

Lois Lane shouldered in and trotted across the room, whining. At the rolled-up rug, she looked back at Jewell, as if expecting orders. Jewell ignored her, so the dog pawed at the rug and then lifted her head, howling.

"Hey, cut that out!" Jewell breathed in and immediately gagged at the stench.

Firm hands gripped Jewell's shoulders from behind, propelling her through the doorway. All four cops jostled into the room, pushing Marco ahead of them.

Winston choked, "Holy shit. I know that smell." He drew his weapon, nodding to the cops fumbling their guns from holsters. "Let's clear the bedroom first." He jerked his chin toward the rug. "We'll tackle that last."

Jewell and Marco trembled against the wall, trying not to breathe while the police moved through the tiny apartment. Lois Lane stationed herself next to the rug, eyes on the bedroom doorway.

"I can't see any furniture," Marco whispered. "Shouldn't there be a couch?" Jewell shook her head. *The kid's stupid drunk.*

"He moved out of here. He might be living upstairs." She peered at Marco. "I thought you two didn't get along."

"He has to tell the cops where Gram is." Marco doubled over, retching.

Jewell knelt next to him, a comforting hand on his back. When she glanced toward Lois Lane the ring appeared, hanging over the rug in a circle of flickering, beckoning light. Lois Lane lifted her head in a mournful howl.

Am I losing my mind? Why do I keep seeing that ring? Go back upstairs where you belong, damn you! Get out of this creepy basement.

The cops emerged from the bedroom, holstering their weapons and moving as a four-man wall toward the rolled-up rug. Winston addressed Lois Lane. "Good dog," he said. "Now, stop howling."

The dog put her ears back, stared hard at him, and then slunk quietly across the room to Jewell.

Jewell shifted to a sitting position, letting Marco rest his head on her shoulder while she cradled Lois Lane's head. *What's going on here? I don't remember a bad smell before, when I talked to Benny.*

She was filled with a feeling she recognized as cold, numbing dread.

"On the count of three," Winston said. "One, Two, Three!" The cops began unrolling the rug.

"What the hell?" The youngest cop squeaked.

In the room's dim light, Jewell could see something small and white against the rug's dark nap.

"One more time," Winston said. "Gently."

"Oof!" Another pull—further unrolling—revealed more of the white object. All four cops leaned in, staring.

"Step back, everyone," Winston's voice was gruff. "We've got a body here."

The other officers backed off, suddenly disorganized and adding a sweaty, acidic component to the room's stench. The youngest cop said, to nobody in particular, "That's an arm. There's an arm in there." He sounded dazed.

Winston spoke quietly into a phone. "Dispatch? Assistance needed here. Eight-eleven Radish. Back of the building."

Marco tensed, pressing his face firmly against Jewell's shoulder. He put his hands over his ears. "Nothing's there. Nothing's there." His voice was high, girlish.

Jewell's brain initially rejected the scene as not making sense. Then, as if she'd been jolted with a cattle prod, her eyes squeezed shut and she gasped. Her arms went protectively around Marco.

Please God, no.

Behind her eyelids, the ring faded and was gone.

"Mrs. McDunn?" The youngest cop crouched next to Jewell. "I'm afraid you're both going to have to come to the station."

Jewell sat up, shaking with shock. "Was that an arm? Where did it come from?" Tears streamed down her cheeks.

Freckles stood out on the cop's ashen face. As he helped Jewell to her feet he said to someone, "Maybe she should stay until the coroner gets here, to ID the vic." He glanced at Jewell. "You live here, right, ma'am? "He jutted his chin toward Marco. "Helluva mess for that guy."

Marco's eyes opened. He stumbled to his feet. "What the fuck? What's goin' on?" He looked around the room, saw the partially unrolled carpet, and lunged toward one end of the rug. It flopped open.

There, barefoot and with arms stretched out on either side of a rose-colored bathrobe, lay Doris. Matted, blood-soaked hair covered one side of her face; on the other side, greenish-yellow bruising above an open, lifeless eye drew attention away from a red line circling her neck.

"Aiee!" Marco jumped back, face radiating horror. "No, no! Get up, Gram! Get up!" He staggered toward the corpse. Two of the cops stepped up and grabbed him.

"Let go! I gotta help my Gram!"

Jewell moved slowly along the wall to the open carpet, barely aware of the melee in the center of the room. Lois Lane stayed at her side, watching anxiously.

At the edge of the rug, Jewell whispered, "Doris." Her landlady's body lay at her feet, sadly battered. Jewell's barely comprehending brain struggled to grasp the reality of the empty, decomposing human shell.

When Doris died, her spirit left her body. The ring must have known. Did it guide us here?

Jewell dropped to her knees and said the only prayer she could think of. "God, help us."

"You need to move back, ma'am." Winston was there, hovering over Jewell. "Can I help you up?" his voice was soft.

Jewell accepted his hand.

"As soon as the homicide team arrives, we'll send you to the station." He guided Jewell from the apartment, watching as she sank down against the house's shingled wall. "Stay right there, ma'am." He went quickly back inside.

With glazed, uncomprehending eyes Jewell watched as Marco was led from the basement. The slamming of a car door failed to register with Jewell. Her hand rested on Lois Lane's head, fingers automatically rubbing between the dog's ears.

Chapter Seventeen

"Mom? Mom!" Carolyn was in Jewell's face and shaking her shoulder.

Jewell looked up, dazed. "Carolyn?"

Her daughter responded by lifting Jewell up and into a tight, tear-filled hug.

At the embrace Jewell relaxed, letting go a heavy sigh. "Doris is dead. In there."

"Shh." Carolyn stroked her mother's hair. "We got here as fast as we could." She gulped. "Doris? When we saw all the cop cars out front, I thought something'd happened to you."

"It did," Jewell murmured.

She looked around 811 Radish's now brightly-lit back yard. Police officers and technicians, bustling in and out of the basement apartment like worker bees on a mission, had transformed the once private lawn and rose garden into an ad for Crime Scenes R Us. With Carolyn to hold onto, Jewell began to see individual figures within the scene. Hank, talking to Officer Winston, stood with his back to them.

"Hank's here?" Her voice came out in a croak.

"Yeah," Carolyn nodded. "Thank God you said where you were before…I guess you dropped the phone?"

A man in a hazmat suit slipped out of the apartment and crossed the lawn to stand by Hank and Officer Winston. After a second all three turned to scrutinize Jewell. She stared dully back at them.

"I saw Marco standing by my car," Jewell whispered.

"Marco? He's here? Where?" Carolyn's voice had a worried catch to it.

Jewell ran tired fingers through her already tousled hair. "Gone, I think. To jail. I'm next. Would you check on that, honey?" She attempted a smile, managed a grimace.

Carolyn pulled away, her pretty face pale. "Jail? You and Marco? What the hell?"

"Long story," Jewell whispered. "Someone told the cops Marco knew where Doris was, and then ..." She glanced at the door of the basement apartment. "I got in the way when Marco escaped the first time they cuffed him."

"Stay here. I'll be right back." Carolyn jumped to her feet and marched across the lawn toward Hank, arms waving.

Jewell watched for a minute—Winston stepped away, probably to avoid a confrontation with Carolyn. Hank swiveled around, attempting to calm his frantic girlfriend.

Without warning, exhaustion claimed every muscle in Jewell's body. She closed her eyes, letting her mind drift. Voices, the rustling of plastic, the changes in energy and light as people moved around—all receded as an image ran over and over in her head: Doris's face, bruised and lifeless, her blood-matted hair forming an ugly halo.

When the ring drifted into the picture, fiery red and glowing, Jewell sighed. *Crap, you're still here.*

Lois Lane got to her feet, lifted one paw, and pointed toward the mansion's kitchen steps.

What in the world? Jewell squinted to see, but everything beyond the perimeter of the crime scene was black.

Screech! Slap! The sound of a screen door closing in the darkness. Two figures took shape on the back steps, a gray-haired man in a wrinkled sports coat—most likely a detective—and a muscular, swaggering person partially hidden within a voluminous hoodie.

Benny Perez. He was in the house all this time?

When the two men stepped into the circle of light, Perez lifted a clumsily bandaged hand to pull the hoodie farther over his face. As the sweatshirt enveloped him, Jewell noted a second bandage on his forehead.

136

His voice drifted across the lawn. "I don't get it. That no-good kid she called her grandson told me mom was in Tahoe, gambling." Perez sounded calm, matter-of-fact.

Front and center in Jewell's vision the ring pulsed fiercely. *Can't deal with you right now. Gotta get moving.*

She eased to a standing position, leaning against the wall on shaking legs. Bile rose in her throat. Moving unsteadily, she crossed the grass to Carolyn and Hank. Hank opened his arms and pulled her into a bear hug. "He's lying about Marco," she whispered into his neck.

"Dude's a fuckin' psycho," Hank muttered.

Carolyn reached for her mother's hand. "He's probably in shock; after all, that's his mom in there." She glanced at Perez. "Marco said Doris texted him from Lake Tahoe. If that's true, how'd she get back here?" A shadow crossed Carolyn's face. "That guy's sure calm."

Jewell gritted her teeth, aware of the ring hovering nearby. *Why won't it disappear?*

"Marco's mistake was trying to talk to his father." A hysterical giggle escaped Jewell's lips. "Perez is selling Marco to the highest bidder."

"Not exactly a humorous situation, mom." Carolyn pursed her lips in an old-lady frown.

"Mrs. McDunn?" Winston strode across the grass. "We'll contact you in the morning for a statement, but in view of the current situation," he shifted his eyes toward the basement door, "there'll be no charge filed against you."

"I should hope not," Carolyn began, her face reddening.

Hank quickly stepped between Carolyn and the cop. "What she means is, thanks, officer. We're pretty shook up about all this." He grabbed Carolyn and Jewell by their elbows. "Let's go, ladies. Any battles worth fighting will still be there in the morning."

Jewell hooked her arm onto Hank's and allowed herself to be shepherded from the backyard crime scene. When they passed the kitchen steps Carolyn muttered, "You're never setting foot in that place again. Ever.."

"Don't blame the house, honey. It's not responsible for this." *I know that now. For sure.*

When they reached the driveway, they came face to face with Perez. At the sight of Jewell and her family, he scowled. "By the way, *lady*—," he sneered.

Jewell returned his stare. Lois Lane stiffened; a growl starting low in her throat.

"She's not cool with people being rude to Jewell." Hank's voice was quiet.

Perez frowned and continued, his tone a shade softer, "With my mother gone, your rental agreement's dead in the water." To the detectives, he said, "No love lost between my mother and that woman. Bitch is a major nuisance."

Jewell tightened her grip on Lois Lane's leash, kept walking, and called back, "Might want to check with your parole officer on that."

The detectives stopped writing. Jewell heard one of them say, "Parole officer?"

* * *

At the front sidewalk—their cars, miraculously, were clear of the many police vehicles—Carolyn said, "I'll drive you back to the Ploughers', mom. Hank can follow us in your car."

Jewell nodded meekly. The take-charge side of Carolyn's personality usually grated on her, but right now exhaustion and shock had rendered her too weak to care. She glanced at the front of the mansion, blinked, and looked again. "Did you see that?"

Hank had already climbed into his truck. Carolyn, digging in her mother's purse for keys, barely turned her head. "What?"

Jewell pointed to 811's second story. The dark sky diffused the building's roofline; the façade, too, was devoid of detail except for a light twinkling erratically in a second-story bay window.

"That's my window," Jewell whispered. "Someone's in my room."

Carolyn's shoulders slumped. She leaned back to rest her head on the car window. "Can we agree, Mom, that whatever—whoever—is up there, it can wait 'til morning? Stick a fork in me, I'm done. At least for tonight."

Desperation-fueled energy coursed through Jewell. She straightened and put a hand on Carolyn's shoulder. "Go on home with Hank if you want to;

I have to find out who's in my room." She looked up at the intermittently blinking light. "The Stone family ring's been dogging me for hours—maybe this is why."

Carolyn turned away, caught Hank's eye, and mouthed, "Help." A second later Hank was out of the truck and standing next to them. "What's up?"

Jewell pointed to her window. "I have to investigate that before I can leave."

Hank shook his head. "Dammit, Jewell, haven't you had enough excitement for one night? Go back to the Ploughers' and get some sleep. Have Leo come over here with you, tomorrow." His tone had gone from irritated to pleading.

"How's this?" Jewell said. "You two wait in the truck; Lois Lane and I'll check out that light and come right back."

Carolyn and Hank exchanged glances.

"I'm not going up there, babe. Not even for my mother." Carolyn's tone was bleak.

"Crap." Hank gave Jewell a calculating look. "Okay, here's the deal: Carolyn stays in the truck with the dog, You and I do a fast recon of the room." He blew out a breath. "Five minutes, tops."

"I won't forget this, Hank." Jewell handed her daughter the leash and whispered to Lois Lane, "Take care of Carolyn."

Lois Lane wagged her tail slightly and led Carolyn to the truck.

"That's a good dog you got there." Hank stepped over to 811's wrought-iron gate. "Let's get this over with."

With a reassuring glance back at Carolyn, Jewell followed Hank through the gate and to the front steps. When he stopped short, she bumped against him and peered around his broad frame.

A cop stepped forward from within the shadows of a cedar bush.

What now?

"This property's part of the crime scene. No entrance." He gave Jewell a worried smile. "Sorry, ma'am."

Jewell elbowed past Hank. "You guys told me to go home a couple of hours ago. Well, this is home. I live here!"

"It's the truth, man." Hanks smiled ingenuously. "She rents a room on the second floor. You can come up with us if you want."

The cop frowned, then spoke into his phone. "I got the McDunn woman out here, wants access to her room." He paused, then said, "Copy that." He stepped away from the door. "You're cleared."

As Jewell unlocked the front door an ambulance rolled down the driveway to the street. She froze, waiting for a siren that didn't happen. The vehicle moved off into the darkness, lights flashing soundlessly.

Doris is in no hurry.

The air in 811's foyer was full of static electricity, as if a storm was coming. Jewell stepped in and stood still, catching her breath. She shivered involuntarily.

Hank, crowding in behind, put his hands on her shoulders. "I'll lead the way," he hissed into her ear.

They quickly climbed the curving staircase to the second floor. The left wing, Jewell's side, was dark, but dim light and the low, staticky sound of a radio playing rap music drifted from the right wing.

"Oh, my God," Jewell whispered. "That music's coming from Doris's room. How can that be?" She stared up at Hank, terrified.

"Sounds like Perez moved himself in. He's not here now." Hank said calmly. "Where's the light switch for your side?"

"Oh. Yeah." Jewell breathed. "Can you believe that creep?" She touched the wall and beacons of light appeared along the corridor.

"That's better." Hank nodded. "Let's get this over with."

They hurried to Jewell's bedroom. While she fumbled for the key, Hank grasped the doorknob. It twisted easily and the door opened.

"What the hell?" Jewell squeaked. "I left it locked!"

Hank pushed the door open wide and stood on the threshold, Jewell squeezing in beside him. The windows allowed some light from the street, but most of the room was in shadows. On the floor at the center of the room, a flashlight blinked off and on.

"Okay," Hank whispered, reaching for the light switch. "Stay where you are. I'll see who's in here besides us." He pulled a pocket knife from his jeans and moved silently to the closet. "Don't touch that flashlight," he said over his shoulder. "It may have fingerprints."

I didn't know he carried a knife.

Jewell stood completely still, moving only her eyeballs. She noted the open curtains (no feet showing under them), and then slowly sank to her knees to look under the bed. *"No dust balls; just the ring. Wait a second: I left it sitting on the comforter."*

She crossed the room and reached beneath the bed: the floor felt sticky. Her hand closed around the ring—also sticky. She palmed it, sat back, and opened her hand. The gold was almost obscured by something dark.

"Nobody in here." Hank turned away from the closet. "Anything missing?" He saw the dresser and stopped, wide-eyed. "What the hell?" The lipstick scrawl across the mirror had been smeared to resemble vandalism.

"That was there before. Not smeared, though. Look what I found under the bed." Jewell opened her palm.

"That your old wedding ring?"

"No. It belonged to the first Mrs. Stone." Jewell studied the ring. "There's something on it. Grease? It's sticky. I can't understand how it got under the bed; It was on top of the comforter last time I saw it."

"Is that the haunted ring?" Hank smiled, his eyes twinkling. "Maybe it hid under the bed when your intruder came in." He took a closer look at the ring; his smile disappeared. "Shit. That's blood."

"Aack!" Jewell dropped the ring onto the dresser. "Oh, my God!" She rubbed her palms against her shirt, whimpering.

"Calm down." Hank stepped over and lightly touched her shoulder. "It's just blood. No need to panic."

Jewell leaned against him and took a deep breath. She noticed a pile of rags in the corner. "Where'd those come from?" She reached down, gingerly lifting up a towel. It fell open to reveal large, red stains. A metal nail file dropped out.

"That's my file," Jewell whispered. "it's bloody, too." Her voice dropped to a whisper. "What is going on?"

"Relax." Hank patted her back awkwardly. "We'll figure this out."

He picked up the towel and held it to the light. "Any chance you cut yourself doing your nails?" He sounded nervous. "You know I wouldn't judge you for leaving stuff on the floor."

"Says the man who leaves piles of dirty clothes all over his house." Jewell sighed. "I didn't cut myself, and I didn't put those towels on the floor. Whoever broke in here, got hurt."

"You think a guy broke in and decided to file his nails?" Hank rolled his eyes. "This would be funnier if the cops hadn't just hauled off a corpse."

You got that right.

"Should I report the break-in?" Jewell opened the top dresser drawer and gave a quick look. "Nothing's missing."

"Maybe tell that cop at the front door." Hank pulled out his phone. "I'll let Carolyn know why we're taking so long."

While Hank was on the phone, Jewell did a more thorough search of the room; nothing was missing.

The cops will probably take everything with blood on it. Not the ring, though. I can't let it be locked up.

She grabbed a tissue, picked up the ring, and slipped it in her pocket. Then she rubbed off the worst of the lipstick smears. *If I tell the cops a ghost wrote on my mirror, they'll haul me away in a straitjacket.*

Chapter Eighteen

Hank turned off his phone and ran a tired hand across his eyes. "Here's the deal, Jewell. We head downstairs and you grab the front-door cop while I get Carolyn from the truck—she thinks they'll listen better if she's here." He held his phone at arms' length, sighted in the pile of bloody towels, and snapped a photo.

When they stepped through the front door, the cop on guard straightened and moved toward them. After a glance at Jewell, Hank nodded to the cop and hurried down the steps.

Jewell squared her shoulders. *Be assertive. He's a public servant, and you're the public.*

"I have something to report, Officer." After the trauma of the last hour, she had trouble raising her voice above a whisper.

The cop's eyebrows went up, slightly. "Yes, ma'am?" He didn't smile, but his face had an encouraging look about it.

Jewell realized how young he was—young enough to be her son. She cleared her throat and said, louder, "Someone broke into my room. I thought of calling 9-1-1, but since you guys are here, anyway …." She rolled her eyes toward the backyard. "It doesn't look like they took anything, but they left the room a mess."

"Yes, ma'am." The officer was suddenly alert. He tapped his phone and spoke into it. Before he'd finished talking—to Dispatch, based on his side of the conversation—another cop came around the house and climbed the steps two at a time.

"I'll take the report." To Jewell, this second cop said, "Officer O'Reilly, ma'am. It's been a rough night for you, hasn't it?"

"It sure has," Jewell didn't even try to smile. She looked beyond O'Reilly to the front gate where Carolyn, Hank, and Lois Lane stood waiting for her nod. "My kids want to come upstairs with us, if that's okay?"

With Lois Lane and O'Reilly vying for point, the four people and one dog hurried inside, up the stairs, and along the hall to Jewell's room.

At her door, O'Reilly drew his gun. "Wait out here while I clear the room." He looked at Jewell. "Was the door locked when you got here?"

"No. And I never leave without locking it."

"Did you touch anything when you got inside?"

"Oh, yeah—Hank did, too. Sorry about that. I didn't notice the blood until we picked up a towel. I never leave dirty clothes on the floor."

"Blood?" O'Reilly's tired-but-thorough demeanor snapped to attention. He spoke into his shoulder phone. "Assistance needed up here, Winston."

Hank spoke up. "Okay if we head home soon? I gotta work tomorrow."

O'Reilly blew out a breath. "Sure. I can't let you back in there tonight, anyway. Blood makes it another crime scene."

"Hank and I were in there, already," Jewell whispered. "I don't see why we can't show Carolyn."

"Yeah," Hank protested. "And we touched everything—the drawer handles, the closet doorknob. What more harm can we do?"

O'Reilly shook his head. "If we need your fingerprints, you'll get a call tomorrow."

Just then Winston came sprinting along the hall. "What've we got?"

"Blood. Get out your gloves." O'Reilly turned to Hank. "Give me your statements, then hit the road." To Jewell, "You'll need some other place to stay tonight."

"Hank said nothing was missing." Carolyn peered earnestly into her mother's face. "Are you sure? Did you check your jewelry box? How about under the bed?"

Jewell's eyes widened. Her fingers went around the ring in her pocket. "Everything's there, far as I can tell." To O'Reilly, "It's still a break-in even if nothing's missing, right?"

O'Reilly's face sagged, working with victims and their families obviously not his strength. "Not my call, ma'am. You'll hear tomorrow." He and Winston drew their weapons and stepped into the room, closing the door on Jewell, Hank, Carolyn, and Lois Lane.

* * *

"You don't have to do this. I'm okay to drive."

"It's no big deal, Mom. And, you're *so* not okay to drive. You're in shock. You really ought to be going to the hospital. Buckle up and shut up." Carolyn gave Jewell a sweet, apologetic smile.

The street in front of 811 Radish was slowly returning to normal as the city's police wrapped up the crime scene. Police units sat on either end of Hank's truck and the bumper of Jewell's car could be seen at the street corner; the rest of the street was quiet, shadowed, and empty of traffic.

Jewell leaned against the headrest, trying to block out the impressions of the past hour: Marco's agonized wailing, the chill, eerie snapshot of post-death Doris, the garishly lit back yard throbbing with macho police intensity. She hardly noticed the stench of human decay emanating from the fur on Lois Lane's foreleg.

Some part of her mind still conscious registered the buzz of a phone and Carolyn's whisper: "She'll be at the Ploughers.... No, you can't see her tonight.... In shock.... Maybe tomorrow."

Jewell forced her eyelids open. "Who?"

"Leo." Carolyn slid her a glance. "Wanted to see you, make sure you're okay. I told him to call in the morning."

Jewell nodded, then opened her eyes wide. "How am I going to tell Mr. and Mrs. P. about Doris—and Marco? It'll kill them!"

Carolyn gave her mother's shoulder a reassuring pat. "It's past their bedtime, right? Deal with it tomorrow."

Jewell stared out the window. *Tomorrow. Unlike Doris, I have a tomorrow.* Tears coursed down her cheeks, meeting under her chin and soaking into her collar. She leaned across the handbrake and rested her head against

Carolyn's shoulder.

* * *

At the Ploughers' Hank parked behind the Civic and escorted Carolyn, Jewell, and Lois Lane to the front door. "I'll wait out here, babe. Take your time."

Jewell sank gratefully into a last hug from Hank before allowing herself to be bundled inside. Lois Lane pushed in first, bounding across the living room to the kitchen. Moments later the house's post-bedtime quiet ended with the sound of water sloshing against a metal bowl.

Jewell noted a lamp left on; fresh tears formed. *They left the light on for me.*

"Lois Lane," Carolyn called quietly, "Come. Let's get her to bed."

The lapping stopped and Lois Lane appeared in the doorway, head cocked. She trotted over to Jewell, nosed her hand, and herded her toward the hallway. Carolyn draped an arm around her dazed mother's shoulder and they followed the dog to the guest bedroom.

"Do you want me to stay the night?" Carolyn looked hesitantly at the room's single bed.

Jewell dropped her sweater on a chair and kicked off her shoes. "I'm not alone, honey. The Ploughers and their weekend sitter are right down the hall. Go home; Hank's already been way more patient than usual." She reached for Carolyn's hand. "Thanks."

"I can at least get you settled." Carolyn stepped into the bathroom and returned with water and aspirin. "These won't hurt, and they might help."

When Jewell was safely under the covers Carolyn planted a kiss on her forehead and tiptoed out. Jewell heard the front door snap shut. Seconds later, Hank's truck backfired as it rumbled away down the street.

Jewell dropped her arm over the side of the bed, reassured when a cold nose touched her palm. With a whispered prayer for Doris's soul, she drifted toward sleep.

She was running along a sidewalk. It was night, and she was in a city—San Francisco—in the Tenderloin. A hypodermic rig and a dirty rag lay in a pile of trash by an old brick building. Fear coursed through her. She tried to run faster, but her legs were like lead. A siren sounded, far away. She looked back frantically along the dark, deserted street and rounded a corner. A man in dirty, ragged clothes stepped from the shadows, a baseball cap shielding all but his grizzled chin. He grabbed Jewell's arm and held out an open palm. A ring lay there, a ring with a woman's face where a stone should be. Jewell reached for it. "Who are you," she asked the man. "Rudy," he muttered.

"Ouch!" Jewell's bare foot stepped on something hard and she came awake standing in the Ploughers' hallway. As confusion and fear engulfed her, she felt Lois Lane's warm, coarse fur against her leg. *I'm sleepwalking!* She brushed off her foot and hobbled back to bed, the dream still with her.

* * *

Tap, tap!

"Time to rise, dear. Ashley made pancakes." Eve Plougher's cheery warble came through the door, bringing Lois Lane off the bed in a flying leap. The dog stood on her hind legs and wrapped her paws around the doorknob, whining.

"Where'd you learn that trick?" Jewell climbed out of bed. "Be right there, Mrs. P."

When she stepped into the kitchen with her red-rimmed eyes and grotesquely tousled hair, Mr. Plougher struggled to his feet and put an arm around her.

"You're not lookin' so hot? Rough night?"

"Coffee," Jewell muttered. "Must have coffee." She managed a sort-of smile and took a seat at the table.

Mr. and Mrs. Plougher looked at each other. "Evidently so, dear." Mrs. Plougher's voice carried the slightest hint of criticism.

The coffee and pancakes Ashley set before Jewell a minute later brought her to full, verbal consciousness. "Thanks. These look yummy." Glancing through the doorway to the living room she saw, splashed across the muted TV screen, the headline 'Body found in Miwok last night.' *Oh, boy. I'd better tell Mr. and Mrs. P.*

"Sorry I'm in such bad shape." She attempted a smile. "Unfortunately, it's not from too much partying. I have some bad news."

"Sounds serious," Nicolas Plougher mumbled through a mouthful of bacon.

"What is it, dear?" Eve Plougher's tone was gentle, relaxed.

"They found Doris," Jewell whispered.

"Eh?" Nicolas shouted. "I missed that. Speak up, woman!" He looked frustrated. "Something about Doris—she's back?"

"Hush, Nicolas. Let the girl finish. Go ahead, dear."

Jewell glanced from Nicolas to Eve. *They didn't know her well. Maybe it won't upset them.* "Doris, my landlady—the cops found her. She's dead. She was at our house the whole time."

Everyone stared at Jewell. Finally, Mrs. Plougher murmured, "Oh my. Are you okay, dear?"

Jewell shook her head. "Not really. I was there when they found her. Her grandson, Marco—they've arrested him."

Confusion spread across the Ploughers' faces. "Arrested that young man?" Mrs. Plougher murmured. "Whatever for?"

Mr. Plougher cut in sharply, "They must think he's responsible, Eve." He raised an eyebrow at Jewell. "She didn't die of natural causes?"

"No," Jewell whispered. "She was murdered."

Ashley, turning pancakes at the stove, gave a small squeak. "You were there? You saw it happen?"

Here we go.

"No, But I was with the cops when they found her. She was in that basement apartment around the back of the house."

"Oh, Jewell! How awful for you!" Eve Plougher's voice quavered.

"That settles it," Mr. Plougher rumbled, "You're not going back there."

"Oh, indeed. You're not safe at that place." Mrs. Plougher nodded agreement with her husband.

Jewell groaned. "Thanks for being protective. It's Marco who needs help. He didn't kill his own grandmother!"

The doorbell rang, startling everyone. Lois Lane dashed from the kitchen, barking furiously; Ashley dropped her spatula.

"I'll get that. It might be for me." Jewell left the table and hurried to the front door. Leo's distorted, smiling face filled the peephole. *Thank God he's here.* She pulled the door open and stepped into his arms.

"I'm so sorry you had to go through that," he whispered into her hair.

Jewell looked up at him. "It was a nightmare, and it's still going on. You know they arrested Marco?"

"I do. Poor kid led them right to the body. How's he going to explain that?"

"He was drunk," Jewell said. "For some reason, he thought Perez could tell him where to find Doris."

Mr. Plougher hurried in from the kitchen. "Leo Stone! Did you hear the latest?"

There was a bounce in the old man's step, and his face was wreathed in smiles. Evidently, murder so close to home was better than a fistful of vitamins.

"Nicholas, behave yourself!" Mrs. Plougher's walker stumped gamely along behind her husband. She reached out and grabbed his sleeve. "Unexpected death is always a tragedy, even if the woman did have a dubious past."

"Don't worry, Eve," Leo's smile didn't make it to his eyes. "I've heard." To Jewell, he murmured, "I'm on my way over to Bob's for a family pow-wow. You want to join me?"

"Sure. Give me ten minutes." Jewell hurried from the room. She heard Leo say, "Doris and I weren't exactly friends—that's no secret—but, I wouldn't wish a death like that on anyone."

* * *

On the short drive into downtown Leo glanced at Jewell several times, but said nothing. She looked much better—she'd brushed her hair and splashed cold water on her face—but a haunted, shocked expression lingered.

"They won't hold your buddy, Marco, for long," Leo assured her. "I talked to Jorgensen. The kid has no motive, no means, and most likely no opportunity, depending on the time of death." His fingers brushed Jewell's cheek. "You may be the closest thing to family he's got, now Doris is gone. From what I heard, that jerk, Perez, wrote him off years ago."

As Jewell digested the words, she felt the cord wrapped around her heart slowly loosen. She took a deep breath, relaxing against the seat. "Thank you," she said. "The image of that bereaved boy sitting in a jail cell is more than I can handle."

"It's still a mess for us Stones. Without the kid to focus on, who do you think they'll look at? Guess who stands to gain with Doris out of the way?"

Jewell turned slowly and looked at Leo, her eyes wide. "Not the Stone family, surely?"

"Bingo."

Comprehension dawned slowly. Jewell finally said, "The mansion? Someone might think you guys killed Doris to get it back? That makes no sense. Doesn't it go to her next of kin—Benny Perez?"

Leo shook his head. "Nope. Benny's excluded from ownership. That's, like, Clause Number Eighty-Seven in my brother's will. The court case'll be dismissed now Doris is gone; the property will revert back to Bob and me."

Jewell stared out her window, letting this information sink in. Without looking at Leo, she whispered, "You guys are in good company on that suspect list."

"Marco?" Leo shook his head. "Like I just said, he's off the hook."

Jewell gulped. When she spoke her voice was thin, tense. "Someone broke into my room yesterday and managed to get cut while they were in there. When we went upstairs to check on things after...." She released a slow breath. "We found blood on towels and on my nail file. The cops are looking at my room as part of the crime scene." Jewell turned frightened eyes to Leo. "So, I'm a suspect, too."

"Are you freaking kidding me?" Leo's truck swerved to the curb. He cut the engine and reached for Jewell's hand. "No way you can be a suspect! My God, woman. When were you going to let me in on this?"

"Now seemed like a good time." Jewell tried to smile, didn't quite make it.

Chapter Nineteen

Leo wrapped her in his arms, clumsily stroking her hair. When she pulled away her eyes were moist. He dug a clean mechanic's rag out of his glove box and handed it to her. Then he started the truck and pulled back on the road again.

"Let's talk about this intruder." Leo's voice was gentle. "How'd he get in? Not through the window. That second floor's at least twenty feet from the ground." When she didn't reply he continued, "Was the door locked when we left yesterday?"

"Yes. And when Hank and I got there last night, it was open." Jewell wiped her nose.

"So, someone came in from the hallway. The place look ransacked? Stuff missing?"

"It was messy—drawers and closet door open, flashlight on the floor." Jewell closed her eyes to revisit the scene. "But I wouldn't say ransacked. More like searched. The worst part was the pile of bloody towels in the corner." She sighed. "The nail file fell out of a towel."

Leo took his eyes off the road for a second to glance at Jewell. "You think someone cut themselves—with a nail file?" He sounded dubious.

"No. It's not sharp. The most you could do is file away some skin if you had, like, time to kill." Jewell groaned at her choice of words. "It does have a pointed end, though," she added. "That could do some damage."

"What I don't get is why your intruder picked it up in the first place. Was it, no pun intended, jewel-encrusted?"

"No. Maybe it was the most available weapon, though, when someone interrupted the burglary." Jewell's eyes widened. "Perez's face and hand were bandaged when he came out of the house last night—fresh bandages."

"You think he surprised an intruder? So, someone breaks into the house and then takes the time to go upstairs, down a long hall, and break into a locked room? I'm not buyin' it." Leo pulled the truck to the curb in front of Bob and Beth Anne's home. "Let's put this on hold 'til we're done talking with the kids. They don't need the extra stress right now."

"Oh. Sure." Jewell looked out the window, feeling discounted. Her stomach clenched as she flashed back to the many times she'd been pushed aside or left on her own by disinterested husbands. She whispered, "Give me a minute to change gears. I'm still pretty shaky." She climbed from the truck. When Leo joined her on the sidewalk, she gave him a tight smile. "You asked if anything was missing, and then you didn't wait for my answer. Here it is: I checked my jewelry, my Princess Grace memorabilia, my shoe collection. Everything was there but your sister-in-law's ring. I found it under the bed."

Leo nodded. "Right. Okay. Put on your happy face now for Bob and Beth Anne." As they climbed the steps he muttered, half to himself, "That ring is driving you around the bend."

Jewell felt a flush of anger. *He thinks I'm making all of this up.*

Slipping a hand in her pocket, she lifted out Maris's ring. "Speaking of which...." It rested benignly on her palm, blood speckles contrasting with the gold. "I didn't turn it over to the cops. I doubt the ghost would appreciate being locked up in an evidence room."

Leo's face paled. "For cryin' out loud, put that thing away." He pressed the doorbell. "Sorry for snapping at you," he mumbled.

"Apology not accepted."

The front door opened and Beth Anne, smiling radiantly, looked out at them.

"Whatever," Leo mouthed as Jewell wrapped Beth Anne in a careful hug.

"How are you doing, honey?" Jewell stepped back for a look. Beth Anne had dark circles under her eyes. Her bandaged arm was in a sling.

Bob reached around them to clasp Leo's hand. "She's got a ways to go, but I've given up trying to keep her on bed rest." He led them into the living room, a cheerful space furnished with a tired-looking floral print couch, a sturdy wooden rocker, and a low, glass-and-wrought-iron table.

"Coffee, anyone?" Bob smiled. "It's my G.I.'s Joe brew without the motor oil."

"Sure," Leo grinned. "I can always drink a cuppa joe."

Jewell shook her head, perching on a corner of the couch. "The burns healing okay?"

Beth Anne nodded. "They are. I have a good immune system, thank God. And, I'm on mega-antibiotics. An infection would put me in deep doo-doo." Beth Anne giggled, glancing at Bob when he came in from the kitchen with the coffee. "Not having to stress about the bills helps, too."

"Your insurance came through? That was fast!"

From his spot on the couch next to Jewell, Leo stirred his coffee. "Nicholas Plougher has a contact at the insurance company. The guy took the brakes off the process."

Bob nodded. "Thank God for friends; you've all been amazing." He turned to Jewell, sympathy in his eyes. "How're you holding up? I understand you were there when they found Doris." He looked away for a second. When he turned back, his face seemed haunted. "No way to erase that kind of memory."

"If you need a place to stay—I doubt you'll want to go back to Radish—our lumpy old couch is always available." Beth Anne's voice was determinedly cheerful.

The anger Jewell had come in with was gone, washed out on a tide of infinite sadness. "Thanks. I'll be at the Ploughers the next couple weekends…" Her voice caught; she stared down at the couch's faded fabric. "I'm going back to 811 Radish as soon as possible, though." Her chin came up. "I know everyone thinks I'm crazy; It's just, well, that place was a dream come true for this trailer-park kid. I'm hanging on as long as I can."

Bob nodded. "I get it. It's special for us, too." He turned to Leo. "I hear they arrested the grandson. You know anything about that? My money would've been on that scumbag, Perez."

"The cops took Marco in. Didn't have enough to hold him." Leo took a sip of coffee. "Be prepared to answer questions, Bob; our family's at the top of Doris Stone's shit list."

Bob straightened, looking startled.

"Not to mention," Leo added, "your loan on the coffee truck. Toni at the bank told me Doris had been threatening to call that in." Leo frowned into his cup.

Beth Anne put her small hand over Bob's larger one. "Don't panic; someone killed that horrible woman, and we know it wasn't us." She looked around the circle of serious faces. "Let's look at this as the second violent act we've sustained. If torching the truck wasn't random violence—and it wasn't—then we're victims just like Doris."

The tension in the room deflated; Jewell settled back into the couch cushions.

"Word is," Leo spoke up, "The van driven when G.I.'s Joe got torched was traced back to Doris's credit card. It—that van—was burned, too, couple days later."

"Let me guess," Bob said. "Doris never got a chance to say who used her card."

"Stateline P.D. was asked to track her down and interview her. Hadn't found her, up to last night." Leo said flatly.

"So," Beth Anne mused, "That links her death to our fire."

"Murder to cover up arson? That's insane." Jewell folded her arms. "It could just as easily be arson to distract from murder."

Three pairs of eyes turn to Jewell. "Just sayin.'"

"Jewell," Leo rubbed his chin. "Whose side are you on?"

Bob stood and paced back and forth across the room's worn beige carpet. "None of this is our responsibility. Hell, we've been making the best of a bad situation—that witch in our family home—for years. If we were killers, we would have taken action long ago." He rested a hand on Beth Anne's shoulder. "PTSD be damned. I think someone's targeting us."

In Jewell's pocket, the ring began to pulse. She wrapped her fingers around it and experienced a slight electric shock.

Crap. Maris has joined the party.

With that last thought, Jewell slipped into a zombie-like state. A shaky, high-pitched voice came from her mouth.

"Leo, Bob needs to know about the For Sale sign. You got your lawyer to quash it, but did you identify the responsible party? It wasn't that floozy Rudolph married; she was dead. And Robert," Jewell's head swiveled so she faced Bob, "did Leo tell you that thug sold the floozy's automobile?"

Jewell shivered, blinked, returned to consciousness. Bone-cold and with a throbbing headache, she turned to Beth Anne. Her friend shrank away from her, looking horrified.

The air in the room snapped with static energy; the silence was almost three-dimensional. Jewell stared at Leo, then Bob. Both showed confusion and, yes, fear.

"What the hell?" Leo's eyes bulged. He groaned, "Maris?"

"Who are you?" Beth Anne whispered.

Bob knelt in front of Jewell, white-faced. "You sounded just like Aunt Maris. And you called me Robert." A tender smile crossed his lips. "Aunt Maris? Is it really you?"

Jewell struggled to process Bob's words. "I did what? The last thing I remember was wrapping my hands around this." She opened her fingers to reveal the glowing ring. "And now, my head's killing me."

"You don't remember turning into Aunt Maris? Let's see if we can bring her back." Bob leaned toward Jewell. "Aunt Maris, we're fresh out of tonic water. How about a vodka on the rocks?" At the mention of vodka, the ring in Jewell's pocket sizzled.

"I don't even like vodka," Jewell whispered in her own voice. "It's the ring." She glanced up at Bob. "Do you have any Advil? If I don't get ahead of this headache, I'll be down with it for days."

Leo got to his feet, scowling. "Enough with the theatrics. I've had it with that damn ring." He turned to Bob. "Jewell and I saw Perez trading his mother's car keys for a wad of cash the other day." He looked somberly down at Jewell. "I think I better take you home."

Jewell let Leo pull her to her feet, leaning heavily against him as they went to the door.

"Hold on." Bob touched her arm. "Will you be okay?" His voice dropped to a whisper. "Aunt Maris?"

Leo's eyebrows went straight up to his hairline. He shouldered in front of his nephew, growling, "You can't afford to act crazy right now, Bob. The wrong person could argue a connection between your PTSD and Doris's murder."

Jewell looked at Beth Anne's scared face. "He may be right." She lifted the glowing, pulsing ring from her pocket. "I was going to give this to you, Bob, but that may not be such a good idea."

As if a switch was flipped, the ring darkened to a lifeless metal circle. Jewell's fingers relaxed and she crumpled, sliding to the floor like a puppet with cut strings. "Catch her!" someone yelled.

* * *

Her next conscious moment, Jewell squirmed against some kind of restraint. Her eyes opened: she was belted into the passenger seat of Leo's truck and he was next to her, driving.

"How's the headache?" Leo sounded worried. "We're heading back to the Ploughers. It was a mistake, taking you with me to Bob and Beth Anne's. You're still in shock from last night."

Jewell moved her head; her entire body hurt. "One of several mistakes." She turned away from Leo and stared out the window at the quiet, tree-lined Sunday morning street.

Leo cleared his throat, but said nothing. A tear trickled down Jewell's cheek; she wiped it away impatiently. *How could I be so wrong about him? I am so stupid.* She leaned her forehead against the cold glass.

"What'd I do?" Leo suddenly barked. "Must've been a doozy. Want to clue me in, so my apology will mean jack shit?"

"No," Jewell murmured. "It's too late for apologies. Just take me back to the Ploughers."

Leo stared straight ahead, white-knuckling the steering wheel.

So, no defense. I'm on my own now with the Stone family ghost.

156

The truck pulled to the curb in front of the Ploughers' house. Jewell climbed out and hurried up the walk, determined not to look back. The truck's engine growled as it drove away. Before she got to the porch, the front door opened and Lois Lane hurtled out, looking happy. After a quick lick at Jewell's face, she headed for a nearby bush.

"Thank God you're back!" Ashley stood in the doorway. "That dog drove us crazy; howled the whole time."

Jewell hugged Lois Lane and got a second face-washing. "Sorry, girl," she whispered into a furry ear. "I won't leave you behind again."

Inside, a TV blared full blast in the empty living room. When she looked through the kitchen and out to the patio, Jewell saw Mr. and Mrs. Plougher with a familiar-looking stranger—the gray-haired detective she'd seen with Benny Perez at 811 Radish last night.

Maybe I can get to my room without being seen.

"Let me get that for you." Before Jewell had time to slink away, Ashley reached around and gave the slider a good pull. The door opened and Lois Lane immediately stepped through, ears back and growling. She walked stiff-legged, almost as if going toward prey.

"Stay, girl!" Jewell quickly crossed the patio and grabbed the dog's collar. "Hi, everyone. I'll take her back inside. I'm fighting a migraine."

"Can you join us, Jewell? This guy's a detective." Mr. P. sounded impressed with his visitor.

"Yes. I know. I saw him last night." Jewell's voice trembled. She hesitated, then walked Lois Lane to a chair and perched on the edge.

"We told him how bad you feel about Mrs. Stone's death." Eve Plougher's tone was gentle.

The detective nodded. "Randy Horton, Mrs. McDunn. Sorry for your loss."

He sounds uncomfortable. Why is he here?

"Thanks," Jewell mumbled.

"Speak up," Nicholas Plougher shouted. "We're talkin' into a mike here." He pointed to a small recorder in the middle of the table. At that moment his cell phone rang. "Who'd be callin' me, for God's sake?" He got up and shuffled toward the house. "I'll take this inside. Don't want to ruin your recording."

The detective suppressed a smile and turned on the recorder. "I have a few questions, Mrs. McDunn, about your relationship with Doris Stone. According to her son, Benny Perez, you were very angry when she gave you notice to vacate your room at 811 Radish."

"What?" Jewell gripped the arms of the patio chair. "That's baloney. The creep! Doris never gave me notice to vacate. He wanted her to move me downstairs, into the library. I told her I wouldn't do that—my lease clearly says I have the upstairs master suite. She wasn't happy I refused—I don't think she liked disappointing him—but we weren't mad at each other. I just stuck to my guns."

Horton wrote something in a notebook. "I'll need to see your lease agreement."

"Sure. I'll make you a copy." Jewell stood. "Just so you know, I've barely met Benny Perez—he arrived at the house shortly after I moved in—but I got the feeling he didn't like having an outsider there. Anything he says about me should be questioned." She went inside, returning moments later with the lease.

Horton took it and gave it a cursory glance. "By the way, we won't need to fingerprint you. Your prints are already on file as a nurse's aide."

"What about my daughter and her boyfriend?"

Horton consulted his notes. "Carolyn Jones and Hank Halverson? They stopped in at the station this morning." He tucked his notebook away. "Tell me about the last time you saw Mrs. Stone before she disappeared. How'd she look? Did she tell you she was taking a trip? Was there luggage by the door, anything like that?" His face was blandly expressionless.

Jewell drew in a breath, involuntarily pressing her fingertips to her forehead. She blinked and looked away.

"Detective Horton," Eve Plougher's voice was shrill, determined. "Our friend has suffered a terrible trauma. She should be inside, resting. Can you do this questioning later? The nightmare of the past hours is still very real."

"No," Jewell's response was sharp. "I'll be okay, Mrs. Plougher." She gave her employer an apologetic smile.

"The last time I saw," she gulped, "Doris, she was sitting at the kitchen table. It was in the middle of last week. I stopped by for a minute. I had my dog with me, and Doris doesn't … didn't … like dogs, but she was nice to Lois Lane that day." Jewell paused, staring at the sparkling clean glass tabletop. "There was no talk about a trip. She wasn't dressed up or anything. The kitchen was messy—usually, it's spotless." Jewell frowned, then whispered, "Doris looked awful. Sad. Tired. Bruised. She had a black eye. It showed beneath her make-up. I felt sorry for her."

"The black eye was present when you saw her? Can you be more specific about the date?"

"Well, I moved in August first, so," Jewell counted on her fingers. "First week in September? Couple days after the attack on G.I.'s Joe."

Horton looked up quickly. "You associate those two because…?"

"Because, I don't know. Maybe because she was hurt and my friend Beth Anne was in the hospital, hurt, too. I take that stuff personally." Jewell sighed and folded her hands.

Detective Horton nodded and pushed away from the table. "Thanks for your cooperation, Mrs. McDunn. We'll be in touch." He helped Nicholas Plougher to his feet so the old gentleman could escort him out.

"Wait a sec!" Jewell called to them. "When can I get into my room? I have to make sure Perez doesn't move my stuff out."

Horton looked back, confused. "Far as I know, any time. It's your residence." He waved the rental agreement. "It's right here in black and white." He added, "Stay out of the back yard, though, 'til we take down the crime scene tape."

"But," Jewell sputtered, "Isn't my room part of the crime scene?"

"Not as far as I know. I'll look into it."

"Thank you." Jewell leaned on the table and covered her face with her hands. The aluminum slider grated as the two men left. There was a soft thump when the front door closed.

In the quiet yard Jewell gradually became aware of Eve Plougher's regular breathing, Lois Lane's panting, and the snip, snip, snip of a garden tool next door. The aluminum slider grated again and Nicholas Plougher's uneven gait added rhythm to the patio serenade.

When Jewell looked up, Plougher stood next to her. "Word is you're havin' a breakdown—seein' ghosts, faintin' and stuff. I just put in a call to our doctor. We're gettin' help."

Chapter Twenty

"What in heaven's name?" Eve Plougher stared at her husband. "Where on earth did you hear such nonsense?"

"It's not nonsense," Nicholas Plougher blustered. "I got it straight from the horses' mouth—Leo Stone. He said she's been seein' ghosts for a while now, in that room of hers over at the mansion. What's more, at Bob Stone's today she had some kind of demonic fit. Scared the crap out of Beth Anne."

Jewell sat up very straight. "Leo called you? He told you I'm crazy?"

Nicholas Plougher shuffled around the table and awkwardly patted Jewell's shoulder. "He's worried about you. Says you're crackin' up under the stress."

Beneath the table next to Jewell's chair, Lois Lane chose this moment to give her mistress's ankle a damp, gritty lick. Jewell reached down to rub between the dog's ears.

Leo didn't act concerned before; disgusted, angry. Not concerned. Feels like he's trying to discredit me. Now I'm really scared.

She lifted her head and looked at her employers. "I don't need a doctor. Some rest, maybe; a few days away from the Stone family, definitely." She looked down at her hands. "Leo has some nerve, telling you I'm having a breakdown. If anyone's crazy, it's him."

"There, there, dear." Mrs. Plougher reached across the table to grip Jewell's hand. "Remember, you've both been through a lot the past twenty-four hours."

"She's right," Mr. Plougher mumbled. "Don't throw the guy under the bus too soon. Another murder at the mansion, with that place's history?

161

Probably shook up the whole clan." His eyes lit up. "Tell us what happened at Bob and Beth Anne's."

It's natural they'd give him the benefit of the doubt. He's been their friend for years.

Jewell sighed. "I'll try. Will you promise to be open-minded? I have to start at the beginning if it's going to make any sense at all." She frowned at the little-girl sound of her voice.

"From my first night at 811 Radish, I had the feeling something awful was about to happen. Lights flickered, there were strange noises—I didn't sleep all night. I thought things would be better after a few days, but it didn't happen. I got a dog, thinking then I'd feel safe." She tried to chuckle, but it came out hollow. "The first day Lois Lane was there, she rooted around in the closet and found that old wedding ring. It glowed, gave off heat, even had a pulse. Almost gave me a heart attack." Jewell paused. The Ploughers listened intently, mouths slightly open.

"Carolyn—she supposedly has a sixth sense—said the room was haunted. When I found the news report of the home invasion and murder years ago, she talked me into organizing a séance."

"A séance? How interesting," Eve Plougher smiled.

"On the Sci-fi channel, maybe," Nicholas Plougher mumbled.

"At the séance, the psychic said the first Mrs. Stone is not only present, she's very upset."

Nicholas Plougher leaned back, his face alight with curiosity. "I always knew there was something fishy about that place."

"Hush, Nicholas." Eve Plougher whispered. "Go on, dear. This is fascinating."

"I was skeptical, but still scared." Jewell took a slow breath. "About that time, Benny Perez got paroled and came back to Miwok. He pressured his mother to kick me out. When I told her I wouldn't leave, she asked if I'd at least move downstairs. I said 'No,' to that, too. I mean, except for the ghost, I love my room. Why would I accommodate that creep?" Jewell looked away for a second. "So, besides the ring acting weird, a few days ago I saw two women huddled in my closet—just for a split second. And then someone jammed the lock on my door, trying to break in."

At this point Mr. and Mrs. Plougher were listening, open-mouthed. "Two women? In your closet? Are you prone to hallucinations, dear?" Mrs. Plougher's voice was little more than a whisper.

"No!" Jewell squeaked. She continued, "Leo went with me the other day, to check my door. As soon as we got in there, he felt the ghost's presence—said he smelled her perfume. Then, right in front of both of us, my lipstick lifted off the dresser and wrote a message on the mirror." Jewell blinked, trying to erase the image behind her eyelids. "He said it was Maris's handwriting."

"Heavens above!" Mrs. Plougher gasped.

Nicholas Plougher's lips clamped together in a straight line. For once he was speechless.

"You can imagine how relieved I was, having the ghost appear to someone besides me. That's why it hurt so much today when he did an about-face—called the ring an 'unholy circle of gold' and said we have more important things to concentrate on." Jewell's voice dropped to a murmur. "I was counting on his support."

"I'm sure he didn't mean it that way," Eve Plougher sounded hesitant.

"Typical male reaction, if you ask me. Probably scared the bejeebers out of him." Nicholas Plougher grinned and winked at Eve, who ignored him.

"What happened when you got to Bob and Beth Anne's, dear?"

"I tried to hide my feelings, but when I went to give Bob the ring, things kind of fell apart. The next thing I knew, I was laying on the floor with three scared faces staring at me. They said I spoke in Maris Stone's voice while I was passed out. That's what Leo meant by the 'demonic fit.'"

The Ploughers practically vibrated with amazement. Mr. Plougher slipped an arm around his wife and she leaned against him, her face drained of color.

"Maris Stone died, but she didn't leave. She's been in the mansion all these years." Mrs. Plougher wiped a tear from her eyes.

My God. They actually believe me. Jewell touched the older woman's arm. "I didn't mean to upset you." She gave Mr. Plougher a pleading look.

He shook his head. "We asked you. And we can take it. We're your friends."

Eve Plougher sat up straight. "What came over you was a trance, dear.

I've heard of them, but nothing like you experienced. It's incredible. A disembodied spirit jumped right into you!"

"So, you believe there is a ghost?" Jewell looked from one to the other, her face pale. "You don't think I had a seizure or something?"

Mr. Plougher nodded. "That's one of the advantages of getting old; you understand that not everything real makes sense." He raised his bushy eyebrows. "Did the ghost say who strung her up?"

"Nicholas!" Eve Plougher turned to Jewell. "Do you have the ring now?"

Jewell shivered. *The ring. Did Bob give it back to me?*

Without meeting Mrs. Plougher's eyes, Jewell checked her pocket. "I don't think so. I didn't see it after...and I must have passed out again because I don't remember leaving Bob and Beth Anne's, or getting into Leo's truck." Jewell pushed away from the table. "I need to find it." As she moved toward the sliding door she fought off a heightened awareness of the green lawn, the bumpy gray cement path, the buzzing of insects in a nearby rosebush. She reached for the sliding door frame to steady herself.

Dear God, is Maris's ghost still here, without the ring?

"Stop right there, young lady," Nicholas barked. "You can't go running around like a chicken with its head cut off. Go in and lie down—I'll call around and find that ring."

"He's right, Jewell." Eve Plougher's voice carried an anxious squeak. "You need time to adjust to everything." She straightened her shoulders. "I sincerely hope the ghost doesn't show up here. I never entertained Maris Stone when she was alive, and I don't want to do so now."

Jewell suppressed a groan. "Okay. I do have a splitting headache." She stepped into the kitchen and got an ice pack from the freezer.

As she went down the hall toward the guest room, Ashley peered around the bathroom door. "Don't tell the seniors," Ashley whispered, "but I can front you a little weed if you want. For that headache."

"I'll keep that in mind if this ice doesn't help." Jewell managed a small thank-you smile and stepped into the guest room, shutting the door quickly. She dropped onto the bed, ice pack on her forehead, and closed her eyes.

Immediately her thoughts flashed on the back yard at 811 Radish. She saw the yellow crime scene tape, the trampled lawn, and the basement apartment's closed door. A bee made a zigzag course in and out of the honeysuckle bush next to the door, buzzing as it went. The yard was empty, quiet. The mansion itself stood eerily silent, empty of life. Jewell saw her hand on the basement doorknob, ready to turn it. *No. I'm not going in there. I refuse to replay finding Doris's dead body.*

Her hand turned the knob.

NO. I'M NOT GOING IN THERE.

Lois Lane, sniffing restlessly around the room, sat back on her haunches and eyed Jewell. Suddenly, WHUMP! the dog jumped on the bed, knocking the breath from Jewell's lungs and pinning her to the comforter.

"Aiee!" The pain in her lungs was awful. The backyard-mansion scene faded.

As soon as she caught her breath Jewell squirmed free of furry dog weight and rolled onto the floor. Lois Lane followed, landing next to her mistress. Jewell twisted away, held the dog at arms' length and peered into anxious canine eyes. "You knocked that ghost right out of me. Thank you!"

Lois Lane emitted a low, earnest whine.

"You're amazing." Jewell held the dog's face in her hands. "If there's such a thing as angel-dogs, you are one."

A paw came up and scratched gently at Jewell's shoulder.

"Is there something we need to do? What?" *Leo and I didn't look in the closet like the ghost asked. Maybe I should get that done. Right away.* Jewell groaned. *Anything to get out of this nightmare.*

Lois Lane's tail wagged; she stood and trotted to the door.

By the way, Ghost, my head's still killing me, and everything about 811 Radish has me scared to death. Jewell held the ice pack to her forehead for a second, enjoying the cool cessation of pain. *There's no choice; if I ever want that ghost out of my life, I have to get back to the mansion and check that closet. It's not like I'm safe here, anyway, with the ghost stuck to me.*

Jewell slipped into her Nikes. She jammed a ball cap low on her forehead, then glanced in the mirror and almost gagged. A pathetically bruised, haggard woman in dirty jeans and a soiled Giants' tee shirt stared back at her. The ice pack, obvious under the ball cap, didn't help.

Crap. I'm a wreck. She shuffled to the door and paused with a hand on the doorknob.

Should I let the Ploughers know I'm going out? No. They're already halfway to having me committed. I'll leave a note in my room. Maybe I'll be back before they see it.

It took less than a minute for Jewell to scribble, *"Feeling better. Making a quick trip home. Back in time for dinner."* She propped the note against her pillow in full view of anyone looking into the room.

"Okay, Lois Lane. Let's hope we sneak out unseen."

The tapping of Lois Lane's nails on the hardwood floor went unnoticed in the quiet household. When they passed the kitchen Jewell saw Mr. Plougher leaning against the counter, supervising Ashley's sandwich-making.

"Easy on the mayo. Remember my heart condition."

There was a *SNAP* when the front door shut behind Jewell and Lois Lane. They hurried down the porch steps to the curb and Jewell's Civic.

Damn! I'm too old to be sneaking around like this.

As the car pulled away, Jewell felt Lois Lane eyeing her from the passenger seat. "I know. Shame on me. But think about it. What choice do I have, with that ghost breathing down my neck?"

The dog looked away, head between her paws.

Halfway across town—light traffic allowed Jewell to notice her surroundings as she drove—a familiar figure emerged through the glass doors of the 7-Eleven. Glancing left, then right, he disappeared around the corner of the building. Lois Lane lifted her head and whined.

"Huh," Jewell muttered. "You saw him, too."

The Civic rounded the corner and entered a parking lot behind the market. At the far end, the side door of an old VW van slid closed.

Marco.

With a groan, Jewell pulled in behind the van. *I don't have time for this.*

She had hardly lifted the driver's-side door handle when Lois Lane scrambled out onto the pavement, barking ecstatically.

Probably no need to knock.

While Lois Lane jumped against the van's side window, barking and whining, Jewell got out and leaned against the Civic. The door slid open a crack. Marco's face appeared, wary. "Whoa!" He pushed the door back and climbed down, wrapping Lois Lane in a hug.

"Can you tell we're glad to see you?" Jewell reached over and gently touched his shoulder.

Marco sat in the doorway, one arm loosely draped around the dog. He glanced at Jewell. "You don't look so good." He rubbed his face. "Me, neither. Spent the night in jail."

"So I heard. Glad they didn't hold you." Jewell tried for a smile, didn't make it.

"Sorry you had to see me drunk." Marco grimaced. "You know they thought I k-k-killed her?" He buried his face against Lois Lane's fur. "Strange, huh? Finding her while we're looking for that creep—my *father*."

"Definitely strange." Jewell nodded. She hesitated, then said, "I didn't know your grandmother very long. Living in the same house, though, she and I connected like, maybe, sisters. Now, especially after last night, it feels like you are part of the family. I hope you know you're welcome any time, at my place or my kids'."

Marco's face reflected sadness. "Thanks." He picked up a pebble and tossed it across the lot. "Why would anyone kill her? She was no saint, but hell, murder? No way." He got to his feet. "I guess you're done at 811 now. Benny's probably already sold it." He frowned. "Sorry end for a beautiful place."

Jewell shook her head. "I'm not leaving." She bent down and snapped the leash on Lois Lane's collar. "Perez has no claim. With your grandmother gone, it goes back to the Stone family."

"No shit?" Marco's face lit up. "That's good news. The Benster'll go ballistic when he hears that." He stroked Lois Lane's fur. "I don't want you worrying about me, Jewell. You've already done way too much. You were smart, you'd get the hell away while you can." He studied a dandelion pushing its way through a crack in the pavement. "It's a little different for me; I'll stick around until I find out who killed my grandmother."

Marco's words had an odd effect on Jewell. Pain and fear gave way to acceptance. At the same time, the air began to sparkle.

Oh, no. Maris. Jewell took a deep breath, struggling to break the ghostly grip. She tensed her muscles fiercely, gritting her teeth. Amazingly, the ghostly presence faded.

"I can't walk away," Jewell whispered. "The ghost won't let me. I have to find out who killed the first Mrs. Stone." She looked somberly at Marco. "Want to help? Maybe we get double the results?"

The disbelief and derision Jewell expected didn't show in Marco's haggard face, so Jewell continued, "Two Mrs. Stones murdered at the same place, ten years apart. Coincidence? I think not."

Marco got to his feet and looked away, toward a row of dusty Eucalyptus trees along the lot's far edge. "You're going there now, aren't you—to 811?" He turned back to Jewell, his face radiating wonder. You're a glutton for punishment. Ah, what the hell? If a curly-haired nurse-lady can do it, so can I. I'll meet you there in an hour."

Jewell let out a whoosh! of relief. "Thanks. It'll be easier going back, knowing you'll be there." She got Lois Lane into the Civic and climbed behind the wheel. As she turned the car around Marco's van pulled onto the street.

Chapter Twenty-One

The yearly Antiques and Curiosities Street Fair brought hundreds of out-of-towners to the usually quiet streets of Miwok. The blocks between the AM-PM Market and Radish Street thronged with pedestrians and slow-driving gawkers. Sitting in stalled traffic while two women hoisted an antique table into a mini-van, Jewell had time to consider the difference between the womens' reality and hers. If she hadn't moved into 811 Radish, her biggest problem, too, might have been fitting an antique table into her car.

I forgot about the street fair. Will the ghost stay docile while we're stuck in this traffic jam? Jewell crossed her fingers.

Maris Stone must have been a very strong person to hang around all these years waiting for retribution. Ghosts are known for that, though. I wonder, was she happily married to Leo's brother? He was a player—the affair with Doris shows that. And he married Doris right after Maris's death. If she was already in a snit about being murdered, the quick remarriage would have been gasoline on an already smoldering fire.

Jewell thought of the marks on Doris's neck, and of Maris's death by hanging. *Both were strangled.* With a shiver, she ran a protective hand across her own neck.

The traffic finally cleared and the Civic began to move along the quiet, tree-lined boulevard leading to Radish Street. As she approached the mansion Jewell saw three vehicles parked next to the wrought-iron fence: a police unit, Leo's truck, and a dark sedan.

I don't want to see Leo—maybe in a few days, when being suckered doesn't hurt so much. Not now.

A figure walking away from 811 on the sidewalk caught Jewell's eye. He—the stride was masculine—darted from one shadow to the next, head down and face concealed by a hoodie. Something about the man's posture was familiar.

That's Benny Perez.

Jewell drove past the mansion at a speed just under the residential limit, scanning the building's façade for clues to any drama unfolding inside. Other than Perez's suspicious behavior—which, knowing him, could have been unconscious—there was no sign of trouble. The house was blank-faced, lifeless: curtains hung at appropriate angles in the windows, shrubs beneath the porch railing stood at orderly attention.

After parking the Civic around the corner by an ancient, gnarled mulberry tree, Jewell turned to Lois Lane. "Eager to get out, huh?"

The dog flicked one ear, her concentration on the nearby door handle.

"Sit," Jewell said, hoping to avoid the inevitable trampling when the car door opened. The command came out in Maris Stone's voice, and harsh.

Lois Lane's eyes widened. She backed away from Jewell and planted her butt on the seat, whining.

There'll be no more of that creature stampeding across our lap to get out.

"Good God," Jewell muttered. "Maris buzzed in, torpedoed Lois Lane, and buzzed away!" Jewell let out a hysterical giggle. She enfolded the dog in an awkward hug. "Sorry. That wasn't me, girl."

Lois Lane licked Jewell's face anxiously.

"Yes. Let's get going."

When she stepped from the car Jewell's feet barely touched the ground before Lois Lane pushed past her. After running the length of the leash, the dog gave Jewell a backward look.

Jewell caught up and put a hand on Lois Lane's head. "Trying to get away from the ghost? Good luck with that."

Lois Lane's posture shifted from loose-limbed to wary. She continued along the sidewalk, slow and cautious.

She understands. Amazing.

As they approached the mansion's wrought-iron fence the front door opened and two cops stepped out. Leo Stone and the Ploughers' lawyer, Mitch Steinberg, were with them, heads together in conversation.

Resisting an impulse to flatten herself behind the hedge, Jewell opened the gate and stepped onto the path.

Leo saw Jewell and stopped in mid-sentence. Steinberg—his back to the street—turned at the click of the gate latch and stared. If she hadn't been so nervous, the surprise in their faces would have been comical.

From somewhere deep within Jewell summoned a carefree attitude; she marched up the steps, smiling. "Hello, gentlemen. What a surprise, finding you here. I'll be in my room."

The officers and Steinberg moved away from the door, nodding. Leo Stone didn't budge. "You really think that's a good idea?" He shifted his weight so he was squarely between Jewell and the door.

With Lois Lane pressed against her side, Jewell locked eyes with him. "Can you give me one reason I shouldn't have access to my *legal* residence?"

For one unguarded moment pain shone from Leo's eyes. Then he looked away. "It's your call, officers. She has a lease on the room, but it's signed by the deceased. Didn't I hear you say this entire property's a crime scene—off limits?"

"Your lease may eventually be in dispute, Mrs. McDunn," Steinberg cut in, "once we get property ownership straightened out. That could take months, though, even years." He looked thoughtfully at the officers. "She's within her legal rights at present."

"You heard him, ma'am." The younger officer gave Jewell a tight smile. "Just stay out of the back yard. And let us know if you see the other resident, one," he looked at some paperwork, "Benny Perez."

Only moments ago. Do I tell them that? I don't think so. That might not have been Benny. And I need to get upstairs right now, away from Mr. Two-faced Stone.

Leo reached toward Jewell, his hand stopping in mid-air when a low growl came from Lois Lane's throat. The dog's lip curled back in a display of sharp, white eyeteeth.

Both of Leo's hands went into his pockets. In a very soft voice he said,

"Looks like I can't keep you from going up there. Jewell. You and I both know that room's got a lot of …" he hesitated, "…problems. For your own welfare you should probably change addresses."

Jewell turned away, shaking her head. "I have unfinished business here. I'm not leaving." She stepped inside and shut the door.

At the second-floor landing, Jewell turned to look down on the entry hall. The light that usually filtered in from the living room windows was absent, leaving the space little more than a dark hole. Heavy, stale air added to the cellar-like quality. *This poor house. It feels shrouded, like death after a long, painful illness.*

The second floor was eerily silent—no air conditioner rumbling, no distant clock ticking. As they moved along the hall toward her room, Jewell noted that Lois Lane was on high alert. The dog seemed to employ all senses with each step. *It feels like we've stepped into a dimension unique to this house, alien to my dog and me.*

"Oh, boy. Gotta snap out of it. The house is not our enemy. We're rightful tenants. Doris is gone. It's up to us to clean out the bad energy." Jewell took a few dance steps and started singing, loud and off-key. "Oh, oh, say, can you see…" Lois Lane looked back at her and raised her head in a joyful howl.

At the bedroom door Jewell dug out the key and, aware of the dog's stare, inserted it in the lock. "No one's messed with it since last time we were here." Her anxiety level dropped a notch.

The door opened with a creak. They stepped inside and Jewell locked the door behind them. She stood still, looking around. *Everything's the same, but it doesn't feel safe anymore.*

Lois Lane slowly circled the room, ears up and the whites of her eyes showing. At the closet door she stopped, backed away, and emitted a low whine.

Jewell stood still, her fists clenched. *Does she sense the ghost or an intruder?*

"Please don't show yourself, Mrs. Stone. If somebody alive is in there, prepare to be bitten!"

In the silence, Jewell could sense the tension easing. She unclenched her fists. At that moment a gust of air fluttered the window curtains and moved toward the closet. Jewell reached for the doorknob and opened the door. With a calming breath, she pulled the closet's stale, musty air into her lungs. *This must be what a tomb smells like.*

Lois Lane squeezed past, straight into a back corner. She clamped her jaws on the carpeting and pulled, laying bare the wood plank subfloor. She looked up at her mistress with a mouthful of carpet fuzz.

"Good dog." Jewell crawled in for a look, running her hand along the seams of the old oak planking. "Should I get my screwdriver and pry these up?" *Do you want to weigh in, Mrs. Stone? What's next?* She turned her head and bumped against the piece of carpet still clenched between Lois Lane's teeth.

Papers, maybe once part of a magazine, were stuck to the back of the carpet. "Huh. Did they use this for padding?" Jewell gently removed the stuff from her dog's mouth and peeled the paper off. "Not a magazine. Maybe notebook pages?"

She sat back, holding the wrinkled paper between two fingers. When a gust of wind fluttered it, she groaned. "Okay. I get it. I'll take a look."

A quick flipping of the pages showed them blank to the last page. There, in smudged pencil, was the handwriting that had been lipsticked across her mirror.

"You wrote this, Mrs. Stone?"

The temperature in the room dropped. Goosebumps formed on Jewell's bare arms and the hair on the back of her neck rose. She blinked back dizziness. "If you want my help, stay out of my head."

Lois Lane's cold nose pushed into Jewell's palm.

"Hi, girl." Jewell took a steadying breath and noticed air circling, cone-like, next to her.

"Whoa! Cut that out!" She pushed through the cone and stepped from the closet, stumbling to a chair. "I'm reading this, okay?" She held up the notebook pages.

The fur on the nape of Lois Lane's neck rose and, without warning, profound sadness washed over Jewell. Brushing back tears, she turned to words written ten years earlier.

Monday, June 2nd

To Whoever Finds This:

That horrible young man tried to kill me. I have no doubt he'll try again. Rudolph laughed, said I'm crazy. Is he blind to the truth? I saw Benny almost kill a child in a fit of passion—I must face the possibility Rudolph and Doris set him on me intentionally.

Just minutes ago I saw Benny in my room, stringing a rope over my curtain rod. I ran downstairs to get Rudolph, but when we got back here, the boy was long gone.

I'm not paranoid. I know what I saw. I also know the boy's mother is furious because I said NO, DEFINITELY NOT, when Rudolph asked for a divorce.

First thing tomorrow, I'm calling Leo. He'll believe me.

The note ended with sharp, angry pen strokes.

Jewell stared at the page, her hands shaking. "You saw Benny Perez in your room, Mrs. Stone? You scared him away? But...."

She squinted at the notepaper for a moment, then reached for her bag and pulled out the folded copy of the home invasion news article. It was dated June 4th, the day after the murder. Mrs. Stone's note was written on June 3rd.

Hollow-voiced, Jewell murmured, "You didn't get a chance to call Leo. Benny came back during the night."

Ten-year-old feelings—terror, rage and despair bounced off Jewell's eardrums and shocked her brain. As she sat there, mist floated in through the open window. It coated every surface it touched, including the mirror.

Grrr!

Lois Lane, growling softly, looked up at Jewell.

Jewell gave herself a shake and put a reassuring hand on Lois Lane's head. Across the room, the mist-shrouded mirror contained a new message.

Stop him—for yourself and us. Maris and Doris.

Moving like a sleepwalker, Jewell lifted the phone from her bag and got photos of the notepaper and the mirror message. She sighted in on the old news article, too, snapping an image of it. A click or two later the three pictures and a hasty, "Taken in my room at 811 Radish. Info on murders," were texted to Carolyn.

Only then did Jewell whisper, "Maris? The two women I saw in the closet the other day: One was you. I didn't see the other woman's face. Was it ... Doris?"

The air in the room was perfectly still.

Oh, God. Am I going to find out who killed her, too?"

The bulb in the Tiffany lamp clicked on. Jewell stifled a sardonic chuckle. "Gallows humor from a ghost."

Thump, thump! Footsteps, heavy ones, on the stairs.

I'm alone in a big haunted house with a psychopath. And I call myself smart. Don't panic; panic makes people stupid.

Lois Lane moved, stiff-legged, to the bedroom door. She stood to one side of it, a low growl rolling in her throat. Jewell reached under the bed, grasped the handle of the baseball bat she'd hoped never to need, and got in line behind her dog.

Three sharp knocks sounded on the door.

Does Perez know we're in here? My car. He'd see it. Damn!

"Who is it?" Jewell squeaked.

Someone blew out a loud breath. Then, "Leo. We need to talk."

Jewell's knees shook so much she had to lean against the wall. "Your timing's lousy, Leo." She stepped around Lois Lane and opened the door.

When he saw the bat and the growling dog, he took a step back. "Whoa, looks like you're armed and dangerous."

Jewell stared blankly at him before opening the door so he could enter. "I'm not in the mood for jokes. What do you want?" She bit off each word trying to subdue panic.

"I need to apologize." Leo looked nervous, but determined. "I was so scared for my family, I lost sight of your feelings." He coughed, seeming to finally notice the room's heavy stillness. "I hope this doesn't sound cold, but Doris's murder couldn't have come at a worse time for Bob. Between his PTSD and bad feelings between our family and Doris, he's top of the list of suspects. Add on her involvement in the firebombing, he's a slam dunk."

Jewell nodded, trying to make sense of his chatter.

"Even so, I shouldn't have ignored your feelings, Jewell. That was insensitive, even for me." His expression reminded Jewell of a guilty four-year-old. "Is there even a remote chance you'll forgive me? You're the best thing that's ever happened to me. Have I blown my chances with you sky high?"

Is he blushing?

"It was more than insensitive," Jewell whispered. "It was mean. You abandoned me when your family's ghost took me hostage." She straightened her shoulders, glaring at him. "This isn't about Bob. You can't handle what's going on here—the ghost, the possessed ring, all that. Forgive you? You have a nerve even asking."

Leo's shoulders sagged. "You're absolutely right."

Lois Lane sidled over next to Leo and leaned against his leg. He stared down at her blankly, then gently rubbed her head.

"You're much stronger than me, Jewell; I don't know if it's life experience, or just who you are. The truth is, things would be a lot easier if Maris's ghost was only in your overactive imagination. But, she's not. I can feel her right now, watching us.

"I know it'll take more than saying sorry to regain your trust, but I'd sure like to try. Not to mention, I'm worried about you. Maris's ghost is too strong for you."

Jewell's legs suddenly gave out. She sank to the floor and sat cross-legged, looking up at Leo. "When you're right, you're really right. She won't let go until I expose her murderer, and I have no clue how to do that."

Leo slid down the wall to sit across from Jewell, his eyes shining with relief. He shook his head. "Remember when I talked to Chief Sorensen about reopening the investigation into Maris's death? He said with their manpower shortage, any new evidence would have to be significant." His gaze traveled around the room to the mirror. "For cryin' out loud. Another message?"

"Yes." Jewell nodded. "Could you get Sorensen to come here? I've found something he should see."

Leo pulled out his phone with shaking hands. "We belong to the same Lodge. I'll lean on his allegiance to a brother." He glanced at the mirror as he keyed numbers into the phone.

The tension gripping Jewell slowly ebbed. She turned her head so he couldn't see the relief in her eyes.

Leo slipped the phone back in his pocket. "Gunnar—Chief Sorensen—was out of the office. When I said it was important, they patched me through. He's on his way here." He frowned. "I hope your new stuff is more than that scribble on the mirror. He wouldn't take that seriously."

"Yeah, we don't want him thinking I'm a crackpot." Jewell's laugh was hollow.

"Even if we can't convince him this ghost thing is real, he should go along with having the writing on the mirror analyzed." He glanced at the dresser. "Is Maris's ring still here? He might be interested in that. Burglars should've taken it during the robbery." He stared at Jewell. "What else do you have?"

Jewell hesitated. *Here goes. Can I trust him?* "I found this journal." She held up the notepaper. "It was Maris's. She wrote in it the night of the murder. Did you know she planned to call you the next day? She evidently considered you a safe friend."

Leo stopped pacing and slowly turned to face her. "Journal? Where'd you unearth that?" He looked scared. "I didn't know she kept one."

A shiver ran through Jewell. *Were you a safe friend, Leo?*

Slipping the notepaper into her bag, Jewell stepped out into the hall. "I think I'll wait for Chief Sorensen on the front porch."

Chapter Twenty-Two

"Wait!" Leo followed her, grabbing her arm.

GRRR! His fingers had barely circled Jewell's wrist when Lois Lane sprang between them, pinning him against the faded wallpaper.

"Whoa! Call her off! I'm not the enemy!"

"Down, girl! Back off."

After giving Jewell a puzzled look, Lois Lane dropped to the floor, paws together and ears forward in a classic sentry pose.

Jewell stared at Leo, slumped to the floor and radiating humiliation. She restrained an impulse to kick him, hard. "What is it you're not telling me? To Lois Lane, you smell like danger. Why is that?"

Looking down the hall toward the stairs, Leo muttered, "That's fear she smells. Probably the same difference to a dog's nose." He sighed. "It's my fault Maris's murder wasn't solved."

At this, Jewell's body became rigid. Her eyes widened and, although she didn't pass out, she felt her spirit shrink. Once again, Maris took over.

"What did you do, Leo?" Maris's words came out soft and breathy from Jewell's mouth.

"I steered the cops away from Rudy—told him to fake being crippled. I thought he was in on the murder." Leo's eyes gleamed bitter agony. "You were dead; nothing could change that. He was my brother. I had to protect him."

"The truth would have hurt the Stone family name." Maris's voice now had a sharp edge. *"Of course. You shielded the family reputation from Rudy's behavior*

for years; It was your job."

"Yes. The goddamn family name. It's been rewritten in blood." Leo pushed to his feet, staying clear of Lois Lane. "What difference does it make now, Maris? Why can't you leave us in peace?"

Jewell felt anger push through her. It seemed to come from the house itself. She felt like a pufferfish, swollen with it. Maris shrieked, *"I'm chained to this house by your lies! Can't you see that?"*

Ding, dong!

From downstairs, the sound of the doorbell shattered the energy-charged air. Lois Lane, barking furiously, ran toward the stairs.

Jewell blinked, panting with the effort to regain her body. She glanced at Leo, slumped against the wall and mumbling.

"That must be Sorenson. Snap out of it!" She ran after her dog.

At the bottom of the stairs Jewell turned to look up at Leo. He moved as if balance and flexibility were forever gone. He seemed to have aged years in the past few minutes.

Poor, misguided sucker. He chose loyalty over ethics a long time ago, and now his marker's been called in.

She forced her mouth into a half-smile and called up to him, "Pull yourself together. We're not done yet."

"Maris was nicer when she was alive." Leo's eyes were vacant.

Jewell shrugged. "Oh, well." She turned away.

The doorbell rang again. Jewell grabbed Lois Lane's leash and pulled the door open, letting in a gust of air. Marco stood there, looking nervous.

I forgot he was coming. "Hi! Get inside, out of the wind."

Looking beyond him to the front yard, Jewell saw 811 Radish's shrubbery bending, twisting in a strange, wind-driven choreography. Tiny blue hydrangea petals swirled across the lawn; dry leaves assaulted a jogger hurrying by.

"It's not supposed to rain, is it?" Marco glanced warily over his shoulder. "Damn wind practically pushed my van off the road." When he saw Leo, he hovered uncertainly at the threshold.

Jewell quickly said, "You two know each other, right?"

"Yeah." A sour expression crossed Leo's face. He turned away, saying, "Sorry about your grandmother. No one should go like that."

Marco acknowledged Leo with a jut of his chin. 'Yeah. Looks like you don't need my help, Jewell. I'm out of here." He stepped back onto the porch.

"Wait, Marco. You have as much right here as anyone." Jewell glared at Leo. "We were just leaving. We'll all go together."

She stepped onto the front porch. When Marco moved to a sheltered corner, Lois Lane and Jewell joined him, leaving Leo in the doorway. Suddenly, from the street a car's engine roared. Gunshots cut through the blustering wind.

POP, POP, POP!

Leo stumbled, clutching his shoulder. "Shooter," he yelled. "Get down!"

"Inside! Inside," Jewell screamed. She threw herself back across the threshold, pulling Lois Lane in by the collar.

A dark sedan revved its engine and took the corner on two wheels.

As Leo sagged against the door frame a bloody red patch bloomed on his shirt front.

"Come on, old man!" Marco reached for Leo and half-dragged him inside, slamming the door behind them. Leo sank to the floor.

"Oh, my God, he's been hit!" Jewell moaned. "What do we do? What do we do?"

"Take a deep breath; count to ten. Don't panic." Marco bit off the words. "I heard three shots. They didn't get me. You?"

"No." Gulping air, Jewell bent to run her hands over Lois Lane's thick fur. "She's clear, too."

"Let's have a look, dude." Marco knelt next to Leo.

"Don't call me dude," Leo wheezed. But he lay back, closing his eyes while Marco unbuttoned the now blood-soaked shirt. Leo's left shoulder, just below the shoulder blade, was a mess of blood and torn flesh.

"Call 9-1-1, Jewell," Marco said quietly. "Then find a towel."

With shaking fingers Jewell punched in the number, blurting out information as soon as someone answered. Her stomach suddenly lurched; she clamped her lips shut, dropped the phone, and dashed for the bathroom.

When she returned, Marco grabbed the towel she'd brought and pressed it against Leo's wound. "If my Boy Scout training's right, this'll slow the bleeding. Relax, old man. You need to slow down that heart." He gave Leo a wicked grin. "Lucky for you it was a lousy shot. A couple inches lower, you'd be looking up out of a coffin." Marco's trembling voice belied his cocky attitude.

A siren wailed in the distance. Lois Lane raised her muzzle and howled.

Jewell felt prickles on the back of her neck. She heard, inside her head, Maris's voice: *Don't worry about Leo. He's not done yet.*

Jewell touched Marco's arm, bending near him to whisper, "Leo's going to be all right."

Marco's eyes slid from staring at Leo's shoulder to a quick, puzzled glance at Jewell. He nodded. "Get the door open. The ER guys will be moving fast."

When she stood, Jewell felt slightly light-headed. To steady herself she scanned the foyer, looking up the staircase and then across to the circular stained-glass window above the front door. Although the second floor was gloomy, a beam of light from somewhere up there blended with the light from the stained-glass window, bathing Leo and Marco in a halo of color. A keen sense of the indomitable heart of this old house flooded Jewell. A tiny smile crept across her face.

When footsteps pounded on the front porch, Jewell yanked the door open and what seemed like a wall of cops swarmed in. Medics were there, too; Marco handed off the job of keeping pressure on Leo's wound and went to help Jewell subdue Lois Lane.

One of the officers, a man in jeans and a sports coat, sidled over to stand a discreet distance from Lois Lane.

"Mrs. McDunn? You'll need to secure the dog somewhere away from here. Immediately."

It registered in Jewell's shocked brain that this man was Detective Horton, last seen in the Ploughers' back yard. "Oh. Okay."

"Can you get her in there?" Horton jerked his head toward the kitchen.

Jewell nodded. With the dog pressed between them, she and Marco moved awkwardly to the kitchen. Only after the leash was securely tied to the kitchen table did Jewell realize Horton and one of the officers had followed them.

"Okay, Mrs. McDunn. Let's have your take on what happened." Horton was irritatingly brusque.

Jewell lowered herself into a chair before saying, "We were all on the front porch—we'd just stepped outside. Leo was in the doorway. I heard, **pop! pop! pop!** Leo yelled—there was a screeching sound—he fell down."

"Shots? Coming from...?" The officer's gentle tone offset Horton's abrasiveness.

"I don't know. It happened too fast." Jewell turned to Marco. "Did you see anything?"

"Hey," Horton barked at Marco. "Weren't you in the drunk tank last night?"

The officer, a slim young Asian man, gave Horton a warning glance and turned to Marco. "Start with your name, please, and tell me what happened."

"Marco Perez," Marco whispered. "I came over to see Jewell—Mrs. McDunn. They were on their way out. Mr. Stone was in the doorway. Jewell and I had our backs to the street. When I heard a loud car muffler, I looked. A black Civic cruised by. Stone yelled; I heard shots; and," Marco gulped, his face ashen. "Stone started bleeding."

Jewell blurted, "Thank God Marco was here. He knows First Aid. If Leo lives, it'll be thanks to him."

Horton, ignoring Jewell, stared at Marco. "Black Civic? You see the driver? The plates?"

Jewell felt dizzy. Through the shock enveloping her, she felt the ghost clamoring for attention.

Please, Maris. Not now. I can't handle all of this and you, too.

After an impatient shudder, a sense of inner calm enveloped her. *Thanks.*

"Stay in here, Mrs. McDunn. Kid, c'mon outside. Maybe the fresh air'll jog your memory."

Jewell stared after the cops and Marco, gradually focusing on a gurney just beyond the open door. Leo lay on it, eyes closed. He was very, very pale.

Dear God, please keep him alive. He made a big mistake a long time ago, but he's sorry. This house doesn't need any more victims.

CHAPTER TWENTY-TWO

She shook herself. *Gotta call Bob and Beth Anne.*

When she keyed in the number, it rang and went to voicemail. "We can't get to the phone right now. Please call back." It was Beth Anne's cheery voice from before the G.I.'s Joe firebombing.

Jewell coughed out, "It's me—Jewell. Sorry to have to leave this message: your uncle is on his way to Miwok General. He's been shot." *Best I can do.*

The paramedics gathered around the gurney and rolled it outside. Jewell followed them, watching as the ambulance doors snapped shut on Leo. Her shoulders sagged. The vehicle, sirens wailing, moved down the street and away from 811 Radish.

Please don't die.

She spotted Detective Horton, Marco, the young Asian officer, and a fair-haired, bulky-framed female cop clustered in the living room and went to join them, perching next to Marco on his grandmother's couch.

"The hits just keep coming here at 811 Radish, don't they?" No one acknowledged Jewell's pathetic attempt at humor.

"Like I asked before the interruption," Horton's glance went from Marco to Jewell and back, "you just happened to accompany Stone and this lady onto the porch?"

Before Marco could respond Horton continued, "This Civic comes by, shooter gets off three rounds, hits Stone. Driver a friend of yours?"

Jewell smothered a groan and spit out, "Three shots, three people on the porch. How can you think Marco had anything to do with it? That's ludicrous! One of those bullets was probably meant for him!"

Marco glanced at Jewell. When he spoke, his voice was quiet but strong. "Half of Miwok drives Civics. But, no, not one of my friends." He abruptly stopped talking and stared at his clenched hands.

Horton made a note, then looked coolly at Jewell. "Leave the conjecture to the experts, little lady. For all we know the guy purposely got off three rounds as a diversion."

The Asian officer cut in, "You're right, though, Mrs. McDunn. Until we know differently, we have to assume you were all targets." He looked solemnly at Marco. "Today's shooting makes two unsolved crimes at this address. You and Mrs. McDunn should be extra careful from now on." He glanced at a recording device on the table. "Just so you know, Mrs. McDunn, I'm Officer Chan. You know Detective Horton. At the far end of the couch, that's Officer Kleiss." Chan added, "We're taping this conversation."

Jewell nodded, glad the rest of the team didn't rubber-stamp Horton's rudeness.

"You and your father don't get along, right, kid? How come you're hanging out here, where he lives?" Horton raised an eyebrow. "You taking a second look at the crime scene out back?" Horton's voice was soft now, confidential.

"Hardly," Marco said through clenched teeth. "Once was more than enough. Mrs. McDunn asked me to come by." He slid a glance at Jewell. "She's not safe here by herself."

Jewell gave Marco a tiny smile. Somewhere in the region of her stomach, she felt an appreciative sigh—Maris evidently liked Marco.

"You say you didn't see the shooter. What kind of car does Benny Perez drive?" Horton snapped.

Marco sat up, startled. "I've seen him in a van and a Civic. I think he uses rentals." He flashed a quick look at Jewell. "I guess you know he hated Leo Stone's guts. The Stones kept Gram from turning this house into cash. Benny was sore as hell about that." He rubbed his eyes, looking miserable.

Horton leaned over, switched off the recorder. "We're done here." He watched as Officer Kleiss stood. "What do you think, Kleiss? Should we ask the chief to increase the patrol along Radish?"

Jewell jumped to her feet. "Chief Sorensen! He should be here by now. Leo—before he got shot—asked him to come by."

"If he heard about the shooting, he probably went straight to the hospital." Kleiss glanced coolly at Horton. "Increasing the patrol is your call, detective, but it makes good sense."

Horton stood, grunting, "Let's roll."

Jewell felt a flash of anger, realized it was coming from Maris, and struggled to subdue it. *I don't like the guy either, Maris, but we have to play nice; he has all the power.*

As soon as the police left, Marco headed for the kitchen. "We better check on your dog." Lois Lane had gone from softly whining to a nervous, insistent yelp.

When they came through the door into the kitchen, they saw Lois Lane wild-eyed and wriggling. She'd run in circles around a table leg and was virtually hog-tied.

"Good Lord, you poor thing!" Jewell knelt and held her while Marco unsnapped the leash. As soon as she was free, Lois Lane pulled away from Jewell and began frantically barking.

"Everyone's gone," Jewell murmured. "Calm down."

With a hurt, accusing look at Jewell, Lois Lane lowered her tail and crawled beneath the table.

"Maybe we should hit the road, too." Marco looked around the kitchen. "That detective has my father pegged for the shooter. If he's right, we're not safe here."

Jewell gulped. "Sit down. We need to talk."

Marco shuffled to the table and eased his angular frame onto a chair. "Make it short." When Lois Lane's cool nose pushed into one of his hands, he muttered, "Yeah, pooch, she probably means you, too." The dog rested a paw on Marco's foot.

"I may be wrong, but I don't think Detective Horton has a clue what's going on here," Jewell began. "I'm not sure myself, and I live here."

Marco turned to the window above the kitchen sink, his grainy, bloodshot eyes slowly focusing on a honeybee hovering close to the glass and landing at the rim of a perfectly shaped, purple morning glory blossom. His face filled with confusion. "There's no dirt below that window, is there? That plant must've come up through a crack in the concrete." He gave Jewell an embarrassed smile. "I'd match your persistence against Mother Nature's, anytime."

Chapter Twenty-Three

He stretched his hands out in a gesture of surrender. "If you have a message for me, let's hear it. Then I'm outa here, with or without you."

Jewell's phone vibrated. She glanced at the screen. "Carolyn. I'll call her back."

Marco nodded, his fingers tapping the table expectantly.

"Your message is from Maris Stone. You know, the lady who died here ten years ago?"

"Get off it, will you?" Marco slouched back in his chair. "No one's buying that ghost baloney."

Jewell pressed her palms together in a prayer that Maris Stone wouldn't reach across the table and grab Marco by the stretched-out neck of his T-shirt.

"The ghost is real, Marco, and she's pissed. She's waited ten years for retribution, and, now that it's in sight, no one'll listen." Jewell studied her fingernails. "Except Leo and me. And look where it got him."

Without warning, Maris took charge of Jewell's voice. A throaty, reptilian growl erupted from her throat, followed by a terse, *I need your help, young man.*

Marco's eyebrows shot up to his hairline. A high-pitched, girlish giggle escaped him. He clapped a hand over his mouth.

"Don't laugh," Jewell gasped as she struggled to subdue the ghost.

"Not laughing—nothing funny," Marco sputtered. "Scary. Listen, Jewell and whoever else is behind those nice brown eyes: I'm well acquainted with being invisible. Hell, that's the story of my life. Even when I found Gram dead in that stinkin' basement, I was invisible until the po-lice needed a suspect."

Jewell reached across the table to awkwardly pat Marco's shoulder. Under the table, Lois Lane sighed.

"Here's the thing:" Jewell glanced around the kitchen. "The evidence I found points to your father for the first murder, and, just a little while ago, the ghost said the same person killed your grandmother."

Marco froze. The spoon he'd been holding clattered to the tabletop. "What? How is that possible?"

"I don't know for sure. Leo and I were taking the evidence to Chief Sorenson when the shooter came by." Her voice softened. "The Chief might've believed Leo about this ghost stuff—they're Lodge buddies—there's no way he'll listen to me." Jewell looked directly at Marco. "Sorry I had to tell you this stuff. I know you and your father aren't friends, but he is your flesh and blood."

A sad smile played on Marco's lips. "It's okay. I kinda knew, anyway. I mean, the guy's the one constant in everything." As he looked at her, his eyes lit up. "Tell the ghost thanks for showing herself to me." He paused. "That slimebag killed Gram, his own mother?" He stumbled to the kitchen counter, grabbed a paper towel, and noisily blew his nose. "He's a psychopath; the county's had their eye on him for years. Gram never listened. She thought they were just out to get him." He hesitated. "How come you're sticking around, trying to help everyone, Jewell? That's the cops' job." He frowned. "That detective's a joke. If you were smart, you'd catch the next plane to Hawaii—or somewhere."

Jewell's mouth opened and Maris Stone's melodious voice flowed out. *She can't leave until I'm free to go.*

Marco sagged against the sink, shuddering. After a moment he muttered, "Next time, warn me before you flip over to channel K-GHOST."

Jewell grinned, shaking her head and speaking with her own voice. "You probably had that coming." Then her smile disappeared. "I tried to get the Stones' help—you know Beth Anne and Bob, right? But they're barely holding it together after the firebombing. Leo—well, he's been shot."

"You still have me; it's the least I can do for Gram." Marco kept his eyes down. "Benny couldn't have done the first murder; he was in prison. Wasn't he?"

Jewell rubbed a hand over her tired face. "The timing was close, but I don't think so. Leo did some checking. Your father was arrested for armed robbery early the next morning, in Eureka." She glanced around the kitchen, with its high ceilings, wall sconces, and sparkling linoleum floor. "Both murdered women stood between him and ownership of this house."

The air turned cold. It flashed through Jewell's mind that, if the mansion had ears, it would not be happy with what she'd just said.

"Is this all my fault?" Marco stuttered. "Gram told me if she ever moved out of 811 Radish, she'd give the place to me."

Exasperation flitted across Jewell's face. "This place's been tied up in court for years. She couldn't give it to anyone. If she said that to your father, though, and he didn't know she wasn't the legal owner…" She took a slow breath. "Don't get mired in self-pity, Marco. Let's focus on the two deaths. How are they connected? If there was a plan, maybe it's still in play. If we know what it is, maybe we won't end up in body bags."

Jewell's phone beeped. A text appeared: *Pages just came through. ????*

"I sent Carolyn the evidence. She got it just now."

"Is she coming here?" Marco hurried to the sink and splashed cold water on his face. "Tear tracks aren't exactly macho." He gave Jewell a twisted smile. "Old plan still in play? Interesting thought."

Jewell opened the refrigerator, removing two Tupperware boxes. "You hungry? I think better on a full stomach; can't remember when I last ate." She opened the boxes. "Raviolis, and a bit of the spinach souffle I made a couple days ago."

"Gram's raviolis." Marco gulped. "Sure, I'll have some. I can't even remember the last time she made raviolis. I bet these were for Benny." He absentmindedly lifted plates down from the cupboard.

Jewell spooned generous portions of the leftovers onto plates, zapped each in the microwave, and set them on the table. "Let's go over the facts while we eat."

Marco paused mid-forkful to mumble, "Let's just eat, for Gram's sake."

Jewell's stomach flip-flopped. *Right.*

She pushed a few pieces of ravioli around with her fork. The kitchen was quiet—Marco's fork clanking on the porcelain plate accentuated the refrigerator's low hum. Jewell relaxed, idling her mind.

Her phone beeped again. Another text flashed across the screen: *Time is running out. Get Sorenson to open my file. You are in danger!!!*

Jewell stifled a gasp.

Marco, scraping the last bits of pasta from his plate, looked up. "What?"

With a shaking hand, Jewell pushed the phone across the table. He read it, his face reflecting wonder.

"That's from your ghost? She texted you? Beyond strange!"

Nodding mutely, Jewell pulled the phone back. "Why does she think I'm in danger? Or, does she mean both of us?"

Clang, clang!

The bell above the dining room door fractured the kitchen's quiet. Jewell jumped to her feet, shaking. "I thought that darn thing was disconnected years ago." She glanced at Marco. He was frozen with a forkful of food in mid-air.

"It's the front doorbell."

Marco carefully set down the fork. "Carolyn?"

"If we're lucky, it's Chief Sorenson."

They tip-toed from the kitchen, Marco in the lead. As they approached the foyer the bell sounded again.

"Don't open it yet," Jewell whispered. "I'll text Carolyn, see if it's her."

Marco nodded, his nonchalant slouch a sad contrast to the perspiration dripping off his face.

That you? texted Carolyn's phone.

No response.

Jewell shrugged. "She must have her phone turned off." She leaned in and peered through the peep-hole. "That's funny. Nobody's out there."

"Let me see." Marco shouldered past and put his eye to the door.

189

Lois Lane growled low in her throat.

Jewell turned and her heart almost stopped. Benny Perez hovered in the hall's rear doorway, looking more like a shadow than a flesh-and-blood person.

"Marco," Jewell whispered.

Behind her Marco pulled in a breath, tensed.

"Didn't mean to scare you," Perez's voice was quiet, almost intimate. "I was down at Seven-Eleven. Heard Stone got shot. Figured I'd run by, do a body count." He stood, hands in his pockets as he leaned against the doorframe. Jewell's skin crawled.

"You sure you oughta be here, Jewell? Doesn't feel all that safe—just my opinion." Perez leered. "Whoever took the kid's granny out could have you in their sights, next."

Lois Lane moved to stand in front of Jewell. A low growl rumbled in her throat.

Within Jewell, the ghost of Maris Stone seethed. Jewell groaned from the effort to control it. *Stay calm, please, Mrs. Stone. I know he's your archenemy, but unlike you, I'm alive, and I want to stay that way.*

"The police want to talk to you, Benny." Jewell couldn't keep her voice from shaking.

"Yeah. You need directions to the cop shop? Oh, I forgot. You've been there before." Marco's tone was quietly challenging.

Jewell shot Marco a warning glance. *Don't provoke him!*

Perez ignored his son to continue leering at Jewell. "I just came from there. They suggested I check on you." He casually scanned the foyer. "This old place could use a facelift. Maybe the next owners will do some restoration, bring back the former pizazz." His eyes were cold. "Or, hell, they might just burn the old dump to the ground."

This got a reaction from the ghost. She grabbed Jewell's stomach in a vise-like grip.

"You were at Miwok P.D.?" Jewell managed to choke out the words. "Did you see Chief Sorenson? He's supposed to be coming by."

"Nope, didn't see him. Matter of fact, the chick at the desk said he's out of town." Perez's grin revealed overly-white, false choppers. "How about we clear out that upstairs bedroom, Jewell?" His voice became soft, menacing. "Take off, kid."

Revulsion and fear fought for dominance within Jewell. *What do I do, Maris?*

Confidence flowed through Jewell. "I'm not moving out of my room," she said, turning to Marco. "You don't have to leave unless you want to."

"Suit yourself." Perez shrugged. He glanced at Lois Lane, his cocky expression disappearing. "That bitch is due for a swift kick." With one eye on Lois Lane he said to Marco, "What the hell are you doing here anyway, kid? You got a thing for old broads?" He sneered. "Or are you making plans for the place, now granny's out of the way?" Hatred shone from Perez's eyes. "You're an even bigger sucker than I thought."

Marco stood tall, fists clenched. "I'm not the slimy bastard here, father."

Jewell let her guard down for a second. Instantly, her mouth opened and Maris's richly elegant voice poured out: *Tell me, little Benny, did Doris beg you to stop, to spare her? Or did she spit in your face, like I did?*

Both men's heads swiveled. They stared at Jewell. Both faces registered confusion and fear.

"Lady," Perez spit through clenched teeth, "I don't appreciate your big mouth." He hissed at Marco, "How many times do I have to tell you? Get the hell outta here."

"Hold on." Marco's eyes were still on Jewell. "Do you believe in ghosts, old man? People who've stuck around after being murdered?"

"You shittin' me? Ghosts?" Perez's voice dripped with contempt. "Hell, no." He moved toward Jewell. "I don't have time for this."

Lois Lane, ears cocked and lips curled back from gleaming canines, lunged. She knocked Perez to the floor and pinned him with her powerful forelegs.

"Call her off, dammit!" Perez screamed.

"Lois Lane! No!" Jewell whispered.

Marco swooped in and reached for Lois Lane's collar. She eyed him, growling. He stepped back.

Jewell pushed past Marco, grabbing a handful of canine neck fur. Lois

Lane's jaws relaxed; Jewell yanked, hard. Dog and woman fell back, away from Perez. As she embraced the trembling Lois Lane, Jewell whispered, "Good girl."

"Get up. You're not hurt—she didn't even draw blood." Marco's tone was heavy with disgust.

Jewell's phone beeped. Reaching for it, her fingers brushed against the notebook.

Good grief. I'd forgotten about the journal. If Benny sees it, he'll kill us for sure.

She glanced at the phone's glowing text: "R u still at 811 Radish? Go to the Ploughers' NOW. I'm fine. Leo." Relief washed over her.

"That was Leo. He's going to be okay." Jewell took a moment to breathe. "I'm going to the hospital." She looked from Marco to Benny, noting that, although they were father and son, there was no resemblance: Marco was tall, thin, and sandy-haired; Benny was several inches shorter, muscular, and olive-skinned. And, while Marco's face mirrored his feelings, Benny's could be carved in stone for all the humanity it revealed.

Perez backed a few feet away from Marco, keeping an eye on Lois Lane. The dog sat quietly next to Jewell, licking her paws. She bore no resemblance to the avenging she-wolf of a moment ago.

"Animal Shelter should have gassed that hound when they had the chance." Perez's hand went to the small of his back, revealing a bulge beneath his leather vest. "Would've saved me some ammo."

That's a gun. Jewell shivered.

Speaking barely above a whisper, Marco leveled a challenging gaze at Perez. "Did you know the first Mrs. Stone? The ghost—that was her talking a minute ago, in case you didn't figure that out—called you 'little Benny' and said something about spitting in your face. Care to explain, old man?"

Perez took a step toward Marco, glanced at Lois Lane, and stopped. His face registered a split-second of confusion, as if he felt cornered. Then he leaned forward menacingly. "I don't explain: not to you, not to anyone. Now, I won't say it again. Get the hell outa here!"

Marco stepped back, his face beet-red. "I'll leave when I'm good and ready," he sputtered.

Leveling a cold stare at Jewell, Perez said, "That ghost scam you got goin'? I don't buy it. Show lover boy the door. You're not going anywhere 'til that room's cleaned out." His tone was low, menacing.

Slipping a hand inside her bag, Jewell turned on her phone and speed-dialed Carolyn. Then, almost as an afterthought, she palmed the phone and dropped it onto the foyer bench.

God and Carolyn, help me.

She squared her shoulders, mentally puffing herself up as if encountering a big forest predator. Then, speaking clearly, she said, "You sure you want him to leave, Benny? It'd be smarter if *you* left."

There was a flash of indecision in Benny's face, the first unguarded expression Jewell had seen from the older Perez.

Her eyes went to Marco. "Go on, get out of here. Find Carolyn."

For a moment Marco seemed hurt, as he'd been dismissed. Then his face cleared. He nodded and stepped outside, shutting the door firmly behind him.

Fear broke a cold sweat on Jewell's forehead. *I have to stall this guy, keep him from getting me upstairs. And talk loud, so the phone picks up our voices.*

"You aren't exactly friends with the Stone family, are you?" Jewell attempted a chatty tone. "Did you know them before you went to prison, when your mother and Rudolph Stone were having an affair?"

Perez scowled, as if she'd stupidly expressed the obvious. "We didn't move in the same circles, did we? They lived here; I had a room on the east side, behind Safeway." His gaze focused on Lois Lane. "Lock your hound in the kitchen. You're wasting my time."

"You must have been pleased when Rudolph Stone died and left your mother this whole, beautiful mansion," Jewell kept talking. "The years you were locked up finally paid off—perfect alibi, by the way: getting arrested miles from here after killing Maris Stone. How'd you feel when Doris changed her mind about selling the house? It had to hurt, being conned by your own mother."

A shadow crossed Perez's face. "Sounds like Mom got chatty over a bottle of wine." He smiled gruesomely. "She's not blabbing anymore. I took care of that once and for all." He stepped toward Jewell, and Lois Lane's throat rumbled ominously. GRR!

Perez stopped. "I thought I told you to lock up that mutt."

Jewell snapped her fingers at Lois Lane. The dog cocked an ear, as if surprised at this unusual version of a command, and then slunk away to a corner.

With the semblance of a smile, Jewell turned to Perez. "Why do you hate the Stones, Benny? Far as I know, they never did anything to you. I can see you being pissed at your mother—I mean, she played you for a fool. I don't see that as a reason to kill her, but then I'm not you. Why shoot Leo, though?" Her voice dropped to a whisper. "I'm thinking it was you that tossed the bottle bomb into G.I.'s Joe, too. Do you think of the Stones as your personal enemies?"

A tiny sliver of surprise, quickly replaced by smug confidence, crossed Perez's face. "You're too smart for your own good, bitch. How'd you put all that together? Now I *have* to kill you." He shoved Jewell toward the stairs. "March!"

Chapter Twenty-Four

As she stumbled forward Jewell glanced over her shoulder and, through one of the front-porch windows, saw a face. The eyes were distorted by the wavy old glass, but it was definitely Carolyn. Deep within Jewell, Maris shuddered. Jewell's mouth opened involuntarily. She gagged, bent double, and vomited.

"Shit!" Perez raised a gun-wielding fist at Jewell as she knelt, retching, on the hardwood floor. She twisted to one side and tensed, but the blow didn't come. Peering up through the crook of her elbow she saw Perez standing over her, stiff as a board and exuding terror.

A whistling sound swept through the small, high-ceilinged foyer, followed by a low, humming noise. Perez's eyes darted from side to side. "Stop it," he hissed through his teeth.

Jewell's first thought was, *Doris never fixed the latch on the garden doors.*

Gusts of wind, whistling and pushing angrily, blew about the room. Curtains flapped and the walls creaked, straining against the whirlwind.

Cowering, Jewell looked around. Lois Lane was pressed against the front door, head down and paws over her eyes.

"Good dog," Jewell whispered.

Following Perez's rigid stare, Jewell looked at the dining room's arched entryway. At first she saw only shadows; as her eyes adjusted, though, the central shadow took the shape of a tall, thin woman in a blood-streaked nightgown. The woman's long, tangled hair and luminous skin highlighted a badly bruised neck.

Maris?

Jewel blinked, thinking the figure would disappear. It didn't; in fact, it grew in size and density.

"No more tricks, Bitch. Cut it out. I mean it!" Perez's voice was high-pitched, adolescent.

"I can't. It's not a trick."

Through immobilizing fear Jewell felt a surge of relief; Maris had left her body. The words, "Don't come back," crossed her mind.

At that moment the blustering wind ushered in a second ghostly form. Bloody hair, a bruised and swollen face, and a ragged green cocktail dress highlighted this apparition as it floated across to Maris.

Doris? Oh, my God. The second woman in the closet **was** *you!*

Perez's eyes bugged out. He gasped, "Mom?" His face changed, flashing from amazed fear to sullen resolve. He snarled. "This is the last trick you'll ever play, Jewell."

When his gun hand came up, Jewell ducked under the bench.

BAM, BAM, BAM!

The wind ricocheted the sound from wall to wall. Jewell shook her head, momentarily deafened. She felt herself take a breath.

I'm still alive. He didn't hit me. Dizzy, she grabbed the edge of the bench and squinted into the room.

Perez stood immobilized by the now swirling wind and, as Jewell stared, horrified, shreds of green cloth blew against his neck. The shreds elongated, becoming a shiny green cord held by two ghostly-white hands. As they pulled tighter and tighter, Benny's face reflected first irritation, then dismay. His mouth opened; was he trying to scream?

Jewell pushed uselessly against the wind trapping her under the bench, then sank back, horribly aware of her helplessness.

The skin on her arm tingled. Her barely comprehending eyes focused on Lois Lane, cowering at her side. Somehow, the dog had managed to crawl along the wall and get to Jewell.

The roaring became a deafening chant in the wood-paneled room. *Your turn, your turn!* bounced off the walls.

Perez flailed helplessly. An awful, gut-wrenching expression of defeat crossed his face.

They're using the wind to hold him so they can strangle him—like he did them.

"Maris! Doris! Stop!" Jewell's screams were swallowed up by the awful chant.

Your turn! Your turn!

Perez struggled to lift his hands. His eyes bulged; his mouth opened, like a fish out of water. Just before his face went slack, Jewell saw something sparkling against his neck. *Maris's ring—she's wearing her ring again!*

Benny's head drooped. He sank to the floor.

As if aware its job was done, the wind subsided. It flowed meekly out through the French doors so that, within the foyer, errant puffs were all that was left of the murderous force.

The two ghostly figures materialized by the front door, and Jewell crawled from beneath the bench. She glanced at the window, seeing only clear blue sky beyond the walls of the house.

Was Carolyn actually there? Have I lost my mind? To the two figures, she whispered, "Are you real?"

The ghost of Doris drifted past Jewell, pausing near Perez's body. It knelt, resting a pale hand on his head, and murmured, *My dear, baby boy.*

The ghost of Maris moved to Doris's side. *He's better off dead,* resounded in the still air. The two eerie faces radiated infinite sadness.

Thank you for saving our house. Maris's elegant voice was hushed. *I'm free, finally.*

She caressed the gold band now on her ring finger.

"You saved my life," Jewell whispered. "I owe you."

All debts are paid, the ghost of Doris murmured.

The house trembled, as if moved by an earthquake. Then, everything was still. The ghosts were gone. Jewell staggered to the bench.

Clack, clack! Lois Lane's toenails on the wood floor broke the silence. The dog gave Perez's body a quick sniff, then turned to the front door and began barking.

Outside, boots thumped on the porch. With a resounding WHUMP! the front door crashed open and the room filled with armed, shouting police.

"Lois Lane! Stay!" Jewell struggled to her feet, then doubled over, unconscious. Her last thought was, *I guess they killed me, too.*

Chapter Twenty-Five

Silence beyond closed eyelids. Correction: not silence. A droning noise seemingly surrounding Jewell, accentuated by a grab-bag of muffled sounds. A throaty whisper somewhere nearby. She involuntarily flexed the muscles in her right arm; winced. One eye opened. She saw, out of focus, a headless robot with hoses instead of arms—no, tubes. Tubes that went from the robot to Jewell.

What in the world?

"Well, hello, darlin'. You at the hospital, in the ER, in case you wondering." The throaty voice, now slightly above a whisper, had a face and a maraschino-cherry smile below sparkling, black-bean eyes.

"Mom?" Carolyn's voice, squeaky with relief, chirped on the heels of the throaty welcome.

Jewell thought of turning her head, became aware of a throbbing headache.

"Hi, baby." She focused beyond the nurse to the haggard, weepy angel at the end of the—*"I'm in the hospital?"*

Her eyes closed. Everything flashed back: The ghosts, the wind, the gunshot. With a very fat tongue she managed to slur, "Lois Lane?"

Carolyn elbowed in past the nurse.

"Don't be puttin' those bony elbows in my ribs, girl. Pretty please works just fine."

Hank's face, stubbled and raccoon-eyed, appeared above Carolyn's shoulder.

"Helluva way to get out of a mess, Jewell." Hank attempted a smile, but it didn't go all the way to his eyes. "For a minute there we thought you'd joined the ranks of the Stone mansion victims."

"Lois Lane," Jewell whispered again. She managed to lift her head an inch. "S'okay?"

"We got her," a voice said from behind Hank.

Marco. He's here, too.

The nurse appeared on the other side of the gurney. "Your dog is fine—unlike you, she didn't pass out and bump her head. If you're up to talking, I got cops out in the hall itching to get in here."

Jewell's eyes, now fully open and focused, took in the IV drip, the curtains surrounding the gurney, and the fear in her daughter's face.

"I fainted? Again?" Jewell suddenly remembered Benny Perez in a heap on the floor. She looked beyond her kids to the slumped, pale figure of Marco standing by the door. "Benny?"

Carolyn and Hank exchanged glances. The nurse sighed, clamped her mouth shut, and stepped away.

"No, Mom," Carolyn whispered. "Benny didn't make it." She gulped. "I saw what happened from outside. It...it was horrible, him shooting at you and getting swamped by that awful wind. If it wasn't for something wrapping around his neck and stopping him, you'd be dead." She squeezed Jewell's hand. "When the cops come in here, keep it simple, okay? If you start talking about ghosts, they'll think you're nuts."

"Yeah," Hank added. "Three guesses who cops tend to blame when they find a dead body alone with a crazy person."

Jewell gave a thankful nod and squeezed her eyes shut. *Does that mean Maris and Doris are finally gone? I think so. Thank God.*

The curtains surrounding the gurney parted to reveal an overweight, gray-haired police officer, Detective Horton, and a man who looked vaguely familiar.

The narrow gurney was now completely surrounded. Jewell felt claustrophobic panic surge through her. She grabbed Carolyn's hand and held tight.

"You better make it quick, boys. This patient's been given meds for shock." The nurse, whose badge, now that Jewell could read it, said, "Shonandra

Parsons, R.N.," folded muscular arms over her ample chest.

After an irritated glance at Parsons, the officer turned to Jewell. "I'm Chief Sorenson, Mrs. McDunn. You've been cleared of all charges, but we have a few questions." His smile was that of a seasoned politician. "You met with Detective Horton earlier in the day. Steinberg's here on behalf of your friends, Nicholas and Eve Plougher. Oh, I almost forgot. We're taping this."

Jewell glanced at Steinberg and smiled weakly. "Tell Mr. and Mrs. P. thanks."

"I will." He expelled a breath and stepped back. "I'm not Mrs. McDunn's lawyer, Chief, but I'll let you know if any of your questions violate her rights."

Chief Sorenson's face went from compassionate to falsely jovial. "Duly noted, Steinberg. Mrs. McDunn—may I call you Jewell?"

As she looked at the chief, Jewell saw his face shimmer and ripple, strangely fluid.

Shock, someone said. Feels like scrambled-egg brains.

With an effort, she switched her gaze to the nurse.

She won't let them hurt me.

"Mrs. McDunn, please." Jewell's voice came out in a whisper; she tried to speak louder. "You're Leo's friend. How is he? Benny Perez shot him; bragged about it." The sight of Benny on the floor flooded her mind and she looked away, trying not to gag.

"Leo's fine. The bullet grazed his shoulder—probably hurts like hell, but the damage was minimal." Sorensen coughed. "We heard that conversation—your daughter's phone was quite effective until that roaring wind came through the house. Mrs. McDunn," he continued, "When we entered the building you, your dog—a young female beagle—and Benny Perez, the deceased Doris Stone's son, were there. Is that correct?"

Jewell nodded, glanced at the recorder. "Yessir."

"Did you see me in the window, Mom?" Carolyn interrupted, her voice an excited squeak. "The guys were with me, trying to get the door unlocked. When Benny pulled his gun out, I thought he was going to shoot Lois Lane." Carolyn gulped. "Instead, he shot you!"

Jewell closed her eyes. "Dear God," she muttered, "that really happened?"

"We need to keep this interview short," Nurse Parsons said crisply. "How about no one else talks until the officer's done?"

"I'd appreciate that." Sorenson's voice was strained.

"Okay. Sorry," Carolyn whispered.

Jewell squeezed Carolyn's hand. *No harm no foul, honey.*

"Until we have more complete information, Mrs. McDunn, we're assuming Perez died as a result of strangulation. We know he shot at you—the gun was still in his hand when he died. We're not clear on how he was strangled. Did you overpower him after he shot at you? Was he overcome by the gale-force wind?"

Steinberg blurted, "You may not want to answer that, Mrs. McDunn."

"S'okay," Jewell whispered. "Never overpowered him. Hid under the bench. Wind blew in and cloth got wrapped around his neck. Couldn't push through the wind to help him." She felt tears oozing past her eyelids.

"There was a helluva wind storm going on. I'll attest to that," Detective Horton mumbled.

Sorenson looked from Jewell to Horton and back. "Did you open the door to let the storm in?" He smiled gently, as if talking to a child.

Marco had been standing next to Hank, his face in shadow. At this question, he shook the sweatshirt hood from around his anguished, puffy-eyed face. "My Gram—Doris Stone— always complained about those doors. The latch was broken; they wouldn't stay shut." He glanced at Jewell. "I was there when my father showed up. He came from the back of the house—probably used those doors. If anyone's responsible for the wind getting in, it's him."

Detective Horton cleared his throat. "Kid's right. I checked those doors when we responded to the shooting earlier today. Houses like that have those glass doorknobs; old as dirt, and the locks don't work worth a damn." He stared at his feet. "Sorry for your loss, kid. I mean, losses."

As Jewell listened, wondering why they were going on about doors and doorknobs, her eyes locked on Marco's face.

I should get off this bed and let him lay down. Don't they see he's the victim, here? His father's greed cost him his whole family.

The air in the small space began to feel thick; voices faded. Jewell slurred,

"The wind twisted a cord around Benny's neck—I couldn't help him." She turned her head away from the wall of inquisitive eyes.

"The rest of this interview will have to wait, boys." Parsons pulled back the curtain and muscled in past the men. "My patient's in no condition for this."

Jewell heard shuffling feet, irritated muttering. Without warning her brain cleared. "Marco?"

The clatter of curtain rings was followed by silence. Disappointment settled on Jewell, causing an ache in the region of her heart. She slowly, tentatively turned onto her side and opened one eye. Marco stood in the curtain's gap, staring at her.

"You came back, with the kids." Jewell's whisper was so soft, she wasn't sure she'd actually said it.

Marco took a lanky step forward and leaned over, resting his face next to her cheek. She felt the shaking of his sobs and lifted a hand to stroke his matted hair.

"You're not like your father," Jewell whispered, "even if you do have his name. He hurt you, most of all." Jewell sighed. "Your mother would be proud of you. You helped break the mansion's curse."

Marco lifted his head. "We did, didn't we? Broke the curse, I mean." His face was somber.

"We did." Jewell smiled from her eyes. "War's over," she slurred. "Time to heal."

* * *

Two days later Jewell sat curled up under a quilt on the couch in the Plougher's living room, Lois Lane sprawled at her feet. Leo fidgeted nearby on a hardbacked chair.

"Are you sure you don't want a vacation courtesy of the Stone family, Jewell? We could go to Hawaii or Mexico—I'd love to show you New York City, but I don't think your nervous system could handle that just now." Leo's smile expressed a boatload of anxiety.

"You might want to step it back a notch, Stone." Nicholas Plougher stood in the kitchen doorway. "She doesn't go anywhere 'til the doctor gives her the go-ahead."

"Sweet of you to offer, though." Eve Plougher, manning a walker, pushed past her husband and made her way to a chair near the couch.

Leo's question finally penetrated the anti-anxiety meds dulling Jewell's brain. She looked at him, puzzled. *Does he really think all I need is a few days in the tropics? If only.*

She wiggled her toes under the quilt. "They're right. Maybe down the road, when I'm done having nightmares. Thanks, though."

Leo nodded, staring at his clasped hands.

"Are you in charge of the mansion now, Leo?" Mrs. Plougher's voice broke the awkward silence. "We'd like to send someone over for Jewell's things."

"That would be Miwok P.D., for now. They'll let me in, though. Give me a list and I'll take care of it."

Leo added, so quietly Mr. Plougher put one hand behind an ear to listen, "I just thought a change of scenery might help clear your mind, Jewell. My family owes you so much. Hell, while we were licking our wounds you faced the bogeyman and saved our lives."

Nicholas and Eve Plougher nodded their agreement; Jewell felt relaxed for the first time in days.

"You made me face my responsibility as head of the family, too." Humiliation shone from Leo's eyes. "It took some bullying. I had my head pretty far up my..." he glanced at Eve Plougher. "I hope better late than never counts with you, Jewell."

"It does. It definitely does." Jewell leaned forward, full of sympathy for this humbler version of Leo Stone. "No one can undo the past, not even ghosts. We're lucky we survived. Let's learn from it."

"I'm glad you're taking responsibility, young man." Eve Plougher's clear, reedy voice cut across theirs. "Beware of selfish habits slipping back when the pressure's off." She looked sharply at her husband.

"I'm not so sure about that, Mother. Life-changing events—and believe you me, that describes what went on at 811 Radish—stick with a person." Nicholas Plougher patted Eve's hand dismissively and turned to Leo. "We never heard what it was Carolyn's phone recorded. Must have been big to impress the cops like it did." He shook his head. "They finally stopped treating that poor Perez kid like a criminal."

As Mr. Plougher spoke, images of the foyer and the murderous, twisting storm flooded Jewell's brain. She whispered, "Perez bragged about hurting the Stones: killing Maris, torching G.I.'s Joe, shooting Leo—even killing his own mother." She put a fist to her mouth and choked back a sob.

Leo and the Ploughers jumped to their feet and hurried to her. Leo was faster, but not by much. While he knelt at Jewell's feet, the Ploughers dropped onto the couch on either side of her and leaned in protectively.

Jewell struggled for control. "Thank God the phone picked up every word. It was a confession he didn't even know he was making." She squeezed Leo's hand. "Maris said she wouldn't leave until her killer was found. Does that mean she's gone for good?"

"What does your gut tell you?" Leo looked hopeful.

The name, 'Maris,' had an odd effect on Eve Plougher. She glowered at Leo. "So, it's true?" Her usually chirpy voice was imperious, cold. "The ghost of Maris Stone haunted your family home...and you encouraged poor Jewell to move in there? For shame!"

"So much has happened since then," Jewell whispered. "Don't blame Leo. He didn't believe in ghosts back then."

He shook his head. "What a shmuck I was."

"That reminds me." Jewell continued. "We were on our way to Miwok P.D. when Benny shot you." She groaned. "Sorenson needs that journal to piece together the details of Maris's death."

Leo sat very still. "You're right. Crap. I was going to let that slide—couldn't face being laughed at about the ghost. Dammit!" He looked at his watch. "I'll go there now, talk to whoever'll listen. Where's the journal?"

"In my bag. I'll get it." Jewell stood and started toward the hallway.

"I'll ride along with you, Leo—keep you honest." There was a rare, alert tone in Nicholas Plougher's voice.

Leo gave the older man a sour look. "You think I'll chicken out?"

Plougher stood there, grinning. Leo nodded. "Fair enough."

At the front door, Jewell brushed her lips against Leo's cheek, then leaned back and looked up at him. "Any idea why Perez was so obsessed with your family? It's almost as if he saw himself as the Stones' personal Grim Reaper." She frowned. "I guess that would be called motive."

Leo put his fingertips tenderly to the spot her lips had touched. A shadow crossed his face. "Best guess? He'd been nursing a grudge since back when Rudy died, when Doris found out the house wasn't in her name. To Perez's criminal mind, that would've made us targets." He blew out a breath. "Living in a quiet place like Miwok, you assume all the bad guys are somewhere else—across the bridge in San Francisco, or in the East Bay."

"Did the family react badly when Rudy married Doris so soon after Maris's death? I could see Perez taking exception to that."

Leo nodded. "We'd been excusing Rudy's slimy behavior for years, but marrying his drinking buddy weeks after Maris's death? That was too much, even for us. We shunned them both until he died."

Jewell suddenly felt exhausted. "With Perez's ego, that was a fatal mistake."

Leo's shoulders slumped. He whispered, "And 811 Radish paid for it."

"But," Eve Plougher piped up, "now you have the chance to move ahead with humility." As she and Jewell stood watching Leo and Mr. Plougher get into Leo's truck, she commented, "Do you have that nice Perez boy's phone number? I'd like to invite him to dinner."

Jewell closed the front door. "Yes, ma'am. I do."

A Note from the Author

Acknowledgements to The Petaluma Thrillers Critique Group.

My Critique Group buddies—Fred Weisel, Thonie Hevron and Andy Gloege—have kept me growing as a writer; my granddaughters—Tiernan and Kaitlyn—have championed the dream.

About the Author

B. Payton Settles lives in Sonoma, California. Stone Cold Dead, her second paranormal mystery and third published novel, draws on the author's fascination with Petaluma, California's colorful history and architecture. In this thriller the town is tactfully renamed Miwok after the original residents of this beautiful area.

AUTHOR WEBSITE:
  B.Paytonsettles.com

Also by B. Payton Settles

Something in the Attic

Accidental Target